ALL OVER IREL

Deirdre Madden is from Toomebridge, Co. Antrim. Her
novels include *One by One in the Darkness*, *Authenticity*, *Molly
Fox's Birthday* and, most recently, *Time Present and Time Past*.
She has twice been shortlisted for the Orange Prize. She
teaches at Trinity College, Dublin, and is a member of the
Irish arts academy, Aosdána.

Also available from Faber

THE FABER BOOK OF BEST NEW IRISH SHORT STORIES 2004–05
Edited by David Marcus

THE FABER BOOK OF BEST NEW IRISH SHORT STORIES 2006–07
Edited by David Marcus

NEW IRISH SHORT STORIES
Edited by Joseph O'Connor

TOWN AND COUNTRY – NEW IRISH SHORT STORIES
Edited by Kevin Barry

ALL OVER IRELAND

New Irish Short Stories

Edited by
DEIRDRE MADDEN

FABER & FABER

First published in 2015
by Faber & Faber Limited
74–77 Great Russell Street
London WC1B 3DA

Typeset by Faber & Faber Ltd
Printed and bound in England by CPI Group (UK) Ltd,
Croydon, CR0 4YY

A CIP record for this book is available from the British Library

ISBN 978–0–571–31103–3

2 4 6 8 10 9 7 5 3 1

To the memory of
John McGahern
1934–2006

Contents

Introduction

Deirdre Madden

WHEN I WAS ASKED TO EDIT this book, the brief from Faber and Faber was straightforward. The anthology was to include a mix of established and new writers. The stories were to be unpublished, and were to remain so until they appeared in this volume. I could include writers who had already contributed to the anthology edited by Joseph O'Connor or to either of the two collections edited by the late David Marcus, but I was asked not to include writers who had had work in *Town and Country*, edited by Kevin Barry, the most recent book in the series.

The above gives a sense of what the book is; but also, significantly, of what it is not. It is not definitive, and does not seek to be. It does not attempt to establish a canon, nor to confirm any canon that might arguably be said to already exist. It does not claim to offer the best Irish new short stories, as that would imply a criticism of stories not included, and perhaps make hostages to fortune those that are.

Anthologising being what it is, there will be regrets and perhaps complaints about the writers who have been omitted. Why nothing from X, Y and Z? What about P, Q and R? No one regrets particular omissions more than I do, and some writers I greatly admire are not included. X no longer writes stories. Y was working on a new novel, and wanted to concentrate fully on that. The stories on which Z was working were already earmarked for publication elsewhere. As for P, Q and R, they are all excellent writers and might well have made the cut had I been able to include a greater volume of work.

*

Turning now to the writers who have been included in the anthology, and looking at the work thematically, it is striking that emigration features in several of the stories – striking, but not surprising, given its constant presence in both Irish life and Irish writing down through the years. What is interesting here is how the stories, by each showing different aspects of emigration and unconsciously complementing each other, point up the extraordinary complexity and multilayered nature of the subject.

Michael Gilligan's story, 'Absent', appears to be the most traditional in its approach, with its father–son tensions and rural setting, but it is also robustly contemporary, with mobile phones and Skype bringing family members closer together even as they confirm the unbridgeable distances between them. While also contemporary, the implied Ireland the central character is leaving behind in Andrew Fox's 'My New Life' is not the same Ireland of Gilligan's story, but one already more secular and urban. Belinda McKeon takes us deep into the mind of a woman no longer at ease or at home in either Ireland or the USA; and Natalie Ryan shows us a group of expats in Ghana, where a child observes how their lives intersect with those of the locals. In Selina Guinness's 'The Weather Project', an elderly Irishwoman on a trip to London remembers her difficult life there in the 1950s; although emigration is only one of the central themes in this complex and original story.

Some of these stories take us to places where we would not wish to be: into the mind of a suicidal young girl in Lucy Caldwell's 'Killing Time'; into the life of a Dublin barber in Sean O'Reilly's 'Ceremony', where the air of latent violence is palpable; or into Eoin McNamee's heart-breaking tale of childhood, 'The Comets', with its bleak seaside setting. In each of these stories, the moral integrity the writers bring to bear upon the subject matter is striking; and this is also true of both Frank McGuinness's 'The Widow's Ferret', about the psychic aftermath of violence and loss suffered by a woman in the Northern Irish Troubles; and of Kathleen Murray's 'They'll Best You with Fun', concerning workmen called in to dismantle a protest against clerical child sexual abuse. The rigour these writers show, their unflinching engagement with sensitive and disturbing material, is courageous, and the stories accomplished.

Colm Tóibín takes as his point of departure a real event concerning real people which has already been the subject of the work of a major Irish writer in the distant past, to create in 'The Journey to Galway' a story which is moving, humane and highly literary, where a woman remembers a trauma 'as a story that had been told and retold rather than a brutal single fact'. Thus, we have a story with a historical setting, which is intertextual but also a free-standing work, complete without external reference.

Mary Morrissy's story, 'Emergency', is also historical, being set as it is in Ireland during the Second World War, as a mother and daughter both find fringe benefits to the arrival in their lives of a parachutist. There is wry humour in this, as there is in Ita Daly's 'Villefranche', which is set at a funeral and points up the fact, seldom acknowledged, that friends for life often can't stand each other.

Finally, Eileen Casey's 'Beneath Green Hills' is perhaps the most redemptive story in the collection, where an elderly Dublin woman faces the end of a difficult life with wit, fortitude and an unexpected interest in Nelson Mandela.

*

I hope that the above gives some sense of the range and diversity of the work included in this anthology. The rude health of the Irish short story and the increasing number of outlets for it at the moment have been commented upon in many forums in recent times, including in the introductions by both of my immediate predecessors, Kevin Barry and Joseph O'Connor. I would commend their texts to you, and feel that there is little point in my returning here to ground that has already been well covered.

Whatever about writing, I would, however, like to comment upon the state of reading, which, I believe, gives cause for concern. I think that the increasing struggles of bookshops to survive is testament to the problem and cannot be simply put down to e-readers and to books being bought online. To value writing over reading is to miss the point, because writers *need* readers. I sometimes feel that there is more and more interest in the process of writing and less and less in the end result. At literary festivals now, panel discussions, interviews and question-and-answer sessions are favoured above readings, and I, for one, regret that loss of the primacy of the text. People seem to be less interested in the finished work than in the path one took to get to it; and any writer will tell you that that path is usually a messy one, littered with discarded ideas and forked with roads leading to dead ends. That direct engagement between a reader and a writer – private, contemplative, born out of silence – is to be valued more and more as the cultural cacophony around us increases.

*

This anthology is dedicated to the memory of the late John McGahern, a true master of the short story, and I am grateful to Madeline McGahern for her kind permission to do so. In their anthologies, both Joseph O'Connor and Kevin Barry paid fitting homage to the late David Marcus, whose uniquely kind and encouraging support of a whole generation of Irish writers made him a legend. I wish to add my own tribute, to register my own gratitude and affection.

The title *All Over Ireland* is a homage to James Joyce and also a quiet theft from his story, 'The Dead'. As someone who ruthlessly raided languages and literatures from all times and places for his own ends, I can't imagine that he would have objected: in any case, I hope not.

My New Life

Andrew Fox

IN MY NEW LIFE, I THOUGHT, I would need to be able to dive. My new classmates – Germanic or Anglo boys with deep tans and bulbous Adam's apples and their own cars – would throw pool parties on Saturday afternoons at their glassy houses, where girls in string bikinis, soft and smelling of summer, would gather to hang their feet in the shallows and ache to be impressed. So, the afternoon before my father met with the lawyers, I asked my mother to teach me.

'Ankles together,' she called from across the milky water, hair sleek against her long and newly red-brown neck. 'Now, stretch out your arms and lower your head between – no, don't look at me, love. *Lower* your head, that's it.'

Back in Dublin, she was a PE instructor, and, so far, on each of our three mornings here, she had got up at dawn to swim laps in the kidney-shaped pool. She had tried to persuade my father to book a hotel downtown with a fitness centre, but he had thought it best to economise on a motor lodge by the airport. This was the City Gardens Inn and Suites, a squat, ash-coloured L-shaped building, with one wing given over to the lobby and the bar and another comprised of two dozen or so self-service rooms. These extended in a flat-roofed line away from the roar of the highway towards a copse of shaggy palm trees, a stretch of waste ground and, eventually, the runway that every few minutes launched another aeroplane howling into the sky.

'Now,' my mother said, miming, 'remember to spring up and – *out!*'

My toes curled at the poolside. The meat of my biceps shook. A paste of sweat and suncream squeezed through the channels of my stomach. I bent my knees and leapt and hit the water hard. My nose and throat flooded, but I stayed down, knifed along the slimy bottom to the other side and came up coughing.

'You're getting it,' my mother said, applauding, and turned to speak with my father, who had appeared at last from the motel's computer room and was staring at his phone. He wore brown slip-on shoes, grey slacks with a hard crease, a soft white shirt that caught the California light and glowed. He was strange to me. For months, he had been the hack of ignition in the driveway at dawn, the slam of kitchen cabinets long after I had gone to bed. But now that the company wanted him to move, everything, he'd said, would be different.

I climbed out of the pool and flip-flopped towards our room, a red welt of impact blazing on my chest. Overhead, palm fronds rattled with the rush of traffic, raining crisp seedpods and the desiccated shells of insects. The room smelled of old sleep, the bathroom of damp grout. I showered and dressed and combed my hair and made it back to the pool deck, where my father now was standing by the droop of the storm fence, a hand clenched in the wire. His arm reached towards my mother, who crossed her legs on a low sunbed, her eyes levelled at a book that I could tell she wasn't reading.

'Your turn,' I said, presenting myself for her inspection.

'You two go ahead and *work*,' she said. 'I'm staying right here.'

I could feel my father's heat at my elbow, hear him suck his teeth as though they were my own. He turned on his heel and strode towards the car, the blades of his shoulders slashing. I lingered by my mother's side. She didn't speak, so neither did I. My father honked the horn, and even still she didn't stir. I turned slowly and edged away and broke into a jog. The car was a blue, shoe-shaped Suzuki with a chrome grille and a matte black bumper and no hubcaps. I climbed inside its air-conditioned cool and shivered. My arms were burnt.

★

Soon, we were on a long bend of highway squeezed between the tight blue skin of the bay and the brawn of the San Bruno hills. SOUTH SAN FRANCISCO THE INDUSTRIAL CITY, a sign set into the hillside read. On their windward faces, the hills were blasted brown; leeward, they were tufted with green scrub. At their feet, low-rise houses shambled away into haze, the gossamer of telephone lines linking each to the next.

'Your mother . . .' my father said, stamping the syllables with an open palm into the rubber of the steering wheel. 'Sometimes . . . Christ, she's just too sensitive, you know what I mean?'

'Yeah,' I said.

He cracked his neck, his shoulders rolling.

'But she'd get used to things, I think,' he said, nodding like his head had been loosened. 'She'd learn to like it here, you know? I think she'd like it here.'

On a narrow wedge of shingled beach, kids were racing bikes. A dog showed the hunting points of its ears for an instant and then vanished. My father broke his gaze from the road and fixed it on me. The spoon-back lenses of his aviators warped the shapes of my face.

'So, what do you think?' he said. 'You think she'd like it here?'

'Probably,' I said.

'And you'd like it here too?'

I shrugged. 'Of course I would.'

He flexed his fingers on the wheel, a pianist limbering up. 'That's really great, son,' he said. 'I'm really glad to hear . . . Although,' his voice lowered, 'I'm sure you'll miss your school and things?'

'Oh yeah,' I said. 'I'm heartbroken.'

He smiled, his teeth like smashed seashells. 'Your friends, then?'

'What friends?' I said. 'They call me *fat boy*. Or worse. And I never get invited anywhere' – which wasn't exactly true. I was by no means the most popular kid at school, but

4

I did have one or two reliables with whom I lied about sex over videogames. But since my father had announced the company's offer, I'd felt myself already begin to drift away from them. In my new life, I thought, I would do better, be better.

With his head bowed, my father eyed a tour bus changing lanes, its rear end woozy on a set of worn-out shocks.

'You shouldn't take that kind of treatment,' he said.

'Okay,' I said.

'You have to stand up for yourself.'

'Okay,' I said.

We left the highway and took to surface streets. Candy-coloured Victorian houses twisted from the roadside. As we passed, I stared up at their tall windows and imagined where we might live, my father and I painting a porch, my mother in a light-filled kitchen. At a stoplight, a double-wide avenue boomed across our path. My father banked the Suzuki and went shoulder-to-shoulder with a city bus. The itch of salt crept back into the air and the city fell away all around us. We turned again onto a cobbled alley of raw brick seafront depots, each of which had been gutted and refitted to accommodate a corporate office. Around the corner and a few blocks away, I knew, was the baseball stadium; and towards it, as we parked, I saw crowds of people moving, all dressed in orange and black.

'There's a game on, looks like,' my father said as he checked his reflection in the rear-view mirror. 'Here.' He turned on the radio and found commentary. 'You can listen along while I'm inside.'

5

I watched him shrink away towards the glassed-in lobby of his building, where he paused a moment to hold the elevator for a woman running in heels. His face was just a blur but I could tell that he was smiling, tell by the angle of her that she was smiling too. Then the doors snapped shut.

★

The air in the car thickened with the sun's heat, and kept thickening. The radio announcer droned something about stolen base percentage, but the murk of the stadium's tannoy conspired to drown him out. In preparation for my new life, I'd been teaching myself the sport, had pored over stats and studied jargon on the Internet. When the Giants smacked one over the wall at the bottom of the second, I could see the batter toss his bat and skip towards first, see his languid jog around the diamond and the ovation at the bench awaiting him.

My father was back at the car before the game restarted. He was frowning, his folded glasses dangling from the open collar of his shirt.

'What's the matter?' I said as he threw himself behind the wheel.

'Ah,' he said, 'some nonsense about a work permit. They have *concerns* about . . . something or other. There are *logistics* to consider, apparently. You know the way lawyers are.'

'Don't get me started,' I said.

He closed his eyes and breathed deeply, white lines

persisting in the red scorch of his forehead. From his shirt pocket he pulled two tickets with 'Giants' printed on them in flowing orange cursive. 'But they gave me these as some kind of apology,' he said. 'What do you think?'

'What do you think I think?' I said.

We swept through evacuated streets and parked in the stadium lot. My father led the way to the gate and ushered me through the turnstile. Inside, the walls and the pillars were of poured concrete, notched and seamed from the moulds. Huge vinyl banners hung from orange rafters, depicting sluggers at the moment of contact or just afterwards, eyes trained upward to track the progress of a ball. There were merchandise stands and hotdog stands, long snaking queues for bathrooms. It was dark, but through an archway on the second level I could see a perfect rectangle of clear blue sky.

'You hungry?' my father said.

'I could eat, I suppose,' I shrugged.

He laughed. 'What else is new?'

I sucked in my gut: a reflex.

In the hotdog line, I watched the people around me, remembering a Millwall match we'd seen on a visit to London some years before. The crowd there all had been young men, skinny and taut with violence, barging and singing 'No surrender to the IRA'– which had made my father quiet. But this crowd was gentler: boyfriends and girlfriends walking arm in arm, old fathers and grown sons joking over beers, parents with little girls in matching oversized jerseys. My father bought a beer for himself, a

Coke for me, a hotdog each. We stood at a counter off to the side and ate together. The meat was warm and spicy, the ketchup tangy and sweet. My father finished his hotdog in four big bites and left still chewing.

'Come on,' he said over his shoulder as he led the way to our section.

I climbed the ramp, heard the crowd detonate and stepped from darkness into light. At the arch, I looked out over a tide of faces breaking against green grass and the white on black of the scoreboard. We squeezed past the bony knees of a little old lady in a short leather coat with a fox-fur collar, who scratched at a scorecard with a nub of a pencil. 'A bookie,' my father whispered.

On the far side of our seats, two men in orange-and-black windbreakers rocked back and forth and booed the Angel on deck. One wore a cap backwards atop a head the shape and hue of an underripe aubergine. The other was bald; his eyebrows were ginger and his eyes aimed ever so slightly in contrary directions.

'Men,' my father said.

Their names were Ryan and Steve. They were brothers, carpenters and 'the biggest Giants fans you're ever likely to meet'. It was Steve's – the aubergine's – birthday.

'Many happy returns.' My father raised his beer. '*Sláinte.*'

'*Sláinte!*' Ryan said and mentioned some distant Sligo connection. And soon he and Steve had become my father's guides, explaining the positions and the scoring and the way that innings worked. In the middle of the fifth, with the Giants up four–nothing, my father bought a round of beers 'to thank our new friends for their hospitality', and poured half of his into my empty cup. He held a finger to his lips.

'Don't tell your mother,' he said.

★

Bottom of the seventh, with a runner on third, a Giant swung wildly at a dipping pitch. The ball popped up and sailed against the blue, froze for a moment at its apex and dropped towards us. I stretched out an arm and knew that I would catch it, but Steve barged in front of his brother and my father to stretch a gloved hand across my face. My father's shoulder jammed into mine; I crumpled into my seat. The ball hit the centre of Steve's glove with a fat *plop*.

'Holy shit!' Ryan said. 'A foul ball!'

'Damn!' I said, rubbing my shoulder. 'I almost had that. Nice one, Steve.'

'Thanks, kid,' Steve said as a white smile opened in his purple face.

'You know,' my father said, 'my son almost had that.'

'Almost.' Ryan clapped the heavy flats of his hands on his knees. 'But didn't.'

'Because your brother took it from him.'

Steve grinned as though there were some joke he wanted to be in on – but there was no joke.

'Dad,' I said. 'It's fine.'

'Hey,' Steve laughed, 'I take nothing from no one, okay? I took it from the *air*, man.'

'Relax,' Ryan said, leaning over my father, the armpits

of his jacket swishing. 'That's my brother's ball. And my brother's going to keep it. So don't make me angry, huh? Just forget it.'

His breath smelled of onions. My father didn't flinch.

'Hey,' Steve said, 'let's just watch the game, okay?'

I stared straight ahead at the mass of faces jumbled in the opposing stand, above them the glare of the sky, below them the glare of the field. Strike followed ball. Line drive followed ground-out. The little old bookie's pencil scratched against her scorecard.

'I'll buy it from you,' my father said.

'Come on, man,' Steve said, 'don't do this in front of the kid, okay? Just forget about it.'

'Name your price.'

'It's not for sale,' Ryan said.

It was then that I noticed the thickness of his neck, the heft and power of his thighs. His boots, I saw, were splotched with something brown; the leather at their toes peeled back to show dull metal caps.

'Hundred bucks,' Steve said.

'Goddamnit, Steve, that's *yours*,' Ryan said. 'It's your birthday gift from the San Francisco motherfucking Giants, who, by the way, are *the* greatest team in all of professional sports – not that the Irishman gets that.'

'I could do with a hundred bucks, bro,' Steve said, half-whispering.

'Fifty,' my father said.

'This motherfucker!' Ryan threw up his hands. 'Now he wants to negotiate?'

'Dad,' I said, but my father wasn't listening. He reached into his back pocket for his wallet and pulled out a crisp, green hundred.

'Here,' he said, and held out the note, his fingers pale and thin.

Steve looked at the ball, and I did too: the white leather and the red stitching, the smeared blue lettering on its face where the bat had connected.

'Deal,' Steve said.

My father handed over the money, took the ball and passed it to me without a word. It felt cold and heavy and seemed to bulge in my hand.

'Lucky kid,' Ryan said and spat at the ground but hit his boot. 'Come on, I need a drink.'

He and Steve rose and shoved past my father's knees.

'Excuse me, ma'am,' Ryan said as he sidled past the bookie.

I turned to watch Steve lay an arm across his brother's shoulders.

★

Twilight fell as we drove back, street lights sucking all colours from all things. Roadside billboards advertised strip clubs, chop shops, divorce attorneys. The strippers had narrow eyes and parted lips, the attorneys piles of hair that seemed as hard as helmets. My father pulled in to the space in front of our room and killed the engine. No light showed between the curtains of the lone window. By the door, a skinny gecko nosed the ground and ambled away. I held the ball in my lap and imagined it to be a massive eye, stitched with red blood vessels, its pupil sightless.

'What are you thinking?' my father said.

'Nothing.'

He cuffed the steering wheel with the butt of a hand. 'Listen,' he said, 'you need to learn something, yeah? Sometimes you just have to do what you *have* to do to get what you *want*. You wanted the ball, yeah?'

'Yeah,' I said.

'So I got it for you, yeah? And now you have it, yeah? Aren't you happy?'

'Yeah,' I said.

'Well, good,' he said and struck the wheel again, this time more softly. 'Good.'

We climbed out of the car and went to our room. I sat on the edge of my bed and placed the ball beside me. The bedspread was patterned in green-and-purple paisley, a swarm of fat crescents that seemed to wriggle.

'She's probably at the bar,' my father said as he unbuttoned his shirt. 'Go find her and bring her back, will you? I'm going to change out of this, and then we'll go eat dinner.'

'Okay,' I said and stepped to the door.

'Wait.' My father picked the ball from the bed and brought it to me. His chest was narrow but hard behind his undershirt. 'Show this to your mother.'

I walked in the shadow of an awning abuzz with fluorescent lights, around which a universe of moths beat their papery wings. Through parted curtains I glimpsed the blue wash of televisions on blank walls. I turned the ball over in my hand and stopped feeling bad for Steve; instead, I felt good about my father, sure that he would take care of us in our new life.

The bar was quiet, just a stooped bartender polishing glasses to the *plinky-plonky* sound of piped-in jazz piano; his nose was stubby, as though redesigned by an upper-cut. I turned down a pink-carpeted hallway whose walls were hung with faded watercolours of wine country. The lobby was cold and scented with the supermarket-freezer smell of old air conditioning. There was no one at the front desk. There was no sign of my mother. But when I stepped through an open sliding door onto the pool deck, I saw her sitting in a plastic chair. She was still in her swimsuit, her legs still bare. Her hair was dry and chlorine-burnt. The skin of her arms was raked all over with gooseflesh. She was shivering.

'Mam?' I said, shoving the ball into the pocket of my shorts.

Her eyes moved lizard-like in my direction. 'Did you eat?' she said.

A breath of steam rose from the pool, lit from below.

'God, Mam,' I said, 'have you been here this whole time?'

'This is where you left me,' she said, her lips blueing at the corners. 'Your father took the key.'

I knelt beside her, grains of sweat-salt scratching in the cleft of my knee. 'Why didn't you ask at reception for another one?'

'And say what?' she said. 'That my husband and son have

13

abandoned me? Do you know how embarrassed I was? Watching all the other families come and go? And they watching me?'

'Come on.' I reached for her elbow, but she pulled away and crossed her arms.

I got to my feet and ran back to our room, the ball jouncing at my hip. I knocked on our door. My father opened it.

'What happened?' he said, though in his face I saw that he understood. 'Wait here. Just wait right here. I'll be right back, I promise.'

For hours, I sat listening to lizards and moths and crickets move beyond the window, rubbing parts of themselves together or against each other. In the morning, I woke to find my mother asleep beside me, my father passed out on the couch with his mouth hanging open in a vague, unspoken vowel. I opened the curtains and sat by the window with the ball in my hand to watch the Suzuki's bonnet flare in the rising sun.

Two months later, my father left Dublin for San Francisco. And a month after that, my mother moved us to an apartment near her sister's on Clanbrassil Street. I don't know if my father took it with him or if I left it behind, but when I unpacked my things to begin my new life I discovered that the ball was gone.

The Comets

Eoin McNamee

JUNE AND KIRSTIE MOVED BACK TO the outskirts of Kilkeel in early autumn and rented one of the chalets. June was already sick with ovarian cancer. The chalets were wooden buildings with flat asphalt roofs. Sand blew against the hedges. The front gardens were unkempt. Troubled lives were to the fore.

June told her daughter that when she was growing up the chalets were the very height of fashion and the whole town stood with their mouths open when the chalet girls went up the town on a Saturday night. When Kirstie asked her why she had left, June said that the town had no inner life.

June told Kirstie stories every day. She said that shooting stars were the spirits of the dead being set free and that you could tell the number of people who died each night if you could count the shooting stars as they blazed through the heavens. When Kirstie asked where she came from June said that she was an angel who flew down from Heaven and that her wings were in a cardboard box on the top shelf of the hot press. There were stories that were just to get you through the next hour and there were stories that were meant for all time.

Eddie had started to come around just before June got sick and he followed them to the chalets. June said that bad taste in men ran in the family and there was nothing she could do about it. Eddie was one of a long line, she said. They were storemen, barmen, migrant workers given to pilferage and absenteeism. Weak-willed princelings of vice.

That autumn June and Kirstie would go for walks down on the esplanade. June wouldn't wear a wig and she said hats were too scratchy.

'You look like an alien,' Kirstie said. June pressed her close to her bony side.

'They'll all be asking, who's the pretty girl with the baldy woman?'

In old photographs June had deep brown eyes and high cheekbones. Now that she was ill her cheekbones seemed to have grown so that her face was all cheekbones with deep shadows instead of eyes above them. Kirstie had her mother's cheekbones but her eyes were blue.

Sometimes they'd stay out until dark and the orange lights along the esplanade came on. At the very edge of the orange glow, before the night sky began, white shapes in flight moved in and out of the light.

'I never saw birds at night before,' Kirstie said.

'That's because they're not birds, they're new souls flying down from Heaven,' June said. They held hands all the way home. Later, when June needed help to walk, Eddie came too.

'I'm a bag of bones,' June said.

Kirstie showed Eddie the white shapes flickering in and out of the light.

'They're the bloody gulls,' he said. 'I don't know what it is about this place. Whoever heard of gulls that fly at night?'

Just before June died the doctors sent her home from hospital. She had a morphine shunt and said she could see birds running up the kitchen walls. June and Kirstie would laugh at the idea of birds in the house.

'Where are the birds coming from?' Kirstie asked.

'I don't know. From far, far away, I think.'

'There's no birds,' Eddie said. 'The morphine is giving you hallucinations. It's bad enough having to cope with you being sick without having to listen to you laughing like fools.'

'What's going to happen to you?' Kirstie said.

'When I die? I'll become a shooting star. Like all the other shooting stars.'

'Where are all the shooting stars going to?'

'To Heaven.'

They took June to hospital, and she died two days later. A lady came to see them and ask about Kirstie and her welfare. Eddie said that he was her father and he would look after her.

This was a lie, but Kirstie didn't say anything. She knew the look in Eddie's eye and she would get to know it a lot better.

Eddie said it would be better if Kirstie didn't see her mother's body or go to the funeral and the lady agreed.

'I want to go to the funeral,' Kirstie said.

'The welfare lady said it would be better if you didn't. It's a cremation.'

'The welfare lady's a bitch,' Kirstie said.

'She is,' Eddie said, 'but I'm worse so fucking watch yourself.'

On the far side of the esplanade there was an arcade called Star Amusements, which was closed for the winter. Kirstie climbed over the sagging fence and walked across the rubber matting where the dodgems ran during the summer. There was a mesh grid overhead and the dodgem cars had comet shapes painted on them. She looked over at the kiosk where they took the money. There was a man standing in it. He was tall and old with a long face. He was wearing a fairground man's coat. He bent down and touched a switch. His voice sounded faraway and hollow. It sounded as if he was speaking from one of the bright comets on the dodgem cars.

'Who are you, and what the hell are you doing here?' he said.

'I'm Kirstie, and I come from down in the chalets.'

'You're the girl whose ma died.'

His booming voice made it sound like he was announcing it so the stars could hear. Kirstie was glad that he said she had died. Other people talked about her passing away.

'She died of ovarian cancer. She saw birds running up the walls before she died.'

'What sort of birds?'

'Colourful ones.'

'At least she never saw a black crow. That would have

been bad.' The man switched off the microphone with a buzzing sound and stepped down from the kiosk.

He came over to her. He was like a bent figure of retribution from an old tale. People would be warned about the error of their ways. They would be told about the sundering to come.

'Is a comet the same thing as a shooting star?' Kirstie asked.

'More or less. I remember your mother from when she was younger.'

'Was she one of the chalet girls?'

'She was better than them. She had a French bob and an aura about her.'

'Did she tell stories then?'

'She'd sit on the rail of the ice rink, and they'd all gather round her. They'd either be bent two double with laughing or crying their eyes out. Who's your father?'

'Mum said I flew down from Heaven and my wings are kept on the top shelf of the hot press. What's your name?'

'Hagan.'

When Kirstie got home that night Eddie had emptied all the kitchen drawers out onto the floor.

'What are you looking for?'

'Insurance policy,' Eddie said. 'She had one somewhere. I heard her talking about it on the phone once.'

'She had a French bob,' Kirstie said.

'I haven't got a red cent after all the time I spent looking after her.'

'And an aura.'

'The hell with her and her aura,' Eddie said.

After that Kirstie tried to stay out of the house. She walked to the hospital most nights. The route took her past the amusements, and if Hagan was there she waved at him. One clear, cold night Kirstie was standing at the hospital railings and realised there was somebody standing beside her. It was Hagan.

'What are you looking at?' he said. She pointed. There was a tall chimney rising from a long dark building in the middle of the hospital complex and every few minutes orange sparks would rise from it to be caught by the winds that blow on high and whirl away into the blackness of the night.

'What's that?' he said.

'Crematorium.'

'Souls?' he said. She nodded.

They watched the sparks blow down over the esplanade where the gulls rode the updraughts, dipping down out of the dark then wheeling back into it as the sparks flew out to sea. They stayed there for some time thinking about souls ablaze in the long black building.

When Eddie found out where she was going at night he told her to stay away from Hagan.

'He turned funny after his daughter was lost.'

'What do you mean lost?'

'She disappeared off the beach. Swept out to sea is the word. He was never right after it.'

'I wonder what it would be like to be a missing girl,' Kirstie said. She would be good at it. She would treat it as a calling. Once she was gone there would be no being found.

Eddie emptied all the drawers in June's tallboy. Her clothes lay everywhere in the bedroom.

'It's for you,' he said. 'The insurance money is for you, so I want you to think about where she hid the policy.'

'I don't know what a policy is,' Kirstie said.

'It's a bit of paper with words on it,' Eddie said.

One evening when Eddie was out she put the stepladder against the pine slats of the hot press and climbed up. At the top she found a cardboard shirt box hidden under blankets. The box was sealed with Sellotape. The corners of the cardboard were foxed and the tape had yellowed. She carried the box carefully down the ladder. She shook it and there was a rustling sound from the inside.

It had been dark all day, cold fronts approaching from the north. The storm struck about teatime. Kirstie wrapped the box carefully in cling film and put it in a plastic bag, then she carried it down to the amusements. It was all she could do to hold on to the plastic bag. It was all she could do not to be blown off her feet and up over the rooftops of the chalets and far, far away.

At Star Amusements, the wind tugged at the roof of the dodgems, and the cars rocked and shook as though they contained comets that were restless and wanted to be released into the wild night. The sea surged over the esplanade and there were hanks of weed caught in the railings. Kirstie didn't see Hagan at first. She looked upwards, but it wasn't a night for winged things. Then she saw Hagan standing in the kiosk. He was staring out to sea. He looked as if he had summoned the storm. The night was full of wrath, and he was its master.

Kirstie climbed up to the kiosk. Hagan turned to her, and she saw his eyes were full of tears.

'What happened to your daughter?' Kirstie said.

'I never looked after her,' Hagan said, 'and she took her own life. Walked into the sea. Teenagers.'

He could see that Kirstie didn't know what he meant about teenagers. That they didn't run away when they saw death coming. They tried to reason. They made pacts with it.

'Will you keep this for me?' She took the box out of the plastic bag.

'I will,' he said.

'Promise?'

'With all my heart.'

Kirstie thought that for all its trouble, it was a great heart and although some parts were ruined others were intact. She handed the box to him.

Eddie was in the living room when she got home. She had left the ladder up against the shelves of the hot press, and he had found it.

'What were you doing up there?' he said.

'Nothing.'

'What did you find?'

'I never found anything.'

'You'll tell me where the policy is or you'll get the back of my hand.'

Eddie kept searching for the insurance policy and he gave Kirstie the back of his hand more than once that night and on other nights. He made sure to hit her where it wouldn't show, but she walked like she was a bag of bones. He pulled up part of the kitchen floor and made her crawl under the boards among the cables and copper pipes.

At school Kirstie was classified as troubled. The teachers were wary. The other girls kept a respectful distance from her. Their mothers said that she was allowed to roam the town all hours of the day and night. Her schoolmates saw an emissary from the land of errant girls.

When Eddie had searched the rest of the house, he broke into the roof space and threw down everything that was there. A bag of babygros spilled on the floor. Kirstie picked up a pink one. It was tiny and faded.

'I probably wore this when I arrived,' she said.

'Arrived from where?' Eddie said.

'From up there.' She pointed upwards.

'What are you talking about?' Eddie said.

'You know,' Kirstie said.

'All I know is that you were born in Newry General Hospital. That's what your ma said.'

Kirstie shook her head and looked down at the floor.

'She never told you?' Eddie was covered in white plaster dust. He looked like a ghost so that Kirstie wasn't sure if she should believe in him or not.

'Your da was a sailor off one of the container boats. A Latvian or some such. He put her on her back then took off and she never seen him again. Did she not tell you?'

Kirstie was quiet for a long time. Eddie started to laugh. It didn't sound the way ghostly laughter was supposed to sound.

'I found a box,' she said.

Eddie stopped laughing. 'Where?' he said.

'In the hot press.'

'What kind of a box?'

'Cardboard.'

'What was in it?' he said. Kirstie shrugged.

'What did you do with it?'

'I took it,' she said, 'and I threw it into the sea. Far, far away.'

When he had finished Eddie knew he had gone too far. He had felt something break under his fist and now there was blood coming out of the girl's mouth, and she was breathing in a strange way. He regretted having got mixed up with Kirstie and her mother and it was time to leave. He walked to the door without making much noise and went out into the moonlit night.

Kirstie looked around the room. Eddie had pulled out the back of the sofa and broken into the walls. The house looked as if it had been turned inside out. She got to her feet. She fully expected to see birds crawling up the walls at any minute and knew what she had to do.

Outside the moonlight shone across the sea, and the heavens were ablaze with stars.

Hagan saw her walking across the dodgems rink. She was walking very carefully as though she was balancing something delicate. When he got to her he saw blood on her cardigan and on her mouth. Her cheekbones were like razors.

'I need my box,' she said.

'You need a doctor,' he said.

'My box.'

Hagan looked at her for a long time then went to fetch the box from where he had left it under the generator. It was always the same when death was around. There was no point arguing.

Hagan brought the box and set it down. He took the Sellotape off and lifted the lid. The tissue paper lining it was old and brittle. He folded it back. Something stirred in the bottom of the box.

'Take them out,' she said. He reached into the bottom of the box and lifted the wings out. He felt them flutter as he touched them, and then they were still again. They were dusty, and the fittings where they went around the shoulders were a little frayed but the tips of them caught the moonlight.

'They're a bit small,' Kirstie said. Hagan turned them from side to side, trying to work out how they went on.

'You're holding them upside down,' Kirstie said. She coughed and dark blood ran down her chin. 'Give them to me,' she said.

The wings were too small to fit over her shoulders but there wasn't much in it. She took off her cardigan.

'You should take off the vest as well,' Hagan said. He helped her take it off. Her skin was translucent in the moonlight and he thought that he could see her heart beating very slowly. This time the wings went over her shoulders. Hagan fixed the straps.

The fastenings were stiff, and it was a little while before she was ready. Hagan looked at her then turned away. The darkness where her eyes had been was so deep that he thought it might devour him if he looked too closely.

They found Kirstie's blood-stained cardigan and vest on the beach the next morning. People gathered on the esplanade to watch the search for the body. They talked about the missing girl as though they knew her. She was proof that the town had an inner life after all. It was entitled to its own imaginings.

The police went back to the chalet and saw the blood-stains there. Eddie was arrested. He said he had nothing to do with Kirstie's disappearance and they had no body but he was sent to prison.

When Eddie got out of prison he drifted north, moving from hostel to hostel and sometimes sleeping on the streets. He drank in parks with others. They took the faithlessness of the universe for granted and when Eddie told them that it was possible for people to just disappear they nodded in mournful agreement.

The grass grew long in the front garden of the chalet. More families moved out. The chalets were cold in the wintertime, and the flat roofs sagged more with each season. Not many people came to the Star Amusements, but when they did Hagan set the cars in motion and the poles struck blue fire from the roof grid and the comets blazed across the rink and when Hagan looked up he could see bright sparks blowing off the land and white shapes riding the night breezes at the edge of the sea.

Emergency

Mary Morrissy

SHE WAKES IN THE ATTIC ROOM to a low drone overhead
and thinks it at first to be a large commotion of the skies,
a thunder roll. She climbs out of the high bed and goes
to the window, low eaves crowding at her shoulders. The
noise that woke her has folded itself back into the night.
The moon is a fat, luminous comma pierced by a single
spear of blue-lead cloud; otherwise, there is nothing to
see; nothing new, that is. Just the stand of bare trees at the
back of the house, their shadows like scribbles on the bowl
of the long meadow that sweeps up to the big ridge. Just
as she is about to turn away, a beautiful white mushroom
floats down, a billowing umbrella. It slowly sails behind the
trees, then faints from view. She throws on a dressing gown
over her nightie, slips her feet into cold shoes and creeps
downstairs. Her mother is already there, standing in the
kitchen, steeped in moonlight.

'What are you doing up?'

'Did you see it?' she asks her mother's back.

'Shh,' her mother hisses.

She wonders why. There is no one else in the house to
wake. Just the two of them, at war. Her mother turns reluc-
tantly, as if the last thing she wants to do is to face Brenda.

In this light, Brenda can see the fine lines etched on her brow and the sour brackets around her mouth. She is in her pyjamas, a striped pair of Brenda's father's that she has taken to wearing since he's been gone. They're too big, of course, so they shroud her mother's figure and make her look slope-shouldered. The collar gapes at her breast, the sleeves graze her knuckles, and the legs are turned up in slovenly rolls.

'What is it?'

'A German,' her mother says in a loud whisper.

'What?' Brenda says stupidly.

'A spy, I'm sure of it.'

It's cold in the kitchen. They used to tamp down the stove overnight, but with the turf in such short supply, they stop feeding it at nine and leave the fire go out. They both stare out the window.

'A spy?'

'Who else would arrive by parachute in the dead of night?'

So that's what it was.

'What will we do?'

Her mother pulls open the drawer in the kitchen table and grabs a pair of scissors, the ones she uses for sewing. Sharpened weekly. Before the Emergency, her mother was a dressmaker, making beautiful things out of nothing. Now she does alterations. Brenda marvels at the transformations her mother achieves: a child's jacket magicked out of a man's overcoat, a dress worn at the arse cut down into a blouse with a tie scarf made from the unspoiled hemline, bloomers blossoming from ballgowns. She admires what her mother can do, while hating the necessity of it. The war, her father gone, and now, the alterations; everything changed.

'Get your coat,' her mother commands as she shrugs on Brenda's father's black mac, pulls on a pair of thick socks and plunges her feet into his wellingtons.

'You're going out there?'

'*We're* going out there,' her mother says. 'What are you standing there for? Gawping?' Everything about Brenda seems to irritate her mother. That she's a girl, that she's fourteen. 'Didn't you hear me? Get your coat.'

Brenda's coat is cut down from one of her mother's – a big tweed yoke with saucer buttons and a rough-hewn look.

'What if he has a gun?'

Her mother raises the scissors and stabs the air, then she marches towards the back door. It creaks as she opens it. It seems a large sound in the silent night. Her mother has a torch, but she doesn't turn it on. They walk gingerly past the outside lavatory. Some of her father's tools are stored in its lee side, and her mother grabs a pitchfork and thrusts it at Brenda. What, she wonders, is she meant to do with it? They go through the wicket gate that leads into the meadow. They climb up the incline towards the stand of trees, and there it is. A parachute, like a cloud fallen to earth. As they draw close, they see the figure of a man. He is stretched out on his back, his top half smothered by the snagged folds of the parachute so that only his legs are sticking out. They stop in unison. There is no sound but

29

Brenda's fearful breathing. She cannot believe they are out here alone in the dead of night with a German spy within feet of them. She has no idea what her mother is going to do next. Drive the scissors through his heart? Her mother darts ahead towards the body – is it a body? – and places her boot under the ribcage and digs in. A groan emanates. She bends over and unveils the man's face by drawing back the parachute with both hands. She shines the torch directly into his eyes. Brenda, hanging back, pitchfork held like a staff, sees the man hold up his hands to shield his eyes from the beam.

'Agh,' he says, and Brenda catches a glimpse of a pale face. She expected him to be in uniform, with crests and epaulettes, but he's in civvies. Brenda thinks of her father; this is how he looked marching off to war.

'Who are you?' her mother barks. 'Where is your gun?'

The man makes a movement, leaning up on his elbow and raising his free hand in surrender. He twists his body slightly and taps a lumpen thing at his waist. Her mother raises the scissors like a dagger. The pinking edges glint.

'Brenda,' she says, 'take his gun.'

Brenda drops the pitchfork and moves forward gingerly. She bends over the German; he looks up at her and smiles. She is not expecting this; she thought he would be fierce, angry. She draws the gun from a stiff leather holster on his belt. He is all trussed up, quartered by the straps of the parachute on his shoulders and at his crotch. Embarrassed, she looks away. The German's amused-looking eyes on her make her fumble, and once she has the gun free, she drops it.

'Brenda!' her mother cries out, and it's the first time she sounds panicky, not in control. Brenda picks the gun up with both hands and points it at the German.

'Watch him,' her mother commands. She lays the torch down on the trampled grass and bends over the German. Brenda trains the gun on him. He's a young man, she can see now in the dazzling torchlight, heavy eyebrows, grey eyes, a pockmark on his cheek. He is grazed and bleeding from his forehead, and his face is dirty. Is that from being dragged through the muck by the parachute, or did he black up for this mission? He doesn't look threatening, or different, or foreign in any way. She doesn't know what she was expecting. He looks directly at her, and she can feel her will quaver and her arms tremble. Who knew a gun could be so heavy? What is her mother doing – scrabbling about like this – when this fella could at any moment leap up and overpower them? He's a soldier, after all, a trained fighter. Just like her father.

No, but that isn't true. Her father's been turned into a soldier by a simple act of will. He used to be the assistant groundsman working for Major Aylward up at the Ballynote Estate. Then he decided to join up, to fight Hitler.

'Mam,' she calls out, as the German reaches one of his arms out towards her. It's not aggressive, it's supplicant, dumbly negotiating. It reminds her of her father, up a ladder in the orchard, his head in a cloud of foliage, dropping down high-hanging apples while she stands on the ground ready to catch them in a basket.

'What is it?' her mother says.

'He's moving.'

Her mother is standing over him now, tugging at the parachute harness. 'We have to get this off.'

'Mam,' Brenda wails, 'he's . . .'

'Stop it, Brenda. He's not going anywhere, not with that leg,' she says, without looking up from her task. One of the German's legs is stretched out straight; the other is twisted under him at a funny angle. But he moves again, and Brenda lets out a yelp. Her mother lifts the torch from the grass and shines it directly into the German's eyes.

'Now look it here,' she says, pointing vigorously at Brenda. 'She'll shoot you if you move again. And don't pretend you don't understand. Everyone understands a gun.'

To emphasise the point, she waves the scissors in his face. She has given up trying to unhook the harness and is now sitting astride him, sawing through the fabric straps with the scissors. If anyone came across them now, they'd think her mother and the spy were a courting couple, going at it in the grass. Her mother and a German spy! The parachute lies beside them, roiling slightly like a cloud that might drift off of its own volition.

'She won't shoot me, ma'am,' the German says, and he chuckles. He sounds exactly like an Irishman, but, Brenda thinks, maybe they teach them to talk like that. 'She won't shoot one of her own.'

'You're Irish?' her mother splutters.

'Local,' he says. 'Moveen.'

Her mother ceases her sawing; Brenda lowers the gun.

'I don't believe you,' her mother says.

'My father's name is . . .'

Her mother puts up her hand to silence him. 'I don't want to hear.'

Brenda feels suddenly deflated. All this time she's been peering at him, trying to discover what a dangerous enemy looks like, and all he is is a boy from Moveen.

'So what are you doing landing down on top of us like this if you're not working for the Germans?' Her mother sounds irritated, as if he'd tracked mud across the kitchen floor.

'I *am* working for the Germans, ma'am; I'd do anything to fix those Brits.'

Her mother disengages and stands up, hands on her hips.

'Are you going to call the guards, ma'am?'

'And why would I do that?'

'For the reward.'

'What reward?' her mother asks.

'Three hundred pounds,' he says.

Brenda has never seen twenty pounds, let alone three hundred.

'I don't care about a reward,' her mother says.

'Mam!' Brenda thinks about what they could do with money like that. They could live out the Emergency without a worry in the world. They could buy a new stove. Her mother could stop taking in sewing. They could stretch to shop-bought clothes, even. Or schoolbooks.

'You be quiet,' her mother warns.

'So?' the German queries. Brenda can't keep on calling him the German, but she doesn't know what else to call him.

'I don't know or care what you're up to with your silly games,' her mother says. 'The only thing I want from you is this.' She points to the parachute, which lies at her feet like a collapsed sail.

'The chute?' he asks, incredulously.

'Yes,' she says, nodding firmly. 'It's silk. Real, ivory silk.'

Somewhere, a dog barks. Her mother freezes. It could be a stray on the prowl, or it could have an owner attached. One of the other groundsmen, or the Major himself taking his hounds for a walk. He's an old man who doesn't sleep and is odd enough to walk a pack of dogs in the dark.

'We've got to get you inside,' her mother says to the German. 'I'll splint up your leg, and then you can be on your way.'

'I have another chute for my suitcase,' he offers. He sounds reasonable now, like a travelling salesman with more merchandise out in his car.

'Go look in the parkland up above,' her mother commands.

Brenda is unsure about leaving, but her mother motions her away impatiently.

'I can handle a boy from Moveen,' she says, and to him, 'What age are you?'

'Twenty-three, ma'am.'

'And what do you think you're doing?'

Brenda hands her mother the pistol; she doesn't hear his reply.

★

The pencil cloud has drifted away, leaving the moon clear, a luscious eyelash. She climbs up the long meadow to the ridge, where it becomes the landscaped grounds of Ballynote. She can make out the grey outline of the house, with its two bowed wings, and the puddled glint of the driveway that winds its way up to the house. She tramps along the boundary for nearly ten minutes before she finds the suitcase, stuck in a midden of ivy and brambles in an area of rough out beyond the stables. It has a smaller parachute attached to it. This one's made of tougher stuff and is khaki-coloured, like muddied grass and rusted leaves. She opens the suitcase. There's a shirt and a jumper and something that looks like a radio, and a little notebook with figures in it. In the rough-hewn pocket under the hinges, she finds cash. She counts it out. Three twenties and four singles. She is about to put it back when she thinks . . . that fella, who's a spy, will just take the money away with him, and why should he? He's the trespasser, the traitor. She folds the notes over and pushes them deep into the pocket of her coat. She carries the suitcase and the parachute further into the rough under the oak trees and stows them away near the stone wall, well out of sight. She makes her way back, fingering the notes in her pocket. If her father doesn't come back, she tells herself, she and her mother are going to need every penny of it.

The only time she heard her parents argue was when her father announced he was volunteering.

'They won't want *you!*' her mother said.

'Major Aylward has fixed it up for me. A reference. All I have to do is get across the border, and I can enlist in Belfast. Hundreds of boys are going.'

'Boys – exactly! You're thirty-seven years of age, Gerry. You're a married man, in case you've forgotten.'

Through the banisters Brenda could see the little bald spot on the top of her father's head and the bulwark of his shoulder. He was standing in the kitchen at the foot of the stairs. Brenda was crouched at the return, invisible.

'The Major said he'll hold my position for me. He'd go himself if he were able.'

The Major had served in the last war and had a gammy leg as a result.

'That's all fine and dandy for the Major, but it's not our war. We're neutral, remember?' her mother said.

Her father had missed his chance in the last war. He often told the story. The marching band trumpeting its way into town. Like the Pied Piper with all the young lads following in their wake. They set up tent on the Fair Green. He and two pals had gone to sign up; they'd filled in the forms and all, lying about their age. His mother had somehow got wind of it and turned up at the tent and read the riot act, shouting at officers and boys alike. Brenda could imagine it – she could easily place the Granny Clancy she knew in the middle of the scene. Crooked and thin, waving her stick in the air. She had died when Brenda was ten, but there was no forgetting her fearsome stare and her whiplash tongue.

'There's no such thing as neutral,' he said. 'We all have to take sides in the end.'

Her mother was out of sight at the sink. Brenda could hear the slurp of suds.

'And what am I supposed to do?'

'There'd be a soldier's salary . . .'

'Oh, I see, I'm supposed to scrimp and save on a soldier's shilling . . .'

There was never any mention of Brenda in her mother's arguments.

'The Major wouldn't see you stuck . . .'

'The Major, the Major,' she mimicked in a sing-songy voice. 'I don't know which one of you is the bigger fool. Have you forgotten Admiral Somerville in west Cork? They took him out and shot him for giving fellas references.'

'Margaret,' her father said. Brenda knew that tone, sensual with a smile in it.

'No,' her mother shouted. 'Don't use that sweet talk on me. What if you end up dead? Then what? All for nothing!'

Brenda could hear the catch in her mother's voice. Then some straightening of mood.

'They'll turn you down, and you'll be back here with your tail between your legs.'

Her father made a move towards her. Her mother had given up on the wash-up and was sitting at the head of the table. Brenda couldn't see her face, but her damp reddened hands were splayed on the scrubbed pine like flayed fish.

'But don't expect a welcome from me when you do.'

They patched things up before he went, but her mother has been angry every day since. It's not that her mother isn't strong; alone, she is the strongest woman Brenda knows. She's had to fight her on everything – staying at school, for one. (Her mother was taken out of school at twelve and apprenticed to a dressmaker.) They've argued about the cost of keeping her shod, as if Brenda is deliberately wearing out her shoes. The price of schoolbooks – four bob for a Nesfield's Grammar! When her father is around, her mother is warm and weak, easier to cajole.

'Your mother's like a teenager,' her father once said to her, foolishly, Brenda thought. 'Still ardent.'

When Brenda gets back to the spot where the German landed, there is no sign of him or her mother. The only evidence is the trampled ground. The parachute is tethered now – two or three rocks have been placed on top of it to keep it in place. She winds her way down to the house. The wicket gate is wide open, and the lamp is on in the kitchen. She can see the German sitting at the table. There is no sign of her mother. When she steps into the kitchen, Brenda finds she is on her knees at the German's feet. There is a tight bandage wrapped around his leg, fashioned out of the straps of the parachute harness, and her mother has managed to get one of her father's wellingtons over it. His left foot is still in his town shoe. She wonders how her mother managed to manoeuvre him into the house without putting her arm around him and allowing him to lean on her.

'He volunteered?' the German is saying. 'The eejit! This is our trouble, always beholden to the bastards!'

'Did you find it?' her mother asks, rising to standing.

'It was too dark. I couldn't see a thing.' Brenda colours as she thinks of the wad of notes in the well of her pocket.

'No sign of it at all?' the German asks.

'It must have been blown further off, or else it's caught in the trees,' her mother says.

The German gives Brenda a funny look. He's been cleaned up. The cuts on his face iodined, his hair damp at the temples. With his face sponged down, he looks less feral. He has clear skin and the beginnings of stubble. The remains of a sandwich sit on a plate on the table, and the dregs of a cup of tea. Her mother has been busy. Brenda feels like she's interrupted something. Like coming upon her parents hurriedly disentangling.

'You should be going,' her mother says loudly, pointing to the kitchen clock. As if, Brenda thinks, he really were German and has to be shouted out. 'It's six fifteen.'

He rises and shuffles to the door, leaning on Granny Clancy's whitethorn stick which her mother has bequeathed to him.

'Show him the back way to the main road, Brenda,' her mother says.

'Me?' Brenda says. 'Why me?'

'I've got to get rid of the evidence,' her mother says, nodding towards the hill behind the house. The parachute. The only things that matters. She peers out at the encroaching light. 'It's nearly dawn. He needs to be gone.

Don't worry – he's quite harmless.'

They leave by the front door this time. Brenda finds herself hurrying furtively with the German following haltingly behind her. They walk in silence for half a mile. The only house they pass is the Morrisons', where the cows are already bellowing to be milked. On the horizon, light is invading the sky. They reach the fork in the road.

'If you take this way,' Brenda says, pointing left, 'you'll reach Shanakyle.'

'You took the money, didn't you?' he says to her.

'I took nothing.'

'Aren't you the cool customer all the same?' he says and presses his face close to hers. His breath smells of whiskey. Has her mother been feeding him drink? 'Like mother, like daughter.'

When he kisses her, his tongue feels hard and cold. It is her first kiss, like that, and when he releases her, he mutters, 'This didn't happen.'

As he hobbles away, she isn't sure if he means the kiss or the entire night.

It is effortful work trying to tame the acres of silk. Her mother measures it – twenty-four feet in diameter. Brenda is kept from school, and they spend the rest of the morning carving it up. It fills the entire floor space of the kitchen with all the furniture pushed back. Her mother cuts along the seams while Brenda holds the sections taut. When they are cut away, Brenda folds the giant triangles and stows them in the blanket box.

'Look at this,' her mother says, reading out the words stamped in large black lettering in one corner of the field of material. 'Richard V. Kehler & Sohn, Berlin-Neukölln.' She leans back on her hunkers. 'Imagine, your father could be there,' she says dreamily.

Brenda knows from the broadcasts that wherever her father is, he isn't in Germany. She feels the old resentment with her mother rising. Only she could see a man falling from the sky as a direct message to her, a message of love.

Her mother makes herself a blouse and three pairs of knickers; she calls them her German bloomers. She makes Brenda a slip and promises when the Emergency is over that she will trim the hem and bodice with lace. Brenda feels funny about the slip and is glad that it is hidden underneath her clothes. It is like being in the secret embrace of a German, which is the only way she can think of the boy from Moveen, the spy from over the mountain. He's in jail now. He made it home to his own people, but then his father reported him to the guards.

'His own people turned him in,' her mother says. Brenda wonders if the spy's father got the reward; she wonders if her mother is thinking the same thing. But her mother doesn't say anything; the silk seems more important to her than anything else. It is the only time they talk about that night. The German must have said nothing about Brenda or her mother when he was picked up. Brenda's relieved. Does kissing a spy constitute treason? She hides the money in a biscuit tin and buries it in a little grave at the back of the lavatory, thinking of the parable of the talents. It is the first secret she keeps from her mother; the first of many.

*

Her father comes home unscathed. He arrives in the late afternoon, walking from the village, looking like a soldier in his khaki uniform and carrying a kit bag. For days her mother has been getting all dressed up, putting on her navy calico dress that was her Sunday best before the Emergency. There is no sign of the parachute blouse. She is flighty and nervous, running to the front door every ten minutes and craning her head up the road. In the end, she's in the lavatory when he arrives, and it's Brenda who sees him first, when, under instruction, she steps out onto the road keeping watch for her mother. It's summer, and the ditches are thick with cow parsley. He drops his bag when he sees her, and she runs to him.

'How's my girl?' he asks, then, 'Where's your mother?'

He disengages and hurries towards the house. Brenda follows him, thinking of the buried box, escape.

They're in the hallway when her mother appears. Flustered, her tawny hair aflame.

'Brenda got there before you,' he says, laughing.

Standing behind him, she sees an expression flicker across her mother's face, a mean, unguarded look.

After tea, her father hoicks the kit bag onto the kitchen table and spills out its moss-coloured contents. Down at the bottom, he finds a slim package, which he gives to her mother.

'Silk stockings,' he says, 'all the way from Paris. Like gold dust these are,' he says, as he slips one of his hands into their feet and rubs them along her mother's cheek. 'Feel that!'

'Yes,' her mother says, and shoots Brenda a conspiring glance as if they're in cahoots with one another. 'I can't remember the last time I saw silk.'

For Keeps

Belinda McKeon

NOBODY LOOKS AT HER ANY MORE because she is ugly.

A woman — she is that woman — walking down Exchequer Street without a single pair of eyes latching on to her. Without that thing; that thing she used to take for granted. When it had stopped, for the first while, it had seemed to her that people were somehow distracted, that it was just another aspect of the business that was pushing in on everything by then; that people had so much on their minds that they could not even look at one another on the footpath, could not even register other people as they passed. And then it hit her. That it was not the economy, stupid. That it was the years.

You are not *ugly*, Elizabeth; that is Philip's voice. Philip is not with her on Exchequer Street just now; he is in his office in a building on the other side of the city. He is getting ready to leave. To meet Elizabeth for a drink in the bar she has chosen for their conversation, the bar in the Central Hotel, where she usually stays, now, when she is in Dublin, since she can hardly stay where she always stayed before. She can hardly stay in the house she chose with Philip;

the house she left. You are not *ugly*, Philip's voice says in Elizabeth's head, and he sounds irritated. Tired of her. Tired of her stories. For a moment, Elizabeth is reassured.

Then Philip speaks again. This time, he starts as though from the beginning. You are not *ugly*, Elizabeth, he says, and then he pauses, and she hears a little laugh. A silent laugh; a breath, really, an exhalation, finding its shape in a smirk. You are not ugly, Elizabeth, he says again, in exactly the same tone. You're just unremarkable. And Elizabeth can see his face, then, and his gaze slides away.

This is how she knows that she was right to end things with Philip. Because she is capable of imagining him saying such things to her. Philip would never; Philip would never say to Elizabeth, you are just unremarkable. Not even after what she has done; not even after all the things that have, after all, already been said. But in her head, she hears him, and that is enough. That may as well be the same.

Earlier today, she thought she saw him. It was in Kilmainham; she was coming from the gallery, nowhere near to where Philip, on a working day, would be. Philip, or the man who was Philip for a mistaken second, was driving a Volvo estate, heading out of the city. It was a new model, or a newish one, not one of the older Volvos which trundled contentedly around the streets of Greenpoint these days, wearing their dirt and scratches proudly, dogs and children and found pieces of lumber propped up in their back seats. A bright yellow 1980s model had been the car of Elizabeth's childhood, its form as familiar, as folded into the family unit, as the forms of her parents, of her siblings. And fuelled, it came back to her, as she blinked after the not-Philip Philip, by a bass cylinder in the boot; by an actual Calor Kosangas cylinder, in matching yellow. *I couldn't take that risk*, she had overheard her father say to her mother, once, when there had been some problem with the cylinder, some danger – what danger, with a tank of gas in the back of a car, could there possibly be? – and Elizabeth, nine or ten at the time, had been dazzled, intensely moved, by his obvious concern. Her father, sounding like a TV father, hectic with the drama of what was happening, puffed up with regard. *I couldn't take that risk; I couldn't take it* – and probably, Elizabeth sees now, he was only annoying her mother's head.

And anyway, that was not Philip, in the Volvo, driving west.

There are shops on Exchequer Street that seem as though they should not be here; as though they should not be surviving. This city has become funny that way. The shops, for example, selling little flecked slabs of soap, and glass jars of cream, and bath stuff in glass bottles with stubby glass stoppers. They are everywhere in New York, these things, as well, these imitation apothecaries. As though you would wander in, with your wicker shopping basket, and someone would weigh the grains for you, or pour the tonic for you, or cut for you the brown paper and the brown length of twine. And in the windows of the cafes, all the cafes, are women who have their mothers' mannerisms, who watch each other, who talk to each other, raising their eyebrows, tilting their chins, thinning their smiles, in precisely the

way a mother must have done, in a sitting room somewhere, thirty years ago. In a kitchen, or in a garden, or at
a school gate, or in the forecourt of a shop that sold milk,
and bread, and Super Splits and gas: that same way of nodding, *Ah, yeah.* That same way of frowning. That same way
of taking some absent person down. *Sure, doesn't she – sure,
she knows damn well. Sure, I heard – wait till you hear what I
heard –*

At least you weren't married, Elizabeth's mother has said.
At least that. Marriage would have made the end of everything so much more difficult. Marriage would have piled
on the details. Marriage would have – *sign here – and here
– and here – oh, and also just here, thanks –* and it is good that
there has been no need for that. They did not marry, and
they did not buy, and thank the gods of jitters and long
fingers and downright uselessness for that.

They rented. It was a nice house. Off the South Circular:
red brick and scrag grass and a chilly kitchen extension in
which it did not make sense to linger too long. The sitting
room was cosy. The bedroom curtains were always drawn.
The couch was shabby – not shabby chic, just shabby –
and the television was ancient, and in winter the peat
briquettes cost €3.50 and in summer you could sit in the
backyard by the bikes and the washing line and the noise
from the Montessori came across the wall. It is the one
part of Dublin now that is capable of yanking her into a
deep pool of nostalgia; it is not a good idea to walk there,
not a good idea to visit that place in her dreams. It is not
a good idea, either, to zoom in on the street corner on

Google Street View, which is something you can do from anywhere; which is something you can do at any time. Her kitchen table in Greenpoint, for instance; her desk in Varick Street. Her bed; Jesus, the toilet, if the notion takes her. And, once a notion takes you, it has you in its hold.

Everything was fine with Philip. Everything was fine.

But then everything was not fine, which was Elizabeth's fault, of course, and she could not very well stay in the house off the South Circular after that. And New York was an opportunity, and Elizabeth took it.

Do you know what you're doing at all? her mother said.

And no, Elizabeth said, in a tone of voice that implied that the insane thing, the unstable thing, was not when you did not know what you were doing, but when you did, or thought you did. And something else came into her mother's eyes, then, a kind of fear, and her mother turned away.

The Central is cheap, or cheapish, and it is close to everything, whatever everything is. Some of the rooms smell of burnt meat, and at night the noise from Dame Lane keeps her awake, but Elizabeth has long since decided that she likes this noise. It is the noise of the Stag's, after all. It is the noise of Rí-Rá. It is noise like the noise of a July night, once, when she sat on the kerb, with Philip beside her, and tucked under the strap of her vest was the head – not much more – of a flower he had pulled for her off a bush in the Green, and tucked into her mind was the certainty of him, and the beginnings of some kind of shape on some kind of future. Eight years; it is astonishing what you can do with eight years. How you can crash on through

48

them without ever, really, looking around. How you can use them up, that way.

How you can blunt the heart. She knows this now. How you can take the edges off it, so that it cannot catch itself on things the same way. It does not hurt the heart, to do this to it. It does not bother it. The heart is almost mockingly resilient. It works out its own new terms, no matter what you do.

Philip is not in the bar when Elizabeth arrives, although she is late; although she has made sure of this much, to be almost fifteen minutes late. She pushes her way in, through the crowd already there, already almost filling the place, at half six on a Thursday. But then, why should they not be here? They've finished work. This is how it goes; Elizabeth remembers that. She walked past her old office on the way here, and she remembered that feeling; work done for the day, and there is someone who wants the pub in the same way as do you. Enablers, yes; enablers, you might call them, if you were so very awful and so very serious and so very dry.

She sits at the bar. She has a book with her, and she intends to read it while she waits for him to arrive, but instead she takes out her phone, and she dives into the tiny moments of other people's days, and this is what she is still doing when something tells her that Philip has come in the door.

Maybe after years with someone it just gets like that. That you can sense their presence; that, even with your eyes directed elsewhere, you can see them move. That your eyes will always go to them. The way, in a block of text, without even reading it, you can see your own name.

Or maybe this is just Elizabeth. Maybe this is just how Elizabeth is about the words that make up her name. About the people that have made up her life.

She waves. He waves. The mortified choreography of it; the smiling, the eyebrows, the looking away, pretending to have something else to see, the looking back, the inability to hold on to one another's gaze. They hug, and it is too quick to feel like anything, to feel like his arms around her, or her arms around him, to feel like body close to body, or warmth pushing in on warmth. He is thinner, she thinks, as he stands back from her, lifting the strap of his bag away from his chest and over his head. Thinner; is that because of her, or is that to spite her? Visceral fat; that had been one of the things, late on, far into the trouble, that she had added to the snag list. Visceral fat, and what it could do to you, ten, fifteen, twenty years down the line. Which was about as dishonest as Elizabeth could get. About as disingenuous. To rag at him, to needle him, about something that might happen years from now, when now was the problem; when the problem was what she was doing to the now.

'Hi,' he says, a long 'Hi', and she knows that he is nervous. He is not really a *Hi* person, Philip. Though does this make him a *Hello* person? Is *Hello* the kind of thing that Philip used to say? She cannot remember. She has found this; this whole experience has been made up of moments like this. What is he like? What, from him, is likely? And does all of that have to shift, for her, into the past tense now, as well? Because it is hardly, really, any concern of hers, now, what he is like, what kind of greeting he is most inclined to use. *How's it going*; is he a *How's it going* kind of guy? She can hear it, in his voice; she can quite clearly imagine him saying the words, but then, that does not seem right, either. It's the new thinness, she decides; the new thinness throws everything off. The new thinness makes the suit look sharper, and the eyes look colder, and it is no longer possible to be sure. *Hi, Hello, All right?* She is staring at him, trying all of them out, as he sits on the barstool.

He nods. He nods at her; nods down at her body, it seems to Elizabeth, though she realises in the next moment that he is nodding at her clothes. Her new coat with the structured shoulders, the coat she had not wanted to take off until he arrived, so that he would notice how good she looked in it – how thin, or pretend-thin, actually – how pretend-devoid of fat, visceral or intellectual or of any other kind. 'You're looking well,' he says, and he instantly looks away.

'Oh, God,' Elizabeth says, 'I don't know about that.' And a doubtful little laugh, and a wince, and it must, surely, be complete now, the thing that is happening to them, whatever it is; whatever kind of bringing-down or humili-ation this is. She has lived with this man. She has done the furniture thing with him. They have opened bank accounts together; those bank accounts, which, it occurs to Elizabeth, really ought already to be closed. They have done together – *done?* – her mother's illness, her father's illness, his mother's illness, his father's death; she can recall very clearly the look in his eyes as he stepped out of his father's hospital room afterwards, the way he reached, so desperately, for her. And grief sex, which is something so good that Elizabeth is not at all surprised that it is something you are not told about, something you are left to discover all of yourself. All of this, she has done with this man. She has walked in front of him naked at night and in the mornings for years now, her flesh soft where it is, according to the websites, a matter of slovenliness and failure to be soft; her hair overgrown where it is a matter of the same things, of still worse things, to be overgrown. She has cried in front of him, and she has cried with him, and she has cried over him. She has ignored him; she has grown so accustomed to the fact of him, sitting in the same room, sleeping in the same bed, breathing in the same air, that she has forgotten about him, in the way that it is fine to forget about someone; in the way that could be thought of, actually, as love.

And now it has come to this; one maiden aunt talking to another. Now it has come to this rote bit of nonsense, this *lie*; that she is looking well.

Which means that she will have to sleep with him tonight. That this will have to be done. One last time, to spread the balance of things back over itself; the room is just upstairs, just on the floor, actually, right over this bar, which cannot, she now realises, be coincidental; which cannot have nothing to do with the fact that she asked Philip to come and meet her here. She needs it; she needs to hear him say things to her, say things about her body, about her skin. About the absence of her, and the things it has put in his mind; she wants them out on the bedspread, wants them laid out between them like things brought home from abroad.

'How are things?' he says, and he leans an elbow on the bar.

'Grand,' Elizabeth says, and she lifts a hand to get the attention of the girl. 'Pint?' she says, because that is what Philip always has to drink, and in fact she has already, now, called the name of it out to the bargirl.

'Oh, no,' Philip says, not to her but to the girl, who pauses now, tap in hand, a frown of quizzical vexation on her brow. 'Just a Coke for me.'

Elizabeth stares at him. 'Just a Coke?'

He nods without looking.

Elizabeth already has a gin and tonic in front of her; Elizabeth, in fact, is already on gin and tonic number two. It is past seven o'clock in the evening now, so it is not as though she needs to feel bad about this; but she does.

'Are you on antibiotics or something?' she has said, through an attempt at laughter that sounds only like panting, before she can stop herself. 'Having just a Coke,' she adds, and she feels how the blush splays itself on her face. His gaze tracks it, as though it is an insect hiking a trail across her skin.

'No, no,' he says mildly, accepting his drink with a nod of thanks. He slides a fiver across the bar.

'I'll get your drink, for Christ's sake,' Elizabeth says, reaching for her wallet.

'No, no,' he says, in the same tone, and he pours out the Coke. The ice cubes crack and settle; he slugs it slowly, neatly. Elizabeth glances at her glass; the naked, lonely lemon. She is ready for her third, but that, now, is hardly an option. The bargirl raises an eyebrow. With a rapid shake of her head, Elizabeth sends her away.

Nobody looks at her any more because she is ugly. On Exchequer Street, the cafes are closing now, but the restaurants are busy, which is the thing you are not meant to comment on, not if you are a visitor, not if you are a returned whatever-you-are; do not say that thing, Elizabeth's sister said to her, the first time she came home, about how the restaurants are all busy and the pubs are all full, and about how the place does not seem to be doing so badly after all; do not, do not dare say that thing. Yesterday morning, when she said goodbye to her parents, when she told them that she would see them on the next trip back, whenever that might be, there was a scene of sorts, a little farce that she had imagined herself and Philip laughing about this evening, maybe over the second or third pint, maybe upstairs in her single bed. Her father wanted her to take a piece of heather – a clump of rust-coloured stuff actually tugged, that morning, from the bog – back to New York with her. The returning Yank, that was how he insists upon seeing her, even though it has been only a year, even though she has been back to Ireland, within that time, twice.

'Can't you take it, Elizabeth?' her mother said, saying something much more forceful with her eyes, and Elizabeth sulked, and Elizabeth caved, and now the bloody thing is in her suitcase, getting its gnarly dried pubes all over her clothes, and in the morning she will probably be stopped and humiliated at customs, and now she will not even have the memory of this evening – not even the memory of Philip – to ease her on her way.

'All right, *all right*,' she said to her father, taking the damp lump, but that was not enough either; that was not, she knows, the correct etiquette, the proper way in which to behave in these circumstances. She should have been emotional. She should have gazed at the heather wistfully, should have announced that it would always make her feel connected to home. She should have hugged. She should have hugged all and everyone around her; hugged her father, hugged her mother, hugged the heather, hugged the dog. Her father would have nodded, would have been unable to speak. Her mother would have had tears in her eyes.

'For fuck's sake, I took the bloody thing, that should be enough for you,' Elizabeth says now, and too late she realises that she has spoken aloud. Someone, some woman, is staring at her.

But she does not live in this city any more.

The Weather Project

Selina Guinness

IT WAS NOT QUITE DAY WHEN she stirred. Helen was dimly aware of doors closing, lifts descending, as her mind drifted through the anonymous places she had discovered were familiar only the night before. The orange street light outside her hotel window buzzed and flickered against the blinds, goading her awake.

Back in April, she had passed through Heathrow without attention, so focused had she been on the journey's end. She had spent most of the flight in the toilet, despite taking Zofran, while Gerry stood outside, trying to deflect the stewards' anxious enquiries. 'It's just nerves,' she'd heard him say. 'She's always fine when we land.'

But last night, passing through the arrivals hall, she'd spotted the exact table where seven months ago she'd sat fingering the spilt grains of sugar while Gerry fetched his breakfast. She'd been trying hard not to think of what lay ahead when a young girl she recognised from the flight had asked to join her.

'By all means,' she'd said and shifted her bag, ignoring the girl's nervous smile, for she had enough of her own to think over.

When Gerry returned with his coffee and croissant, he'd asked the girl if she wanted anything from the counter. 'No thanks,' she'd replied, 'I'm waiting for *him*.' She'd nodded towards a man in a Kilkenny shirt, standing in the queue.

Helen had assumed *he* must be her father, yet when the man set his tray down, he'd spoken roughly to her.

'Move,' he'd commanded, cramming onto the bench beside her. His tray took up most of the table. He hadn't got the girl anything to eat or drink. It seemed she hadn't expected anything. With the man's fry in front of her, Helen had felt sick again, prompting Gerry to take her hand and ask quietly if they shouldn't get going. She'd looked up then, to find the girl staring at her, a look of revelation in her kohl-lined eyes. That's all it had been: a fleeting moment of recognition at the fasting and the hand-holding, before they separately had risen to resume the journey. But to this day she regretted she had not spoken. 'This is not an end, but a beginning,' she'd wanted to tell her. 'This is your chance to begin again.'

Helen lay on her back in the smooth plump linen, thinking through it all as the day crept in. Her hand settled for comfort on her belly's soft and empty pouch. She still felt relieved by their decision. For, in the end, a decision it had been, not a choice, with all the time for consideration that implied. It troubled her that even in the quiet of a London hotel room, even as the objects round her acquired a cold and lucid stillness in the rising light, she could still find herself rehearsing the arguments that no one, in the end, had required her to make. Hyperemesis gravidarum – the excessive vomiting of pregnant women – most likely a 'curse of heredity', her GP had announced on her first pregnancy as, head down, he wrote out the prescription for an anti-emetic that would take little effect on the sickness that would see her hospitalised through the second trimester. The one saving grace of carrying twins, the nurses had joked, was that she would not have to suffer it all again to provide a sibling. And they were right.

She didn't often have time for reflection – brooding, her mother would call it. She could take a few hours to herself before meeting her mum and sister outside the Tate Modern at eleven. She could do all manner of things; walk down through Soho and have breakfast in Patisserie Valerie, sit there, read the papers and reminisce on what it was to have once lived in this city where she'd always felt nostalgic and lost.

But instead she lay on, enjoying the rare absence of Mara and Jess, only to let her head fill with their never-still bodies, the shiny and complicit laughter of her three-year-old girls.

★

Maureen was leaning against the railing at Bankside, smoking. She appeared lost in thought, staring down at the brief shore of shingle cast up at low tide. Helen sidled along the railing and gave her mother a nudge.

'Hi, Mum!' she said, quickly returning the startled smile.

'Oh, Helen! You made me jump. When did you get here?'

'Just this minute. I spotted you from the bridge. Is Laura not with you?'

'She's gone inside,' replied Maureen, 'She wanted to buy you a catalogue.'

Helen leant on the railing next to her mum. Together they looked out at the river. The low November clouds had turned supernaturally golden. The dome of St Paul's stood opposite, grey and sombre as the mind of God.

'So, tell me, Mum, how's it been? All calm in Camberwell?' It had been a long time since her mother had visited Laura, something Helen had risked pointing out to her sister when they'd made their arrangements over the phone. 'I see her every week. It's not going to bother Mum flying out on her own. If you want the boys to spend time with her, then let her come early and stay with you, and I'll book a hotel.'

'No, I wouldn't say calm,' replied Maureen drily, 'but then how could it be with builders, three boys, and Mark never seems to get home before nine? It's amazing how Laura copes.'

'And did you sleep OK?'

'Hmmm.' Maureen attempted to nod. It was better not to chase the night's lost hours and just to get on with the day. Though she guessed the strain must show.

'Don't they look like wishbones?' she asked, instead, glancing across at the Millennium Bridge. 'What's that you call them, the supports?'

'Those Y-things there?' asked Helen, pointing. 'You'll have to ask Laura. To me they look like catapults set up to fire the ungodly through the doors of St. Paul's.'

It gratified Helen to make her mother laugh. She wasn't always the easiest company. She bent down and gave her a kiss on the cheek.

'Happy Birthday, Mum,' she said softly. 'It's great to be here with you.'

'Thank you, love,' said Maureen. 'And you.'

'Come on, let's find Laura before she gives up on us. You know what she's like.'

★

Laura was standing at the base of the Tate's tall tower like the point of an exclamation mark. She looked appropriately hip in an expensive red bomber jacket and jeans, her ash-blonde hair scooped up in a ponytail. Helen felt a surprising rush of warmth at the sight of her.

'Helen! God, it's great to see you,' Laura said.

She returned the catalogue she'd just bought to the bag and embraced her sister enthusiastically. Helen drew back to appraise her again. 'Well, would you look at you? Isn't this city treating you well!'

'Oh, I don't know about that.'

'Well, I do. You look lovely.'

'Ah, stop!' Laura protested, pleased that the hour spent deciding what to wear had been worthwhile. She always liked to impress her sister.

They hadn't seen each other so much in recent years. Laura had come home with Mark for the first few

Christmases after they married. But when her second son, Patrick, was born, the prospect of travelling with two boys under three had sent them instead to Godalming, where Mark's parents lived. With Conor's arrival, Laura had felt she could finally concede to Mark that, yes, she preferred to spend Christmas with his family. On the last trip home to Dublin, her mother had finished off dinner by handing round yoghurts that were a week out of date. 'They're grand,' Maureen had insisted. 'Look, the lids haven't domed.'

Mark's warning glance had stayed her tongue, but she'd felt angry and silenced as she'd watched Owen manfully swallow down each clotted spoonful. Patrick had simply replaced his spoon on the saucer and left the table. When they'd finally got home, she'd cried at the out-of-date food in the fridge, the unaired beds with their damp, fitted sheets and the overall lack of care they'd been shown. 'I'm not hiking them back to Dublin again. *She* can make the effort next time,' she'd told her husband, flinging the boys' clothes into the laundry basket.

'Fine,' said Mark. 'Whenever suits.'

Helen was more reasonable, more forgiving. *She* always had been. And although Laura no longer missed Dublin so much, she missed her big sister. They had ground to make up this weekend.

'Wait till you see this now,' she said, linking arms. 'Everyone's talking about it.'

★

Maureen's two daughters disappeared ahead of her through the narrow entrance. It came as a relief to be momentarily forgotten after a week of almost constant attention. It had been Laura's idea to come and see this show. It seemed to her odd that something called 'The Weather Project' should be housed indoors, while outside the Thames continued to make its own dramatic weather. She would have preferred to amble along the embankment in the clear and sallow light and explore this stretch of the city so changed from when she had lived here more than fifty years ago. She remembered how busy the wharves used to be. She remembered the water slicked with oil and tar, loud with the chug and whistle of barges and the roar of men. Since then, the river had been tamed for idling. It seemed to her a loss. She found a bin for her cigarette stub and followed them inside.

Maureen had come with no expectations of the Tate Modern, but she had assumed white walls and identifiable rooms would make up a gallery. Instead, there seemed to be just this yellow light, emanating mistily from deep inside the building. It took her a moment to locate its source: a huge, fluorescent sun hung on the far wall, illuminating everyone below in the vast and vaulted space. A wide ramp led down towards it into the depths of the enormous hall. She wondered if she could look at this sun directly, or whether, like the real thing, it was better to catch it obliquely out of the corner of her eye. But the sun seemed to demand her gaze, until she could do nothing else but stand and look, and look. She couldn't decide whether she felt warm or cold, whether it shone like the sun in summer or in the depths of winter at the end of the world. She began to move forwards down the ramp, a little unsteadily, her eyes fixed on the people ahead of her, straining to hear, in the hubbub and shuffle, the reassuring sound of her daughters' voices.

★

Laura had read about it all in the catalogue. What you did was lie down on the floor and wave at your reflection high in the ceiling mirror above.

'We're all constellations,' she told her sister. She unyoked her ponytail and lay down.

Helen, still standing, craned her head back as far as it would go. Sure enough, up there in the galaxy, her sister waved. Beside Laura, her own figure was inverted, her shadow puddled briefly behind her, a tiny moon face staring out. The effect reminded her of when she used to angle the hinged mirrors on her mother's dressing table to see herself multiply: a succession of little girls infinitely receding from the cold bedroom.

A sudden dizziness caused her to stagger.

'Are you okay?' asked Laura, who had seen her lurch in the galaxy above. She sat up and offered her hand, which Helen refused. She should sit down but feared not being able to rise again.

'It's just vertigo,' she said. 'It'll pass.'

Helen stood still: all was rush and blur and echo. She couldn't think of a cultural event in Dublin that would attract such a various crowd: the laughter of all nations rippled in her ears. Was it the spectacle itself that provoked such wonder? Or was it that the artificial sun had made of strangers a new congregation, though assembled to worship what, she did not know? She fixed her gaze on the figures ahead and waited for them to resolve into distinct strangers, only to discover the one face of faces missing.

'Hang on, Laura, do you see Mum anywhere?'

'No.' Laura got to her feet. 'Did she not come in with us?'

'I'm not sure. I thought she was following right behind.'

A sense of alarm out of all proportion to her age washed over Helen. She knew what caused it was adrenaline, not loss, or abandonment; it was just her body in shocked flight from its diminution above. Nonetheless her heart would not settle now until she had found her.

'I tell you what,' suggested Helen, as evenly as she could, 'I'll go up to that balcony, and see if I can spot Mum from there. You can stay here and I'll meet you back at the entrance at twelve.'

*

Helen had to jostle people aside to get to the rail at the top of the stairs. Below in the Turbine Hall, the crowd stood around in clusters, staring up at their own reflections or turned in collective awe to gaze at the false sun. Off to the side, a man and woman were performing yoga, while a large group, strangers or friends she could not tell, had joined hands to form a circle. There were very few figures standing alone.

What, she wondered, feeling increasingly anxious, would make her mother stand out? Any daughter should just know, shouldn't she, when she saw her mum? She would know her by the jut of her head, her tense detachment from those around her, the weight of her bag tugging at her right shoulder. She scanned the crowd again, trying to pick out each distinct individual. As she searched, it struck Helen with sudden force that she could no longer picture her mother's face. Were anyone to ask her to describe her now, she wouldn't be able to tell them much. Nothing beyond: my mother's eyes are not brown, but are blue or green, or maybe hazel; her hair is grey. The startling thought occurred to her that Maureen Brown might have chosen this moment to resign being a mother and to resume her anonymity. Lost to her daughters, the woman who bore them might in fact be any woman at all in the crowd below.

★

When she got to the end of the ramp, Maureen realised she did not wish to proceed further. The gallery's confident, young crowd brushed past her through the dark underpass to enter the main chamber. Each face seemed to lose all trace of character in this spectral light. She could feel herself becoming upset as she began to imagine that if Helen or Laura were to appear, as she wished they would, she would not see the daughters she loved but the shades they must one day become. The thought surprised her, the words were not her own. It was akin to claustrophobia, or vertigo, this familiar sense that she was falling out of herself into an element where she became nothing. She moved to the wall and waited for the momentary panic to subside. It didn't. Still feeling fluttery, Maureen turned slowly around, and began her dazed climb back up the ramp, against the flow of the crowd, towards the narrow slot of the day at its close.

★

The ferry ride to Greenwich that afternoon was the only part of the trip that Maureen had planned. She had never, she announced grandly to her eldest daughter, been out on the Thames and seen the city as the poets had intended.

'Oh, lah-di-dah!' Helen had teased. 'What's all this "as the poets intended"?'

They had been standing at the kitchen window in Stillorgan a fortnight earlier, mugs of tea in their hands. They'd been watching the twins play on Laura's old slide: Mara, more confident, plunging down, while Jess lingered at the top of the steps, a hesitant eye on her sister.

'Don't you remember?' Maureen replied, with a smile. And still watching the girls, she'd declaimed the lines from the school play Helen had rehearsed many years ago:

The barge she sat in, like a burnished throne,
Burned on the water: the poop was beaten gold.

Purple the sails, and so perfumèd that
The winds were seasick with them . . .

'Seasick!' Helen had interrupted, 'I'm sure it was "lovesick",
Mum, not "seasick"!' And the vision of Cleopatra regally
vomiting over her golden poop-deck had them doubled
up in laughter.

'Well, you would know,' her mother had conceded,
going out to fetch the mop and bucket from the utility
room to clean up the tea they had spilled.

It had astonished Helen that her mother could remember her big speech, almost word for word, when she had
long since forgotten the names of her school friends. Her
father, Eugene, had fallen ill during her inter-cert exams.
For two years, he'd mooched around the house in his dressing gown between his sickbed and the living room, unable
to do much except help his daughters with their homework. And it was he who had first read her Shakespeare,
insisted on it, when she was only interested in *Top of the
Pops* and boys. It was because of him then, she'd assumed,
that her mother had remembered the lines.

That morning, though, lying in her hotel bed, she'd
considered her mother's mistake again. Maureen had never
visited her in hospital when she was pregnant with the
twins. It was true that the hyperemesis had made Helen
acutely sensitive to ordinary perfumes – deodorant, shampoo, unguents of all sorts, the faintest trace of cooking. But
it was possible to prepare for this, as Gerry did, by washing thoroughly with non-scented products. Only once

had her mum appeared in the doorway and smiled at her, calling that she would keep her distance, it was safer. And Helen, tethered by her drip, had tried weakly to persuade her in, knowing at heart that if her mother drew up the vacant chair she would soon become anxious and run out of things to say. It was useless to press her, Gerry had said. Hospitals reminded her of Eugene's last days. You couldn't blame her for staying away. But Helen sensed that it was more than that. No, what made her mother nervous, she thought, was not illness *per se*, but pregnancy.

★

The clouds had turned black above St Paul's. The sun shone in bursts aslant the steely water. As they waited for the next ferry, Laura pointed out Norman Foster's new skyscraper butting the clouds above the city.

'Don't you think it's pretty, Mum?'

Maureen wished Laura would stop asking her to admire the architecture. She knew she should be more gracious and acknowledge her daughter's professional expertise, but all she could hear was the persistent demand of a six-year-old child: 'Look at me! Look at me!'

'Lovely,' she agreed, barely glancing that way.

She remembered these streets a boarded wasteland, filled with debris. London seemed such an unsettled city, bombed and rebuilt by successive generations. She supposed that Laura had to believe in these brash structures, being an architect, even though the shape of this snub-nosed building suggested it too would one day shatter. Her daughter's confidence in these glass blocks as monuments of a sort, to design or ingenuity, disappointed her.

When the ferry docked, Maureen made directly for the cabin while her two daughters dithered over whether to join her or to take the two free seats in the stern.

'Go on, you stay out and enjoy the city. I'm going inside to keep warm.' The door swung shut, the choice made for them. Laura sighed wearily.

'Helen, what is up with her today?'

'She doesn't seem to have slept much, but that's nothing new. To be honest, I think turning seventy is hitting her hard.'

Helen didn't mean it flippantly. She'd hunted inside and out, till she'd found Maureen beside the pier, looking lost and shaken, drawing shallowly on a cigarette.

'Just let me get on the ferry and I'll be fine,' was all she'd said.

The two sisters watched the water churn as the ferry pulled out into the main channel and nosed under the Millennium Bridge. The Thames expanded like a road in their wake. All air, and glint and shining surfaces – the thunder withheld – that's what London is, thought Helen. And, as her mind wandered, the counsellor's phrase came back to her, as if by repetition in the backwash of the river, a husk of meaning might be conferred on an event that had none. 'It is not your time; that time is over for you now.' And as her sister continued to point out the new skyscrapers rising through the city, Helen finally allowed herself to consider that today her time would have come. Her womb should be rotund and ripe as a pomegranate ready to split and shed its seed.

★

Maureen had decided back at the pier before Helen found her that, over lunch, she would tell them all. It was not the first panic attack she'd suffered in recent years. She bought a bottle of water from the cabin's coffee dock to wash down a Xanax. She needed to steady herself before they reached Tower Bridge and the Bermondsey wharves.

She had not told her daughters much about her early life in London. Like all children, their interest in her story began with their own origins: the moment when Eugene Brown had ascended the wooden stairs to Mr Porter's office, perched high above the warehouse floor at Butler's Wharf.

It happened fifty-two years ago today: 8 November 1951. That autumn, the London Auction had resumed its trade in Mincing Lane, and there was talk of the tea ration ending. Maureen had not been working as Mr Porter's filing clerk for very long when Eugene, a tea merchant from Dublin, opened the glass office door. She was not a girl used to feeling pretty, but she'd noticed the appraisal in his cool grey eyes and knew what it meant. He'd taken the chair she offered and matter-of-factly asked if it would put her out if he waited for Mr Porter there. He would descend below, if she preferred. 'You can stay,' she'd said.

He was here, he'd told her proudly, to find out wharfage

fees for Victor Bewley, now that tea was on again. Before the war, all the Irish firms had bought their tea at Mincing Lane, but now the Irish state had set up a company to deal directly with India, Kenya and Ceylon, cutting London out. The trouble was that the prices fetched here for the finest Assam blends were substantially lower now the auction had resumed, and the Irish importers were unable to negotiate such good deals directly with the producers. National pride, he'd told her, was being allowed to interfere with simple market forces. Victor Bewley hoped to petition the Minister, Mr Lemass, for a change in policy on the basis of his report.

He was clearly a man, she'd told her daughters, who liked women – a rarer thing than they might suppose. She didn't mind his self-importance, for it flattered her that he spoke as if she were clever enough to follow all the intricacies of his profession, which she'd been surprised to find she could. And so they'd moved on from tea, to Dublin, to Monaghan town where she grew up. By the time Mr Porter arrived, more cross than apologetic, Maureen Sweeney had agreed to meet Eugene Brown outside the Oxford Corner House at 7.30 p.m. It was her nineteenth birthday, and he would take her out to dinner, to celebrate.

That evening had represented a fresh start for her as Maureen made a pitch for the respectability she'd assumed a lost cause. She explained to Eugene how first she'd arrived in Greenwich to work as a nanny for the three Moriarty children, who reminded her so much of the brother and two sisters she had left behind in Monaghan. By night, she solemnly told him, she had taken a Pitmans' correspondence course and learned to touch-type till she was proficient enough to pass her secretarial exams. What she really wanted was to find a secretarial job in an advertising company. Mr Porter had offered to give her a start on Mr Moriarty's recommendation, for he was in the port and docks. She found the warehouse loud and dusty, but she'd come to find the exotic scent of tea a consolation for the noise.

None of this, except the last, was true. And she'd never told Eugene, whom she married the following Easter, why she had declined to go out dancing after, earning her the teasing reputation of being a cold and heartless virgin for packing him off that November night without so much as a kiss to warm his frozen lips.

Above the Monument, the sky looked bruised and heavy. The first drops of rain began to fall, dimpling the river's surface. Funny, thought Maureen, how each dimple seems to invert like the end of a bottle. The golden fish on top of Billingsgate Market swam upstream in the crowded air.

Outside, in the stern, her daughters quickly gathered up their bags. They appeared in the aisle beside her, Helen holding out a miniature bottle of red wine and a plastic glass.

'I thought we could all use an aperitif,' she said, already untwisting the cap and pouring. 'Here, take it.'

'*Sláinte*,' announced Laura, raising her glass to her mother.

'Cheers,' said Maureen, 'chin-chin.'

'Your health,' echoed Helen.

They passed quickly under London Bridge. Phrases flickered in Maureen's head as they emerged into the rain. Through the far window, the Tower of London appeared a child's fortress, a plaything of the city. Without the throng of ships gathered in the lower pool, Tower Bridge seemed to have lost its majesty. It now appeared the equal of the three-dimensional jigsaw her grandson, Owen, had wanted her to build with him. Even so, she experienced a rising sense of dread at the sight of it. She had to say something soon, she thought, venture some explanation to close the growing distance among them all.

'That's where I worked,' she said. The old warehouse loomed above the river, seven storeys high, BUTLER'S WHARF spelt out in tall, black letters across the top. Black iron balconies scaled the building, some with plants, some with satellite dishes clipped onto the side. Maureen imagined financiers gliding through their harried lives in the same space where once she'd watched the forklift trucks move in and out, among the stacks. She imagined the hoists and pulleys that used to squeal all day long, silently left in situ, replaced by the swoosh of lifts ascending through newly created foyers. Perhaps the air still smelt of tea. Cafes and restaurants lined the river. Outside one, a pair of waiters were attempting to wind in the drenched and heavy awnings, water sheeting off the canvas, like linen in a mangle.

'I bet it didn't look like that, Mum, when you worked there,' Laura remarked with a wry smile.

They were waiting, her two girls, waiting for her to begin the old familiar story. And, of course, it dawned on her, both of them would have assumed the purpose of this ferry trip was to remember their father on this anniversary of their meeting, so many years ago. How stupid she'd been, not to think of it sooner. 'No, it didn't look like that at all,' she said. 'London was a very different city when I lived here.'

★

As soon as the war was over, Maureen's father, Joseph Sweeney, had gone to work with a demolition team to clear the London streets of fallen masonry. He'd been operating the pile driver on a site in Walworth when it accidentally detonated an unexploded bomb. He was only thirty-seven. The loss of his wages was the better part of his widow's grief.

His ganger-man had written to her mother within a month of his burial. He offered to advance her eldest daughter the fare to London and to find her lodgings there with his niece. The job, he'd written, though likely hard, would be well paid and regular and should enable her girl to send some money home. Maureen saw the gleam of hope in her mother's eyes and understood that this offer to her eldest child was the only compensation the family were likely to receive.

And so, in June 1951, as the crowds flocked downriver to saunter around the Dome of Discovery at the Festival of Britain, Maureen had pitched up in a sour Bermondsey tenement to ask for a Miss Kathleen Moriarty. And the following Monday morning at eight, Kathleen had taken her down Tanner Street to join the throng of pinafored women waiting at the gates of Sarson's Virgin Vinegar factory. Kathleen knew everybody for she was the union shop steward. Maureen was greeted with a chirpy solidarity that reassured her she'd done right to take up work in the factory's bottling plant.

That first night, Kathleen had laughed as Maureen scrubbed herself raw in the zinc bath, trying to get rid of the smell. 'Give up, love,' she'd said. 'If you're that bothered, you could try the jam factory, but Hartley's pay a shilling less. Besides,' she'd added slyly, 'all the Bermondsey boys take liquor on their mash; they'll not be minding it on you.'

Maureen had soon learned to make herself scarce on Friday nights when Kathleen's young man used to call. She longed to escape the broken, bombed-out terraces with the broken, footsore navvies who reminded her of her own father, Christmas being the one extravagance he had scrimped to spend at home. As the summer passed, she began to explore further up along the river and found her way out onto the wharves through a narrow entry at Shad Thames. She used to sit there and watch the cranes delicately pick their cargo from the red-sailed barges in the Lower Pool and imagine what each haul contained: sticky figs from Smyrna, seedless grapes from Cyprus and, as the days grew shorter, the fragrant oranges and lemons in from Spain and Israel.

That is where she'd first encountered the wharfinger, Mr Porter. He used to come and sit with her and tell her the names of the ships newly docked, where they hailed from, and what cargo they were carrying. He explained too what a neap tide was, how it relied upon the sun and moon being at right angles to the earth. Back at the bottling plant, sticking label after label on the scalding bottles of vinegar, she'd dreamed of the scented territories she some day would explore.

Then, one day, he spoke of his time in the navy and his part in the Dieppe raid.

'It was sheer, bloody hell, all our men on the landing crafts, screaming and dying in the dark.'

After, he'd gone quiet, and placed his hand on her arm, and when he'd gone to kiss her, though she was not eager, she had felt that he was taking no more than his due for all that he had said. And the feeling that she owed him allowed him to lead her deep into his domain. In the quiet of the late evening, they had climbed the stacks of tea chests in a far corner of the warehouse, where she'd found a mattress hidden, to make a kind of crow's nest. And, though she hadn't wanted to, she'd lain down as he commanded, and when she rose, her throat felt as if someone had forced it to constrict, for when she finally spoke, her voice sounded narrow and fluted as a bird's.

It was Kathleen who had noticed first when the smell of vinegar began to make her sick. 'You're pregnant,' she'd announced flatly, through the shut privy door, 'and you won't survive it here. All the women will talk.' There was a pharmacist over in Rotherhithe who had the pills to bring it off, depending, of course, on how far she was gone. She could take a week off with the flu, and Kathleen would make sure that no one was any wiser. It happened a lot. But Maureen had been too scared and too ill to imagine how this could occur.

She'd left it a week. Then she'd gone to Mr Porter's office and had told him she was pregnant. He had put his arm round her and led her to his chair.

'You silly cow,' he'd said. 'You should have come to me sooner. How do you fancy working here as my filing clerk?' He'd moved her out of the shared lodgings while Kathleen was at work and into a back room, over a bookmaker's in Weston Street. He'd pay her, he promised, the same wages she'd got at Sarson's, minus her board and lodging, so there'd be no change in her remittance money home. But there would be no more talk of her having a baby. He didn't trust the pills for they didn't always work but he would send a woman round who knew how to do these things. It would be all right. No harm would come of it. His good lady wife had used her when they'd decided five kids were enough to rear.

In all their years of marriage, Maureen had never confided these things to Eugene. Only when they'd learned his diagnosis did she feel ready to set her burden down and ask to be forgiven, but she could not find a way of raising it without the truth seeming petty now. Out of mercy, she remained silent, or so she told herself. She tried to ease her husband's suffering in between the long bouts of chemotherapy and focused her remaining time exclusively on their girls.

*

None of them felt like eating by the time they reached Greenwich – it was still too early – nor did they feel like

walking far in the rain. A blue-framed shelter stood empty
on the jetty, and there they decided to sit, cocooned from
the shower. The wind had got up a little, and it was loud
inside. The pontoon rocked up and down with the turning
tide. The shoreline of the Isle of Dogs appeared indeter-
minable from the water. The ribbon of the river blended
with the rain.

Maureen's daughters sat down either side and waited for
her to speak. She pulled across her bag and reached inside
for her cigarettes and lighter. Helen noticed she was trembling as she tried to find the plastic strip to open the pack.

'Here, let me do that for you,' she said.

Helen unwrapped the packet efficiently and took out
a cigarette, but instead of returning it to her mother, she
placed it in her own mouth and lit it.

'Here, Laura, take this,' she commanded. 'It's for you.'
Laura hesitated, looking confused. 'Go on, take it, you used
to smoke.'

Helen lit another, this time for herself. Only then did
she hand the pack back to Maureen, and, leaning against
the glass, inhaled deeply as she had not done since she was
a teenager.

'Mum, what's the matter?' The shelter resounded with
the noise of the pontoon sawing against the gangplank, the
slap of the water against the struts.

Maureen had always found herself stranded at this edge,
unsure how to phrase the things no woman surely should
have to tell her daughters. Her own words seemed to slip
away on the verge of speech, decaying with imprecision,

and yet their silence could be felt, heavy as drops in the glistening air.

She began. 'Do you remember when your grandmother died, I went up to clear her house out on my own? Laura, you'd just started college, and Helen, I think you were in your last year of teacher training. Well, I found a letter there, tucked in behind the dresser drawer.'

Maureen reached down and retrieved her purse from her bag. From an inner pocket, hidden behind her library card, she pulled a piece of furred notepaper. She unfolded it and handed it to Helen.

23 Paradise Street,
London SE 16.

25 September 1951

Dear Mrs Sweeney,
I'm sorry to be writing to you with bad news. Maureen is no longer working at the factory. She has got herself into difficulties. I don't have her address, but I know how to find her. If you wire me the fare, I promise I will get her home.

Yours sincerely,
Miss Kathleen Moriarty.

Helen passed it to her sister, wordlessly, and took her mother's hand. She wished that she could turn away now, step back onto the ferry and find her way back to her own daughters without being any the wiser. But it was too late for that.

'Tell me, who's Kathleen Moriarty?' she asked, as gently as she could, but her mother ignored her question.

'Kathleen mustn't have got an answer to that letter. I didn't even know she'd sent it till I found it there. My mother never sent that money, and she never asked what had happened. All she was concerned about was losing the remittance money if I had to come home. When I found that letter . . . well, believe me, then I understood my worth.'

★

Helen negotiated the boisterous crowd spilling out of the Hermit's Cave at Camberwell Green. Any other night their rowdiness would not have bothered her, but tonight she felt vulnerable and scared. When the 68 bus came, she chose a seat upstairs at the front and wiped away the condensation. She gazed out at the passing shopfronts on Camberwell Road and the orange lights – white, red – wetly flickering their code. She recognised the antiques shop where she and Laura had once drunk coffee in a secret garden out the back while the cousins chased each other among the wild clematis and lilac bushes.

She knew she'd disappointed Laura by leaving so soon after dinner, but she simply did not have the energy to provide the conversation her little sister would demand. Their mother had gone up to read her grandsons a bedtime story.

The two sisters had left it half an hour before creeping upstairs to find her asleep on Conor's bed, her mouth open, snoring gently, his little blond head resting peacefully in the crook of his grandmother's arm.

Their mother had always had trouble sleeping. You can't swallow all that darkness and expect to hold it down for ever, Helen thought. Her earliest memories were of her mum sitting at the kitchen table, the window dark, nursing a mug of tea, listening to the repeat shows on the radio. 'Come on, I'll take you back to bed, love,' she used to say, leading her by the hand back up the long corridor. It was her father who used to wake Helen and get her dressed most mornings, plait her hair, give her breakfast and take her to school, quietly closing the front door behind them to let his wife sleep on, tucked up with their youngest daughter. She missed him.

'It was over very quickly, but the pain after was excruciating,' their mother had told them, prompting Laura to get up and leave the shelter, to walk up and down the pontoon in the rain.

'I nearly couldn't have you. Whatever she did caused me to prolapse whenever I fell pregnant,' she'd continued to Helen. 'I miscarried four times till they found a way of propping me up inside.'

Some coldness of her own had allowed Helen to stay and listen to revelations that struck repeatedly at her own silence. She imagined the core of the girl her mother once was, burned away at sufficient heat to anneal a new person from the elements of Maureen Sweeney. It had created the woman who could marry their father and consistently maintain the tale she'd once told, without shattering.

And what of herself? Would she one day sit down with the twins and explain how she'd travelled to London because she could not face the trauma of hyperemesis again? At seven weeks, she'd bent to kiss Mara goodnight, and the scent of her shiny hair had sent her running to the bathroom. When she and her mother boarded the flight home tomorrow, would she tell her then of her own journey back in April? With her cheek pressed wetly against the window, she remembered how her mum had shied away on the threshold of the ward.

Her mother's story had set the same arguments, allayed this morning, tumbling round her head again. She wondered when they would end. The fumes of the bus, its stop-start motion, the memories of getting sick, made her feel suddenly nauseous. As the bus swung round a corner, Helen rose quickly and pressed the bell. The middle doors clapped open and set her down at Waterloo. She made it the few steps to a doorway, and vomited. Trembling, she fumbled for a pack of tissues and some water from her bag and mopped herself clean as best she could. She was fed up being betrayed by her body in every particular.

She entered the station concourse and located the Ladies. She had to pay in through a turnstile. The cubicles were lit with blue, fluorescent tubes. She washed her hands, face and neck and put her mouth to the tap to swallow more water. She cleaned her shoes with toilet paper and dried them at the hand-dryers. *The old drill*, she thought bitterly. At the mirror, she applied concealer, powder, lipstick, attempting to replace her broken face with one she wouldn't recognise as her own.

Unsure of which exit to take, Helen decided to follow the signs for the South Bank Centre. These led her out to a busy road and pointed on the far side towards a tunnel under the railway bridge. As she hesitated, wondering whether at this late hour it was safe to enter, a crowd emerged on their way home. Reassured, she stepped briskly into the orange glow.

'Hey, would you look at that?'

A man was standing in the exit, his bald head tipped back to stare at the sky. He'd intended his comment to be overheard. Helen kept her pace and prayed that someone else would come along before she reached him.

'Excuse me!' she said firmly, as she approached.

'Sorry. I'm in your way,' he answered, immediately stepping aside.

She hurried on in what she trusted was the direction of the river. She crossed a busy road and took a broad pedestrian path beneath another railway bridge. On the far side, the bold blue lettering of the Royal Festival Hall beckoned to her left. There were still plenty of tables occupied in the restaurant.

She hesitated before deciding to continue on to the embankment. The rain had eased off, and the sky had cleared. She felt too self-conscious to hail a taxi or to enter one of the South Bank bars and order herself a drink. So instead she climbed the steps from Queen's Walk up onto Waterloo Bridge.

Helen had forgotten how spectacular London was at night. The Thames curved around her and gleamed with liquid fireworks: the London Eye, a Catherine wheel, the Hungerford Bridge frozen in a shower of white sparks, and beyond glowed Westminster, lit up like a candelabra. The water below Blackfriars Bridge burned petrol and amber. All the lights in the city seemed to have been left on.

Across the road, she noticed people had begun to congregate against the railings. She feared what might have brought them there, though they were not looking at the water. She crossed over to check what was going on.

'Do you see it now?' a familiar voice asked.

She whipped round. The man from the tunnel was standing at the rail. He looked friendly, eager to share his news.

'Sorry, what am I meant to be looking at?' she replied.

He nodded towards St Paul's. 'The lunar eclipse. I thought we wouldn't see it, but the clouds have begun to clear. It started a little over an hour ago.'

Helen looked up. If the moon were a face, it had lost its left eye to a small patch of dark. She thanked the stranger and moved away to find a spot at the railings on her own. She knew she would stay and watch this spectacle until she grew cold.

Last season's fruit was being eaten. It was turning umber up there, the bottom half unpeeled and shining white like the pith of some exotic fruit. She wished she could believe herself pardoned, as if this end had been preordained for the child whose time had never come. She felt a pang of grief contract inside her for the impossibility of ever having that child stand beside her and watch the moon briefly lose out to the swell of the earth. This end she now knew had always been there, kernelled in the mother to begin again in the daughter, predicted in the tea leaves that had set the omens aswirl. Helen craned her head back as far as it would go and stared up straight into London's fluorescent sky. Just as tomorrow, the moon would pull out from the shade of the earth, so tomorrow the words she never thought she would speak might just come and illumine mother and daughter on their journey home.

Absent

Michael Gilligan

AT THE REMOVAL, NOBODY HAD MENTIONED his absence. James had stood in the living room with his family, shaking hands with everyone who walked by. He wasn't sure at first how to respond to the repetition of 'I'm sorry for your loss', so he just said, 'Thank you for coming', which was what his mum had told him to say. At the wake the night before, it might have come up once or twice, James couldn't remember. He was told to go to bed when the house got busy, full of solemn-faced men and women he had never seen before and was sure had never visited when Frank had been alive. Upstairs, he stayed awake as long as he could because he thought that was the point; and he felt guilty when he found himself on top of his bed the next day, his clothes still on, having fallen asleep sometime after the voices downstairs had started to grow quiet. It was finally brought up after the funeral when a little old woman in the car park outside had said that she was sorry for his uncle.

'My dad, you mean,' James had replied.

'Oh, yes, yes. I'm awful sorry. I must have been mixing

you up with your cousin – you all look so very alike . . . and your name is?'

'James.'

'And do you not have a brother?'

'I do. He's in Australia.'

'Oh, right, I see,' she had said, hobbling away apologetically.

That was the only time it was mentioned to James, but he was sure most people knew Dara wouldn't be back for the funeral. These things had a way of getting around. It would have been brushed off with sentences like, 'Ah, it's terribly dear to get a flight back from Australia. And at such short notice. Sure, it's the other side of the world, the poor lad.'

But nobody, except those close to the family, knew that Anne had fully expected him to come back, that she had even planned to hold off the funeral for a few days to give him time. James had been in the room when Dara Skyped home, the two of them huddled close to the glow of the computer screen. Dara's face appeared, tired and bleary. It was five in the morning in Brisbane, the call only manageable for him because of the long hours he worked in a bar.

'I was looking at flights yesterday,' Anne said.

There had been a long pause. Anne thought the connection was bad, so she said it again, louder, but James knew what was coming. He could see it in his face.

'Listen, Mum. I don't think I'll be flying back.'

'What on earth are you talking about?'

'I've only just got this job, and they might not let me

back if I go. And when you think it'd cost over a grand to get there and back . . .'

'Christ, Dara, what loss about the bloody job? It's bar work – you could be doing that in Ireland. The least you could do is be there, after six months of not talking.'

'Well, I can't very well talk to him now,' Dara had said, his voice rising slightly. There was another pause. Anne said nothing. 'I'm sorry,' Dara muttered quietly. 'I shouldn't have said that.'

It didn't matter though because Anne had tears in her eyes. The conversation ended shortly afterwards. There were many more, just like it, over the next few days. One morning, James woke to the sound of Dara and his mother speaking downstairs. His voice rang out so clearly through the house that for a moment James was convinced that his brother had returned. He would be sitting in the kitchen with a mug of tea, James thought, too late for the funeral, but not so late that Anne wouldn't forgive him. But when he was halfway down the stairs he could hear behind Dara's words the distinct whirr of the old computer from the corner where his mother was sitting, and he could see the green light of the Internet router that was blinking madly.

As James returned home after his first day back at school, the bus pulled away, and he noticed his uncle's jeep outside the house. Standing in the utility room, his bag still on his back, he could hear them talking in the kitchen.

'He's a quiet lad, always was. It's you I'd be more worried about.'

There was the thud of a mug being placed down on the

kitchen table. It sounded louder than usual, as though the house had been in some way hollowed. Cahal's voice came again, deep and serious. 'You'll be all right though?'

It was more a statement than a question. And James got the sense that it was awkward for his uncle in there, sitting with Anne in the kitchen. There was a long silence, and the trickle of tea being poured into a mug, so James presumed she had just nodded.

Later that night, in the milking parlour, Cahal asked James the same question.

'How's Mammy been?'

James said she was grand but he could hear the uncertainty in his own voice.

'She'll probably be off for a wee while, but now I suppose the lot of us will. Although poor Anne might struggle more than most,' Cahal said.

For an entire week after Frank died, Cahal had come every night and every morning to work on the farm. He took the time off his own job as an accountant in Galway city, and James came out to help in the mornings before school and in the evenings after tea, like he used to with Frank. Cahal had organised an auction for the following week. James got the sense that he didn't mind looking after the place until the animals were sold; that the way he'd quietly smoke a cigarette when standing in the pit with the buzz of the milking machinery around him and tell James stories about Frank when he was younger was all part of his own peculiar way of dealing with the loss of his brother.

On the first night, Cahal struggled with the equipment,

but it didn't matter because James knew how to do most of it already. Cahal had stood behind him in the pit, watching him handle the milking clusters, like dangling metal jellyfish, and telling him about what the farm had been like when he was growing up. 'Serious changes,' he would say, marvelling at the equipment. He had a habit of taking out his phone every couple of minutes and pressing a button so that the screen would light up for just a moment. Once, when James came back from throwing lime on the cubicles, he caught his uncle taking a picture of the dairy with the phone. Embarrassed, he put it back in his pocket and then nodded towards one of the cows, who was placidly eyeing the two of them. 'There's not a loss on them, is there?' he said.

But for most of the week the cows were nervous with the unfamiliar sound of Cahal's voice in the parlour. Cahal cursed loudly when a younger heifer, who had recently calved, kicked back its hind legs as he tried to put on the clusters, knocking the equipment onto the floor, where the suction gasped loudly through the parlour. There was a special order in which Frank used to bring in the cows, so that the younger ones were never at the back and didn't have the leg room to get restless. When Dara helped out on the farm, Frank would point specifically to which one he wanted brought in next. One time, James remembered, he had pointed vaguely to a group in the corner, and Dara, picking one and glancing at the yellow tag on its ear, had yelled 'Is it 337P you want?'

'I don't have a clue what the bloody tag is,' Frank had

shouted back, 'but she's the scrawny one with the big white spot in the middle of her forehead.'

The last night before the auction, as they were siphoning off milk into steel buckets for the calves, Cahal asked James whether he had ever considered taking the place over when he was older.

'I suppose I wouldn't mind,' said James.

Cahal laughed. 'A right wee diplomat so you are,' he said, and James didn't understand what he meant, so he smiled up nervously. 'But there was always more of a chance with you than with that brother of yours. Never had an iota of interest, Frank used to say. And do you know he might have been right.'

It was true, James thought, thinking back to the time Dara was asked to catch and hold one of the cows so that Frank could dose it for fluke. Frank showed him how to do it first, sticking his middle finger and his thumb firmly into the cow's nostrils and yanking its head back hard, exposing the mouth. The cow's eyes darted wildly, its pink gums bared and its breathing heavy and panicked. Frank stepped aside to pour a creamy, viscous liquid into a small plastic bottle while Dara stood with his hands in his pockets. 'Right,' Frank had said. 'Now for it.' Dara had stepped forward, and the cow retreated back as far as she could, pushing against the animal behind her in the aisle. Dara's face squirmed as he stuck his fingers up the cow's nose, and once the head was pulled back, he closed his eyes, unaware that his grip was loose; and the cow jerked hard as Frank approached, knocking the bottle onto the ground, where the bright, white liquid spread slowly across the mud-covered floor like a cracked egg on a pan. Frank had cursed loudly and told Dara he was as useless as they come and that it was impossible to believe he was a farmer's son at all. There was no real anger in it, James remembered. But Dara had taken it to heart, and shortly afterwards, when he started university in Galway, he stopped coming out to help in the evenings, and it was left to just James and Frank.

The first of the steel buckets was almost full with the milk, frothy and bubbly at the top, so James placed another underneath the stream that poured from the recording jar, and over the heavy sound of the milk hitting hard off the steel, Cahal continued.

'You know, Frank and your grandfather usen't to get on so well either. Funny, isn't it, how history repeats itself?' He wore a grim smile on his face and ran his hand through his thinning grey hair. 'That's why all that silly bickering with Dara used to cut him to pieces, God rest him. And why it's hard not to feel for that lad out in Australia. I don't know what's going on in his head now, but believe you me, it'll get to him sometime.'

The calves were kept in a shed on the other side of the farm. On the way there, James stumbled, and the buckets lurched, milk spilling onto the legs of his overalls and seeping through to the skin underneath. He was familiar with the warmth and the dampness and the sour smell which would linger on his leg until he showered the next day. He left the buckets down outside the shed. There was nothing but an empty blackness inside and the bustling movement of the calves from inside their pens. This was always the scariest part for James: his arms stretched ahead of himself in the darkness of the shed, finding his way to the wall without bumping into any of the machinery or tripping over a toolbox or bag of fertiliser on the ground. When he reached the wall, he would fumble for a few moments before he found the light switch. It was high up, so he would have to stand on his tiptoes, moving his hand along through the cobwebs until they met the white plastic. And it was then that James's imagination would get the better of him, and he would imagine all sorts of phantoms and ghosts creeping in the darkness. The crunch of someone's footsteps on the gravel outside. Or the sharp whetting of the scythe that James knew was in the corner. His heart would pump fast in those moments, and he would feel a sudden rush, until the switch was flicked on, and he was just in an old shed, where the only sound was the banging of the calves against the wooden pallets, and where the scythe would be resting safely against the brick wall.

But tonight when James left down the buckets, he walked slowly over to the wall; he reached calmly for the light switch, and when he didn't find it immediately there was no familiar panic. The thoughts he used to have in those moments suddenly seemed silly and childish. The shed would no longer conjure up his old fears to scare him. And when the light flicked on, all he saw was a dreary place with bales of hay stacked up on top of each other, a rusty transport box attached to a small red tractor and a neat pile of straw he would shake over the calves' pens as bedding. He would have preferred it to be a few weeks previous, when he was still jumpy with the excitement of fear, but he carried out his task quietly, and with a heaviness he hadn't felt before.

When he came back into the house each night, he found that the rooms were strangely dark. One night, he decided to go in and join his mother in the living room where she disappeared to every evening. The only light came from the television – a bluey glow that lit up the wall and empty sofa – and the red of the Sacred Heart lamp which still hung above the table where the coffin had been placed at the wake. On the windowsill there was a statue of Our Lady, beads in her hands, and a portrait of a smiling Padre Pio. James was reminded of the older people murmuring decades of the rosary beside the coffin the night of the wake.

His mum was sitting on the armchair, not watching the television. There was a half-drunk bottle of red wine on the coffee table beside her. She watched him looking at the Sacred Heart lamp and the statue and the portrait, and suddenly she put her hand on her forehead.

'Ach, Jamesie . . .' She closed her eyes, and there was a pained expression on her face. 'Did I even make you dinner today?'

The next day, she brought him into town. She held his hand as they walked up the grey pavement of Shop Street. They were standing in Eyre Square when she asked him what he wanted, told him that she would buy him anything as long as it wasn't dangerous or too dear. He tilted his head slightly to one side and looked up at her.

'Could I get a mobile?'

'A mobile phone? But sure you're only just gone twelve years old! What in the name of God would you do with a mobile phone?'

'But everyone at school has one,' James said.

Anne sighed and said all right, all right, but that it had better not be too fancy a one. It would have to be the cheapest in the shop – one that could only call and send text messages.

In the car on the way home she asked him how things were getting on in school, whether he was having any difficulty concentrating in class and how his friends were.

'Grand,' he said.

She frowned. 'And what about that lad you used to be pally with a while back, the little dark-haired fella, Gearóid?'

'No, we don't really hang around with him any more.'

'Oh. Right.'

Up in his bedroom he sat playing with his new phone, but there was only the one game on it, and he soon got bored. He didn't have his friends' numbers, so there was nobody he could text. He lay there, his school books unopened in his bag, thinking about how busy the house had been a year ago. When Dara was still around and his friends would call over, he could hear them playing loud music in the room next door, or downstairs on the PlayStation in the living room. When Frank was alive, there used to be Joe Brady, who called over for a cup of tea most weeks, or Sean Mulrooney from up Gort. They both stopped by once since the funeral to drop off a mass card, and none of the neighbours had called over at all. Best give Anne and the young lad some peace and quiet, they must have thought.

★

There had been fights before, of course, but no more than James had thought normal. Ordinary conversations that became heated arguments which left behind tense, fuming silences. In the beginning, Anne had made small efforts, here and there, to bring about a reconciliation. She had suggested a weekend trip to Donegal, but Frank maintained that he could find nobody free to work the farm. She had planned lunch in Galway city an afternoon that Dara had no lectures, but Dara arrived late and sat absorbed in a book as they waited on their food. And so Anne took her distance, rarely interfering. James noticed that she never spoke of the conflict when he was in the room. It was only on Dara's last day in Ireland, with Frank grumbling in the kitchen, that he had ever heard her refer to it in his presence.

'Listen, he'll have the car back this evening – can't you use mine if you need it? And if there's one day the two of you should be able to keep a lid on it then it's today. He's only gone to get some drink for the party.'

'He could have done that down the road! He didn't have to travel halfway up the country to Enniskillen. Besides, today's a day he should be spending with the family.'

'It's much cheaper up there.'

'Cheaper, my foot! He'd want to be buying it by the keg to get it any cheaper than here if you think of the price of petrol.'

And sure enough, at half seven, when the red Toyota pulled up outside, James saw Dara open the boot of the car and, in one exaggerated motion, hoist out a metal keg which he let down with a clang on the driveway before rolling it along the tarmac to the front door.

'What in the name of God,' said Frank, sitting up from the sofa and peering out the living room window. 'I thought it was only a couple of friends he was having over tonight.'

The cars started to pull up from half nine. Some of them were flashy, with spoilers and engines James thought sounded far too loud. Soon the house was full of girls in make-up and high heels, and tall lads, some of whom smelt strongly of aftershave. Anne was rushing around asking people if they wanted anything to eat, that she would have put on some food had she known there was going to be this many. Frank was sitting quietly in the corner of the kitchen while the music from the living room blasted out into the quiet countryside through the open windows.

It wasn't long before Joe Brady popped his head in the door, a wide grin on his face.

'I would have put something more decent on if I'd known there was a shindig happenin'', he joked, plopping himself down beside Frank. 'Tell ya though, it'll have the animals up in those sheds scared stiff, that racket.'

'And do ya think he gives a hoot about that?'

'Here, Frank, lighten up – isn't he only right to have a bit of fun before he leaves. It might be a while before we've him back under this roof again.'

Dara came into the kitchen shortly afterwards, a pint glass in his hands and small beads of sweat visible on his forehead. His dark hair was ruffled, and his eyes wide and excited-looking. Joe leaned forward and shook his hand, and then handed him an envelope.

'Now, Dara, I wish you the very best of luck. There's a few Australian bob in there to get you started.'

'Wow, Joe – thank you so much.'

James thought Dara's voice sounded strange. There was more emotion in the words, and he was saying them slower than usual, as if being careful not to slip. When he turned to Frank, his tone was suddenly serious.

'We'll be off with ourselves to the club in about half an hour.'

Frank nodded, and Dara disappeared off into the party. James was holding an abandoned glass under his nose, sniffing it. He watched the group of boys gathered around the keg in the other room. It was hooked up to a small canister and a tap, from which pints were flowing freely.

'This lad will be off to the club himself yet if he's not put to bed soon, Frank,' Joe said, winking at James.

Later, from upstairs, James heard the sound of cars and taxis leaving. The voices in the kitchen gradually started to grow quiet, until it was only Frank, Anne and Joe Brady that were audible. When Joe left, his booming laugh and loud shout of 'Goodbye and good luck!' fading from the doorway, there was silence for the first time all night. No cars drove on the roads of Cloon at this time of night. There was only the occasional wail of a calf from the sheds or the rush of wind in the pines.

He was woken by voices arguing in the driveway. An engine was running, and he could hear Dara saying, 'It's okay, it's okay – I have some money inside.'

Then a second voice. A girl's.

'How about I pay the taxi driver, Dara, and you can get me back later?'

There was the sound of the taxi driving away. The door banged, louder than usual, downstairs. Giggles. The door of Dara's room closed softly. More giggles.

James rolled over in his bed and tried to go back to sleep.

There was the screech of a door handle being turned vigorously. A light in the hallway came on, and a shadow of feet passed by the gap under James's door. Frank could be heard muttering fiercely in the hallway.

Another sound of a door being opened, Dara's. There was a yell of fright. 'Jesus, Dad, get out! What the hell are you doing up?'

Silence. A low, serious voice.

'Where do you live, miss?'

'Cregboy.'

'Come on, and I'll drive you.'

The sound of the car driving away. James heard Dara get up, leave his room and go downstairs. Silence, for some time. The car came back up the driveway, the headlights shining through the curtains and lighting up James's room for a moment. The room was pitch-black again, and James was left staring wide-eyed into the darkness. There came a flurry of voices in the hallway, hushed and excited. They grew louder and louder until James stopped trying not to listen. He was sure Anne was also awake in the other room. He could imagine her, hand on her forehead, fretting over whether or not she should go out and attempt to stop them. Lying there, James felt a sudden sense of relief. He was glad for the first time that he was the youngest, that both Frank and Dara, as long as they'd been arguing, as long as the fights had been building up and getting more frequent and more bitter, that nobody had expected him to do anything about it. And the next day, when Anne had come back from driving Dara to the airport, she had never been able to begrudge James for doing nothing when she knew that he, like her, had sat through the sound of the scuffle in the hallway, the shrieks of curse words, the thunk of Dara's body hitting against the wooden banister. If he were older, James thought, though he wasn't sure how much older he would have to be, she might have expected more.

His father never spoke of Dara after that. Never asked for him, or asked to talk when his mum was on Skype with him. And every Wednesday evening, for six months before Frank had the heart attack, Dara Skyped home. He and Anne would talk for an hour, and James would sometimes be called downstairs, but Dara, likewise, never asked for Frank.

Eventually, after the first two months, Frank could

be found hovering near the computer during these talk sessions. Walking idly around the living room with the television on mute, or sitting in the kitchen, listening. Sometimes he even pulled a chair into the hallway and sat just off the edge of the screen. James caught him smiling once when Dara told a story about escorting a drunken Australian from the bar. He wondered whether Dara had ever seen the legs of a chair being placed softly down on the red carpet or made out the sleeves of his jumper off the corner of the screen.

★

He didn't ask his mother for Dara's Australian number. When she was watching the news one night, a time he knew she wouldn't leave the living room, he found her handbag in the kitchen, took out her phone and copied it down.

Upstairs, from his bedroom window, James could see that it was raining outside. Thin sheets of rain that were barely visible except that the tarmac of the driveway was slicked black and the grass in the fields glistened wet. Even though it wasn't yet fully dark, the moon could be seen clearly above the bare, spindly branches of the elm at the end of the garden. James looked beyond the tree, to the red corrugated-iron roof of the byre and the cold grey of the milking parlour, which had been silent for a few days now. The auction had been a serious, orderly affair: groups of men in long raincoats and wellingtons, with tractors that sloshed through the puddles in the lane, bringing the cattle away in trailerloads from the byre. Most of the livestock had been sold for well under what they were worth, Cahal said, but it was better to get rid of them.

'I tell ya,' he said afterwards, as he was stepping into his jeep to leave, 'it'll be a changed place if Dara ever comes back to see it.'

After school the following day, James sent his brother a text: 'How r u? Mum finally let me get a fone! Not much news here, da house is pretty quiet. James.'

He left the phone down on the bedside locker. When it started to ring out fifteen minutes later, James jumped with fright: nobody had called him on it before. He picked it up.

'Hullo, Jamesie?'

'Hi.'

'How are ya gettin' on? I couldn't believe that was you when I got the text! How are things back home? You doing all right, yeah?'

The connection was bad, and his voice sounded strange, like it had been on the night of the party. There were people talking loudly in the background, and music.

'I'm fine.'

Dara let out a shout, which was followed by laughter.

'Jesus, James, this is some place so it is.'

He told him about how he went surfing at the weekend, how there were waves ten times bigger than anything you would see in Fanore. Then he talked about someone named Rogers, who was also from Galway. He had met him in the bar, he said, and they were going to travel to New Zealand later in the summer. He spoke so fast that it was hard for James to contribute anything of his own. A moment came when Dara slowed down, but it was only to say, 'You might come out at some point, Mum and yourself.'

'We might,' James said.

Dara hesitated, and then he was off again. There was an urgency about him, but there was also something else that had crept into his voice. At one point, thinking that James had been cut off, he sounded almost panicked.

'Are you there James? Are you there?'

James waited a few seconds before responding. Listening to his brother had left him feeling tired. The conversation continued in the same manner as before, with James offering short replies, until it seemed that Dara could find nothing more to say. Towards the end he spoke with less ease, and there were frequent pauses. He began to repeat himself, telling James again about his plans for the weekend. And his voice grew more strained and distant, and wilted over certain words, as though he had been crying.

Killing Time

Lucy Caldwell

I try to kill myself on the first of March, a Sunday. I haven't planned it. I somehow just find myself standing in the bathroom, my heart beating fast, watching the watery light through the rippled windowpanes, knowing I'm going to, and suddenly it all makes sense. I kneel to reach right to the back of the cabinet under the sink where the medicines are kept, rooting through plasters and sanitary towels and sticky bottles of herbal cough syrup, and next thing I'm sitting cross-legged on my bed pushing the paracetamol tablets from the blister pack, shaking out what there is of baby aspirin, until there is a little heap that I line up on the duvet.

I have no idea about the dosage. My mum, a keep-fit addict and health freak, doesn't believe in painkillers except in the direst of emergencies. My brother and I have grown up on clove oil for toothaches, arnica for bruises and camomile tea for upset stomachs. She buys the camomile flowers in dusty bags from Nature's Way on the Upper Newtownards Road, along with dried feverfew leaves for her headaches and Chinese tea that is meant to be an appetite suppressant. I tried it, once: it is thin and bitter and brown-tasting and makes your tongue feel dry in your mouth.

My mouth is dry now. Time is catching and skipping, and yet I've been methodical enough to fill the toothbrush mug with water and bring it back into my bedroom with me. I lift it and take a sip. The lip is thick, and the water inside is slimy and mint-edged. But I don't trust myself to go downstairs and get a proper glass, or even to go to the bathroom to rinse out the tooth mug and refill it. I swallow and try to read the instructions on the paracetamol packet. *Children below the age of twelve*, it says, *should have no more than four tablets in twenty-four hours.* Adults can have up to eight. There are eight tablets left, and I have only just turned thirteen. Taking them all at once must surely make a difference, too. I study the baby-aspirin packaging. It is cherry-flavoured, chewable and years out of date. The most it can do, I decide, is nothing. I straighten one of the tablets on the duvet, aligning it with its partner. There is a sort of ringing in my ears. I take another sip of the swampy water. Then I begin to swallow down the paracetamol, a pair at a time. A song starts playing in my head: part of a song, a silly nursery rhyme from years ago. *The animals went in two-by-two, hurrah, hurrah.* I swallow the final pair of paracetamol. *The elephant and the kangaroo.* The baby aspirin are sharp and taste nothing like cherries. I have to stop myself from spitting them back out. I sit for a moment. The song and its animals are parading around my head, over and over, their thumping insistent feet. *The unicorn got there just too late for to get out of the rain*. I brush the trail of white dust from the duvet and get up. I look at my face in the mirror. My fringe needs cutting. I take the tooth mug back to the bathroom and carefully replace the toothbrushes in it, bright and stiff on their plastic stalks. Then I brush my teeth to get rid of the synthetic taste and return to my bedroom and lie down on the bed.

This autumn, we studied *The Crucible* in English. For months I haven't been able to stop thinking about the scene where Giles Corey refuses to answer ay or nay and so is pressed to death. *Peine forte et dure*, it was called, where they laid you down and stone after stone was put on your chest until under the weight of it you could no longer breathe. Sometimes it took minutes, but sometimes it took days. Giles Corey, the real Giles Corey, was an actual person. He was the only person in the whole of the United States to die by pressing, but they used to do it in the UK and France, all the time. I looked it up in an encyclopedia in the library after school. The first day you were allowed bread; the second and subsequent days, foul water. There was a difference, Miss Gibson said, between saying that someone died and someone was killed. Saying that someone died was a way of reneging on your responsibility if in fact they had been killed, or murdered. She wrote it on the blackboard, 'to renege on', and underlined it. Then she wrote beside it a ladder of words, from 'murdered' at the top to 'passed away' at the bottom. We were to be alert to the strengths words had, and most of all to their shadows, the ways you could use them to mean or to not mean something or to wriggle out of having to say something directly. We should listen to the news with our eyes closed, she said, so that we could hear more clearly. A few girls giggled when she said that. She pretended she didn't notice but a web of colour inched across her face. Ashleigh McAuley said that when she turned away to put the books back in the store cupboard she was crying. *Peine forte et dure.* You could feel the weight of the stones as you said it, each of them.

An hour or so later, my father calls me down for dinner, and I sit up, straighten my fringe with my fingers, tighten my ponytail, and go downstairs. We sit there, the four of us, forking potatoes and nut roast, the scrape of knives on china, asking and answering questions about school, friends, neighbours. Afterwards, I go back up to my room and get into bed again, still fully clothed. I close my eyes and try to breathe. I can't tell if my liver hurts – or even, when I think about it, where it is supposed to be hurting. I read the back of the packaging again, and all of the small print in the leaflet inside. I assumed an overdose would make you drift off into a marshmallowy sleep, but paracetamol isn't designed to send you to sleep, so it must be your liver. Or maybe your kidneys. I'm not sure of the difference: all we've done in Science so far this year is food chains and plant reproduction. Carpels and anthers and stamens. I got good marks because my drawings were so neat, and I'd colour-coordinated them. I lie there. I listen to the sounds of the TV, shrunken and muffled through the ceiling and carpet. I listen to my dad taking Sheba out to the back garden. My bedroom is right above them, so I hear him talking to her, calling her Sheebs and Shub-Shub and Old Girl, teasing her about next door's cat, who Sheba's terrified of. I hear her bark, as if they're having a conversation, and the sound of the door slamming as they go back inside. I know that two hours have passed when 'Boogie Nights' starts playing: my mum does her Rosemary Conley video every morning and evening, but you have to wait at least two hours after meals. Sometimes I do it with her. *One two three four five six seven eight. And out.* The video finishes, and then it's Sheba to the garden one last time and doors being locked and footsteps on stairs and calls of 'Goodnight!' The taps running, the toilet flushing. 'Goodnight!' My little brother's piping voice. 'Goodnight!'

I lie awake for a long, long while. Eventually, I somehow sleep.

And, to my surprise, I wake up, and things go on as usual: school, viola practice, homework. I tidy my room and learn my French vocab. The weird thing is, I feel better than I have done in ages. It's like a safety valve has been released, and for the first time I can breathe again. Monday, Tuesday, Wednesday, Thursday, Friday. The week passes. It's sort of as if things matter less now: and because they matter less, they are more bearable.

On Saturday, my parents have a wedding reception to go to, a late lunch at the Park Avenue – a friend of theirs who got divorced and is now remarrying. They've decided we're old enough, for the first time ever, to be left home alone: it's during the daytime, after all, and only down the road. They leave just after two. I watch the taxi pull away from the kerb and turn onto the main road and give them five minutes in case they've forgotten something. Then I yell out to Niall to stay in his room and not to move until I get back.

It's a wet, blustery day, not a day to be outside. But it's been burning my mind all week: and I might not get another chance.

I walk fast, through the residential streets, my collar pulled up for warmth – and to hide my face. It is only a ten-minute walk to the main road and the shops, but I've never felt so visible, so naked. Cars whoosh past, some with their headlights on already, spraying dirty puddled water up onto the pavement. Every time a car sounds its horn or backfires in the distance I nearly jump out of my skin. Our parents laid down the law before they left: no fighting, no answering the door, and absolutely no going out, under any circumstances. My mum panics about us when she doesn't know where we are. It's a relief to reach the newsagent's, push open the door to the sound of the bell and the babble of voices and steamy warm fug.

'What can I do you for?' the newsagent says when my turn comes. He is a nice man: Mick, and his wife is Alanna. I suddenly think that despite everything I should have gone elsewhere, somewhere up in Ballyhackamore, further afield.

I take a breath. I hope he can't see the weird guilt I feel written on my face. As soon as the painkillers are back in the cupboard, I tell myself, it will be like nothing ever happened.

'I need a packet of paracetamol,' I say.

'Well, you're out of luck,' he says, winking over my head at the old man shuffling up behind me. 'And do you know why that is?'

I blink at him.

'Because the parrots in the jungle have them all eaten. Parrots-eat-em-all: d'you get me?' The old man behind me hacks out a phlegmy laugh. Mick looks disappointed that I haven't laughed. I force a smile. He reaches behind him and takes a box from the shelf. It's a different kind than the ones we had, but I hope that by the time they come to need it, my parents won't notice.

'Anything else?' Mick says.

'A bottle of baby aspirin?'

'No can do. Don't stock it, only the normal stuff.'

I'll have to do without the baby aspirin. But that's okay: they can't have used it since Niall was wee; they've probably forgotten it was even there. The paracetamol's the main thing. I hand over fifty pence, and he rings up my change.

'How many . . .' I hear myself saying, and the words come out of nowhere. 'How many can you take at once?'

Mick frowns, and picks up the packet. 'Says here no more than four doses in twenty-four hours.'

'And four doses is eight tablets?'

'That's what it says. These for yourself, love?'

'They're . . . for my mum. Her headache. She gets these headaches.'

The old man leans forward and taps my shoulder. 'You'd want to be careful, but,' he says.

'I'm sorry?' I say.

'I said, you'd want to be careful, but.'

I turn to look at him. His face is thin and lined, and his eyes are milky, and there are plugs of yellowish-white hair in his ears. He puts his face right up to me, and I can feel his warm, wet breath.

'Woman the wife knew,' he says, leaning in even closer, 'got this terrible headache. Kept popping the pills, every couple of hours. Headache passes, she thinks no more of it, goes about her business. Few days later, the vomiting starts, and her skin turns yellow. Then she swells up like your Michelin Man. By the time they got her to hospital, it was too late.'

'What do you mean?' I say. I try to take a step back, only my back's right against the counter, and there's nowhere to go. 'What do you mean?'

'She'd OD'd, you see,' he says, flecking me with spittle. 'She'd overdosed. It had her liver and whatnot destroyed, and her organs were packing it in one after the other. Oh, you wouldn't wish it on your worst enemy, what that poor woman went through. It's the most painful way to go, they say, for they can't give you anything to help with the pain once your liver's packed in. And the tragedy is she done it without realising. Her family was in pieces. In pieces. A *Telegraph*, Mick, and a packet of B&H, if you please.'

I stare at the old man. He looks like . . . what's the word. A harbinger.

'Is that true?' I say.

'Sorry, dear?'

'Is it true – what you said? About the woman.'

'God rest her soul. It was a terrible tragedy. Terrible.'

'And it was definitely the painkillers, it wasn't anything else?'

'Oh aye, it was the headache pills for sure. They should come with more warnings, if you ask me. The cruellest part is she thought she was fine. The headache lifted, and she was right as rain for days. Or so she thought. When all the while the damage was being done. God rest her soul.'

His milky eyes glide over my face again, searching to meet mine. A great rush of heat and then cold goes through my body.

'Don't be scaremongering there, Eddie,' says Mick. 'You've put the heart crossways in the wee girl, look at her face.'

'I wish it was only scaremongering,' the old man says. 'They say it happens oftener than you'd think. They should put warnings on the packets. You wouldn't wish it on your worst enemy.'

'Come on, Eddie. I'm sure her mum knows what she's doing. Don't mind him, love. Now then.' Mick rings up the till. The old man is still peering at me. He knows, I think. I don't know how, but he knows. I squeeze past him and manage to get out of the shop and into the dank fag-end of an alleyway around the corner.

I try to tell myself the old man was mad, or lying. I scrabble to recall what we did in Home Economics, when we studied First Aid. Don't touch someone you suspect has been electrocuted. Never use butter to treat a burn. ABC stands for Airways Breathing Circulation. The rules ping, neat and useless, around my head. We didn't mention painkiller overdose. The closest we came was when Mrs McAneary was talking about tying a tourniquet, and Kelly Clark put up her hand and asked was it true that cutting your wrists across didn't work, you had to cut them down. Mrs McAneary told her not to be so morbid, and if there was any more of that sort of talk she'd be in detention.

I feel a kind of numbness come over my body. I put a hand on one of the dustbin lids to steady myself. I try to think logically. I try to think Miss Gibson-style. A few days later, the old man said. How many is a few? Three, four? Surely no more than five? *A couple* is two or three, and *several* might be longer, but *a few days*, surely, has to be less than a week, has to be fewer than – what has it been? – six days.

Slowly, I calm myself down. It is raining more heavily now, and I'm getting soaked, but I stay there in the vomit-spattered alleyway until my legs feel strong enough to take me back home.

I go up the Holywood Road this time. As I pass the Park Avenue, I suddenly think about going inside, up the driveway and into the lobby and through to the restaurant, finding my parents. But what would I say? There's nothing, whatever I say, that my parents can do. I stand across the road looking at the gates of the hotel, my hands clenched into fists so tight that blood wells up in half-moons under the skin where my nails dig in. When I wrench myself away it feels as if years might have passed.

When I make it home, Niall is in his room, the door shut, a skull-and-crossboned NO GIRLS ALLOWED sign Blu-tacked up. In smaller letters he's written, AND THAT MEANS YOU!!! I tap on the door.

'Go away,' he says. 'I'm busy.'

'Niall,' I say, nudging the door open a crack. He's hunched over, gluing something.

'I thought you were meant to be good at English,' he says. 'Can you not read?'

'Niall,' I say, but the words won't come out.

'What?' he says.

'Niall,' I try again.

'*What?*' he says, and when I don't reply, he rolls his eyes and goes back to his gluing. 'Give my head peace.'

'Do you want to play Lego?' I blurt out.

He stares at me. 'Do I what?'

'Do you want to play Lego? We could build the Pirate Ship and the Space Rocket, have a battle.'

Niall shifts in his chair and looks at me.

'It'll be epic,' I say. 'It'll be huge. It'll be like – carnage.'

'I don't know,' he says. 'I don't really play with Lego these days?'

'Since when?' I say. 'Not even the Pirate Ship?' It was his Christmas present the year before last, and even I was jealous of it.

'I don't know,' he says. 'I just don't. Sheba ate some of the pieces anyway, I think.'

'Oh,' I say.

'Not that I care anyway,' he says, turning back to his gluing. 'But if I tell Mum and Dad you went out, you're in such big trouble.'

'Niall?' I say, and I hear my voice crack a little. 'I don't know what to do.'

He frowns at me. 'Do you mean, like, now?'

'Now – for the rest of the day – please, Niall – can I sit in here with you?' I say, and my voice is barely a whisper now. 'I won't get in your way, I promise.'

'Wise up,' he says. Then he sighs. 'Look,' he says, pushing his cardboard to one side. 'You can watch me play *Paperboy* if you want. I almost got a Perfect Delivery the other day on Middle Road.'

When I try to thank him, he looks at me like I've gone mad, so I shut up and just follow him downstairs.

We boot up the Amstrad and sit side by side while he fires the newspapers at the doors and crashes into flowerpots and dodges the stray rolling tyres and remote-controlled cars and tornadoes. It's banal and repetitive and weirdly hypnotic. Gradually, I feel my breathing lengthen and my heartbeat slow. I stop watching the computer screen after a while and watch Niall instead: his pale, creased forehead, his flicking thumbs. We sit there for hours. By the time he gives up on the elusive Perfect Delivery, it's almost teatime, so I micro-wave the jacket potatoes Mum has left cling-filmed in the fridge, three minutes each plate, and grate cheese carefully over. Niall eats his and most of mine. After we've finished, I do the washing-up, drying each knife and fork individually, eking them out. So long as you keep moving, I say to myself. It's like in the game: you can speed up or slow down but you have to keep moving, because as soon as you stop, it's over. I line up the last knife in its compartment and close the cutlery drawer. Niall is back up in his room by now, at work on whatever he's cutting and gluing. I wet the dishcloth and wipe the table, then wring it out and drape it over the tap. I am more tired than I can ever remember being; more tired than I even knew was possible. I want to go to bed, but I don't dare – in case I don't wake up this time. As I wonder what to do next, I hear Sheba whine by the back door and I realise we haven't let her out all afternoon.

'Come on then,' I say, and she gives a little thump of her tail, or tries to. I unlock the door, and she hauls herself up and pads outside. The rain still hasn't let up. She makes it across the yard and to the edge of the garden and squats: to make her puddle, I suddenly think, that's what we always used to call it when we were little. I don't remember a time without Sheba. I don't remember when she was a puppy, except in photographs. She's always just been there. She shambles back to the house, and I let her in and kneel down on the floor beside her. She was really blonde once, platinum-bright, but now she's kind of an ashy colour, and her muzzle is grey. She's getting on: that's what my parents say. Poor old Sheba's getting on. I stroke her and see how knotted her undercoat is. So I tease her soft drifts of tummy fur until they untangle and brush through her damp topcoat with my fingers. It isn't dirty, exactly, because she doesn't go outside much any more, but it doesn't feel clean. She's too stiff and cumbersome to climb into the bath, and it seems cruel to blast her with a cold hose in the middle of winter, so she hasn't been properly bathed for weeks. My dad wipes her down with a facecloth and soapy water from time to time, but she needs a proper shampoo. Maybe we could all make a sort of hammock, I suddenly think, out of a sheet, and all four of us could lift her into the bath and out. I could blowdry her coat afterwards, on the lowest gentle setting, so she doesn't get a chill. Maybe we could do it tomorrow afternoon; maybe that's what we could do. And by then, a whole week would have passed, seven whole days, and that was surely more than *a few*, and then I'd know I'd made it safely through. Surely a week was enough, surely? I curl up with Sheba, there on the linoleum tiles of the utility room floor, and close my eyes and breathe in her warm, sour, biscuity smell, exhausted suddenly with something almost like relief.

The rest of March passes. March turns into April, and in the middle of April Easter comes, and on Easter Monday Sheba dies. Mum bought her doggy chocolates from Supermac, but she didn't eat them, only licked at them and wagged the tip of her tail, and the next morning she's stiff and cold against the utility room door. We all cry, even Dad. Later that night, I hear my parents talking on the landing. Niall has been inconsolable all day, and Mum's had to sit with him until he's sobbed himself to sleep.

'It's good for them,' she says. 'That's what they say. It teaches them about mortality.' But she's crying as she says it – I can hear. Then she says, 'That's a joke. Isn't that a fucking joke?' Mum never swears. I have never in my life, ever, heard Mum say anything stronger than *sugar* or *flipping* or *fudge*. I hear Dad shush and soothe her, as if he's the only parent and she is a child. I think of the things they said to each other and to us when we found Sheba this morning. 'She's gone to sleep'; 'she's passed away'; 'she's gone to a better place'. They are all gentle, cloudy phrases. Right at the other end of the scale from 'murdered', 'killed' or even 'died'. And somewhere off the scale entirely is the poisonous word for what I tried to do. I try to make myself whisper it aloud, but I can't: the word just sits on my tongue, too terrible to say. Miss Gibson didn't so much as mention it when she wrote out her ladder of death words.

As I lie in bed, I listen to them on the landing and wonder. I try not to, but I still can't stop wondering, how many more tablets it would have taken: another whole strip of eight, or maybe four, or maybe only two or even one. For a sudden long moment I can't seem to breathe. And then I breathe; and then I concentrate only on breathing.

Villefranche

Ita Daly

THEY HAD BEEN FRIENDS FOREVER, FROM those first days at secretarial college and on through jobs, marriage, motherhood. The Three Musketeers they had called themselves – *all for one and one for all!* Never mind that the three musketeers had been men: women were the ones who were in for the long haul when it came to friendship. For forty years they had met at least once a month – coffee, a drink, a walk in summer. Sometimes one or other of them would be en route somewhere else, but that hadn't mattered as long as they met, however briefly.

And now there were two.

Paula's melancholic thought was halted and replaced by a wave of irritation as Siobhan leant over and nudged her: kneel. She had eyes in her head; she could see. And, anyway, she was confident that she could go up there and conduct the funeral service herself, so many of them had she been to over the past few years. She settled her knees more comfortably and hunched over the pew. The priest spoke clearly in a young, country voice. Our friend, Rosemary, he said, as if they had been best buddies.

That's what the three of them had been for over forty years, best buddies, although it was against the odds that the friendship would survive. They had come together as unformed girls, eighteen-year-olds, fluid, like water, changing, swirling, taking different paths.

On the altar the young priest now motioned them to sit. Homily time.

Who had decided to bring in the Druids? Rosemary hadn't been inside a church for forty years – none of them had been believers until Siobhan had caught respectability and returned to the fold a year before she married George. Good-Catch George with a mother who played tennis and a brother who was on the missions – you couldn't be parading your atheism in front of such a family, though rumour had it that the brother had since jumped ship and got himself an African wife. Of course, you'd never hear that from Siobhan, who was good at pretending frankness but only ever told you stories and gossip that reflected well on her.

Paula sat back, relieved to be off her knees.

A slight young woman was walking up to the altar. Must be one of the nieces. She had a look of Rosemary about her, something about the way she held her head.

'Were you asked to speak?' Siobhan whispered.

'No.'

'Me neither.'

The girl had a strong voice, and she faced the mourners with confidence. She spoke lovingly of her aunt, how she had been like a second mother to her, a guide, a confidante.

Paula looked up at the stained-glass window where sunlight was transfusing an angel's golden wing. Strange that Rosemary had never married. She had been the prettiest of the three of them, the one with the boyfriends circling round. But maybe that was why, maybe knowing that she could pluck a husband from the air any time she wanted, she just hadn't bothered. And she had been happy and generous in her life – a godmother many times over, even to Paula's unbaptised daughter.

'This is the first time I don't have to explain myself,' she had said. 'It's so awkward because it's an honour to be asked to stand for a baby, but I always have to explain that I don't really believe in God.'

'And they still want you.'

'Well, I think Siobhan has started a novena for me.' And they had both laughed.

Paula sniffed and began to search her bag for a tissue.

'Here,' said Siobhan. 'And stop it or you'll start me off.'

Up at the altar the girl's voice wobbled. 'Auntie Rosemary was the one I told when I didn't get enough points for college the first time. I remember how she made me a pot of tea – she never used tea bags – and she said that I'd be fine, that I could try again, and if I didn't go to college it wasn't the end of the world. Look at her. And she was right. She never went to college, but she had a brilliant career.'

Paula closed her eyes. The girl had got it almost right. Rosemary had had a brilliant life but a lousy career.

No career, in fact. She had hopped from office to office, never settling long enough anywhere to make a mark. That was until fifteen years ago, when she had found a job she felt perfectly suited to, as a dogsbody, a gopher in a small art gallery. She had loved working with artists, loved selling their work, loved the launches, loved even the long, empty days when nobody came in to look at the paintings and she could sit and muse and stare out the dirty Georgian window at the street below.

'It gives me a licence to be idle,' she had told Paula, 'and when someone does come in, it's always someone nice or interesting, someone you can talk to.'

'But can you afford to work in a place like this? They can't be paying you very much.'

'Yeah, but they won't make me retire when I'm sixty-five. I can go on working here till I die, that's the bonus.'

And she had.

The mass dragged on. At least the church was warm, not like the old days, but in the old days everyone shivered, the nation had been tougher or more masochistic then. Siobhan swished past, her backside smug and stylish inside the camel coat, en route to receive Communion. The last time Paula had received the sacrament had been at her father's funeral. Not wanting to add to her mother's pain she had stood with the rest of the family, and when she put the wafer onto her tongue, she was seven years old again, terrified that she might, somehow, let the body of Christ fall from her mouth. Paula rubbed her eyes and thought about the strangeness of belief, how wars were fought and men and women killed because they had different takes on God.

She pulled her knees in as Siobhan shuffled past, kneeling now, her head bowed. Paula noted the inclined head, the creased chin just visible. We're getting old, she thought. Those of us left, we're getting old. She felt a sudden affection for her friend. She wasn't a bad old stick, and they had been through so much together. The three of them had grown up together, for you did more growing up in your twenties than your teens.

They had gone to their first dance together, on their first foreign holiday. Paula had imagined that she would be a hit with the Spanish boys because of her red hair, but none of them had eyes for anyone but Rosemary..

'It's because she gets a tan,' Siobhan had said one evening after Rosemary had disappeared on the back of a scooter and the two of them were pretending to enjoy their paella, which seemed to be a mixture of yellow rice and prawns, but prawns with crackly coats on their backs, not like the ones that came in jars in Dublin. 'You'd think they'd be interested in something different for a change – the pale look – but they just seem to want more of the same.'

The week before she had shown Paula an article in *Vogue* that declared that pale skin was in fashion. But nobody seemed to have told the Spanish boys.

The congregation stood as the priest began to walk around the coffin, sprinkling it with holy water. Then men in suits moved forward to take up their positions and began to roll the coffin down the aisle. In front of them a young boy seemed to stagger under the weight of the giant crucifix he was carrying.

Presumably there were lots of these crucifixes in sacristies around the country, but where had the boy come from? Few parents were happy to have their children function as altar boys since all those scandals.

The coffin moved slowly past.

Paula tried to imagine the body inside but couldn't. Yesterday, at the wake, she had kissed the forehead of her dead friend and was shocked by its cold. That's what the absence of life was: a unique, a shocking, cold.

The congregation shuffled out after the coffin and reassembled on the steps of the church as the shiny black hearse opened up to receive its load. Friends were finding one another, seeking out the family. Laughter rose here and there, hugs were exchanged. The Irish mightn't make much of a fist of living, but they really did death well. Neighbours from her apartment block, friends from years ago, acquaintances from various stages of her life had come out to see Rosemary off. Paula had once been to the funeral of a cousin in Scotland, and it had been a pallid affair, a small, self-conscious gathering. The mourners couldn't wait to get back to their lives. People lingered at Irish funerals, everyone with a tale to tell about the deceased.

Now a man in a tweed overcoat was making his way through the crowd.

'Siobhan, Paula, thanks for coming.' It was Patrick, Rosemary's younger brother. 'Are you going to the graveyard? Do you need a lift?'

'Thanks, Patrick, we're grand,' Siobhan answered for them both.

'Mount Venus Cemetery, not far from Rathfarnham, and then we're all going to the Yellow House for something to eat. I hope you can come.' He rushed off to talk to other mourners, offering thanks, issuing invitations.

Siobhan took Paula's arm. 'I'm just over here.'

Paula climbed into the jeep, glad to be out of the wind which had suddenly risen, coming down off the mountains where the highest peaks were still blotched with snow. She ran her hand over the leather upholstery and stretched her legs, pushing a pair of runners out of the way. Siobhan had always been untidy. Before a date with George she would tear around the flat dropping hair irons, make-up, shoes, underwear all over the flat, leaving Paula and Rosemary to tidy up after her.

'I never asked you to. Did I tell you to tidy up when I had gone?'

'We can't all live like pigs.'

'Girls, come on. A glass of wine.' Rosemary had always been the peacemaker.

The hearse moved off, and they waited as the long, black funeral limousine fell into place behind.

'I hate those cars,' Paula said. 'I don't understand why people don't use their own cars – get a friend to drive if they are too upset. Those big long black things give me the willies.'

'It's for appearances. Appearances are important at a funeral – just the same as a wedding.'

'Why? The corpse isn't complaining.'

'Is it really our business, Paula? I'm not inclined to tell other people how to conduct the funerals of their loved ones.'

Paula stared out the window and clamped her lips together. My God, but she was so annoying. It was that effortless complacency, the way she always ended up looking down at you from the moral high ground. Paula shrugged herself into a more comfortable position. What did it matter? It was Rosemary's funeral. Rosemary was dead. She couldn't get her head round it, Rosemary not being there. With her eyes closed, Paula could see her, not as a sixty-year-old woman but as a girl in a flowered dress, on a sunny day, sitting in Stephen's Green, eating sandwiches.

They came to the park at lunchtime unless it was raining, for the secretarial college was just a few doors up on Harcourt Street.

'Where would you like to work – I mean, if you could pick? What would be your ideal job?' Siobhan had asked.

'Anywhere, as long as it's not the Civil Service.' Paula, happy in the sunshine, was folding the greaseproof paper and putting it back in her bag: you could use the same paper a second day and maybe even a third.

'Well, you needn't worry about that because you wouldn't get into the Service – you have to have all sorts of honours in your Leaving.'

'I'm going to work where there are lots of interesting people.' Rosemary had plucked a daisy from the grass at her feet and was busy pulling off its tiny white tongues.

He loves me, he loves me not.

'Not just men, people. If you're surrounded by interesting people you won't be bored, no matter how dull the stuff you have to type.'

Siobhan had stood up, shaking crumbs off her dress. 'I'm going to be a legal secretary. I'll have to do extra exams, but it'll be worth it.'

The other two had smiled.

And three years later, she was engaged to the Junior Partner of Hayes & Spencer, Solicitors. Yes, Siobhan had always known what she wanted. But how did she manage to get it? How had she managed to end up with a well-heeled, solicitous husband, two children (a boy and a girl, naturally) and a neo-Georgian house?

'Neo-Georgian. What's that when it's at home?'

'All the advantages of the real thing but none of the draughts or rising damp.'

'Oh you mean mock. Mock-Georgian.'

'No, Paula, I mean neo. That's what I want, and that's what I'm getting.'

Paula screwed up her face, irritated all over again by a conversation that had taken place over thirty years ago. Why on earth was that? She had grown old, so why couldn't she grow up?

Because Siobhan was still infuriating – you couldn't put a dent in Siobhan. She sailed through life like a giant balloon puffed up with self-importance. Paula didn't want Siobhan's life. She wouldn't take George home if she won him in a raffle, and she was happy, yes, happy, with Dermot. After all, he was a professional man too: he had been to university. And Dermot loved his job. He said you had to have a vocation to teach and that he wanted to make a difference. And she agreed: what was more important than teaching the next generation? Certainly it was way more significant than drawing up people's wills.

But who believed that, apart from teachers themselves? It was society that was at fault, society that undervalued teachers. Paula was always furious at the manner in which teachers, nurses and guards were lumped together when it should have been teachers, doctors and solicitors. They had all been to university, they were graduates. She knew that nurses now got some sort of Mickey Mouse degree, but it wasn't the real thing, not like an Arts degree, followed by a higher diploma; that's what teachers had. Four years Dermot had spent at university, and look at his salary now compared with George's, for example.

No wonder teachers were always going on strike.

Paula scowled at the passing world as the suburbs fell away and the road began to rise.

'Have you ever been to this cemetery?' Siobhan asked.

'No. I remember passing the signposts, but I've never been there at a burial.'

'Lovely name, though.'

'Somehow it suits Rosemary.'

'Do you remember that first time we went to Spain, and she wasn't on the beach five minutes when she was as brown as any Spaniard?'

'And I got burnt.'

'And I got pissed off. None of those *señors* knew we existed when Rosemary was around.'

'I often wonder how we escaped melanoma. We were so ignorant in those days.'

'God, we had no idea. It's the curse of that white Irish skin; look at how many Australians get skin cancer. It's their Irish heritage. But Rosemary was always okay because her skin was naturally dark.'

There was a sudden awkwardness in the car as they both realised what had been said.

Rosemary hadn't been okay. Rosemary had got another cancer – a woman's cancer. A cancer that was caused by a virus transmitted sexually. The more sexual partners, the more likelihood of picking up the virus. The Wages of Sin.

'We should have been born ten years earlier or ten years later,' Paula said.

'Why?'

'Oh, I don't know. It would have made things easier.'

It was too hot in the car now. She began to open the buttons on her coat. 'Why do you think she never married?'

'Search me. Timing, I suppose, meeting the right fella at the right time. And luck.' Paula looked across at her, at the face that had seemed heavy in youth but had now achieved a certain handsomeness. 'You know, Siobhan, you can still surprise me.'

'Well, we have been lucky, haven't we? I think we have.'

Except that they too would end up in Mount Venus or some such place, so where did the luck come into that?

It all came to the same thing in the long run. Paula smiled out the window. There was something consoling about that – equality at last.

They shot through a red light.

'Siobhan.'

'It's a funeral procession, what did you expect me to do?' She began yanking off her gloves, throwing them in Paula's direction. Her hands moved down on the steering wheel, relaxed and easy.

They were old hands: loose skin, thick, twisting veins, a splatter of brown spots.

'We are old women, Siobhan.'

'No, we're not. Sixty is the new forty – didn't you know that? Anyway, you're as old as you feel.' Siobhan was never stuck for a cliché. Rain had begun to fall – another cliché.

Paula stared out at the landscape, which looked battered still, with no signs of spring, though they were halfway through March.

'Could you turn down the heating? It's too warm in here.'

'Why didn't you say? You're always so cold I had it on high. But this little beauty is happy to oblige.' Was she talking about the car or herself? With Siobhan you couldn't be sure. Paula felt her resentment grow again. How much had the damn thing cost her? And it had to be a jeep. Her whole life was a cliché – even her wedding. Especially her wedding.

'You're getting married in white, and your father is giving you away?'

'What's wrong with that?'

'You are such a hypocrite, Siobhan. How often have I heard you sneering at all that, laughing at those idiots who went in for such shows?'

'A girl can change her mind.'

'A girl? A girl? We're women, not girls.'

'Oh, give it a rest, Paula, you're giving me a headache.'

Yes, she had somehow always managed to end up in the right, making Paula seem the strident one. How had she done that? She had expounded principles to the other two and then abandoned them when it suited her, and still she had managed to end up vindicated.

After the wedding, there had been the move to the mock-Georgian suburbs. Paula might have raised an eyebrow except that she had ended up two years later not in one of the lovely little terraces along the South Circular Road but in a poorer version of Siobhan's suburb, further out and mocking nothing but its own shoddy semi-Ds.

And then there had been that whole business about Jonathan's school.

They had met for an early drink, ending up in Grogan's, though Siobhan had suggested the Shelbourne.

'I'm not paying those sorts of prices,' Rosemary had said. 'Let's go to Grogan's. It'll be a return to your *temps perdu*, Siobhan, your bohemian youth.' Escaping the suburbs, working with artists, Rosemary had become the sophisticate among them, and Paula remembered feeling surprised at this metamorphosis.

They had sat around a table, smoking. The ban hadn't come in yet, and they had bought a packet of cigarettes, just for old times' sake. None of them had ever been serious smokers, but they had affected the habit for a while when it had been fashionable. They had chatted and laughed together, and when they were ready to go, Siobhan had said, 'This one's on me – I'm celebrating.'

They waited to hear what new triumph she would

unveil; her long face was flushed and smiling.

'We just heard today: Jonathan has a place in Gonzaga.'

'Oh, congratulations!' Rosemary exclaimed.

As they got to the door of the pub, Paula had stopped, and planted herself in front of Siobhan. 'You are such a hypocrite you take my breath away.'

'Oh, here we go, waving the red flag.'

'No, you really take the biscuit, Siobhan. It's nothing to do with the red flag, it's about our principles, the ones you were so hot on. Fee-paying schools, equality of opportunity, elitism. What's happened to all of that?'

Siobhan had stared down at her for a minute. 'Paula, you don't have to worry. There are scholarships, and your Eoin is a bright boy.'

And Rosemary had hurried them out and begun to prattle about some painter who was showing in the gallery, and Siobhan had smiled, and Paula had glared but allowed herself to be calmed down.

Rosemary, the peacemaker. If she hadn't been there, Paula feared that she might have struck Siobhan. That remark was way below the belt, even for her.

Oh, Rosemary, how were they going to survive without her?

'Here we are.' Siobhan swung the jeep through the gates of the cemetery. 'It's not as far as I thought.'

'This is the bit I really hate.'

Siobhan nosed the car into a narrow space, and they got out into a colder day, though the rain had stopped. Paula could see, up at the far end, the mound of newly dug earth.

People were quieter now as they followed the coffin to the grave. They gathered round, huddling together. The priest, who had put a coat on over his vestments, stood, waiting for them to settle. Paula stared at the broken earth. It was not brown or black, but a sickly yellow. A worm that had escaped the gravedigger's spade slithered across a sod and disappeared. The hole itself had been covered by an oblong of faux grass in lurid green. She felt her stomach contract and turned her head to stare at the mountains beyond. She reached out and took Siobhan's arm and felt a reassuring pressure.

She had no principles any more. The world was a far bigger puzzle to her than it had been when she was young. But how foolish to squander time on squabbles and resentment, when there was so little time left. They were sixty years old, and Rosemary was dead.

The priest had begun to pray now, the final prayers before the coffin was lowered into the ground. Later, when the mourners had left, the gravediggers would come back and finish their task. Rosemary was dead, but they were alive. The two of them would go on for another few years, maybe longer, maybe a decade or two.

And Siobhan would surely outlive her. She would present herself to a grieving Dermot, who would also outlive her, and take over as head bottle-washer, explaining to all who would listen how much she had loved her dead friend, how central she had been in her life.

And I won't be here to answer her back.

Siobhan would buy a new outfit for the occasion –

another Nicole Farhi coat, or maybe Armani this time. Had she left her coat folded back deliberately in the church so that the label was visible?

Paula stared at the grave, willing herself to a consciousness of the moment. There must be something wrong with her, there must be something missing to have her obsessing about Siobhan, resenting her and all her worldly goods when she was standing at the grave of her beloved friend.

On the journey back, the traffic was heavier. Paula could feel a sense of relief in the car – they had seen their friend off, they had acquitted themselves well. They began to chatter about other things – family, work, how tired they were. Again, Paula felt an affection for her friend – after all, she wasn't perfect herself.

'We really must make an effort to keep in touch,' she said. 'It's more important than ever now that . . . well, you know.'

'And we will, we definitely will. I hate going out in the cold, but the worst of the winter must be over by now. Roll on summer, I say.' Siobhan took one hand off the steering wheel and began to wave it about. 'Have you and Dermot made any holiday plans yet?'

'Ah, you know, it's hard to decide,' Paula said. 'Probably somewhere in France, maybe Italy, though it's got very expensive. Or the north of Spain – do you know the north of Spain? It's such a surprise, really lovely. What about you two?'

Siobhan glanced across at her. 'It's France for us for the foreseeable future.'

'You mean . . . ?'

'Yes, we finally took the plunge and bought a place.'

'Well, good for you. I'll expect invitations, mind. What part of France?'

'Villefranche. Do you know it? It's near—'

'I know where it is.'

She had been there once, years ago, when they had motored down through France and Dermot had been too tired to drive over the border to Italy where they had booked a room in a hotel in Genoa. She remembered, now, her delight when they arrived. She saw again the lovely coast, the mountains that protected it, the gentle curve of the bay, the benign sun that shone but never too fiercely. She thought of the little town itself with its narrow climbing streets, its odd assortment of shops, its station where the train from Nice stopped and took on passengers to chuf-chuf them all the way to Italy.

She remembered holding Dermot's hand and thinking, *I'm happy*. Can a landscape make one happy?

'It cost us a few bob, but as George says, you can't take it with you. No pockets in a shroud.'

In the pub a section had been reserved for the mourners. There was the smell of coffee, and a fire was lit.

'Look, there's two places there,' Siobhan said, 'beside the cousins – what are their names? Bill and Angela.'

But Paula knew she must get away. If she had to sit down now beside that woman she wouldn't be responsible for what she said. 'Just excuse me for a minute, will you, Siobhan. I'll just . . . the Ladies.'

In the Ladies, the hand-dryer was roaring, and the air

was dense with the smell of chemicals, but Paula gritted her teeth and stared at her reflection.

Rosemary is dead, she told herself. *Don't you get it? You'll never see her face again, never hear her voice. That is what matters, that's what you should be feeling.*

Yes, but . . . Villefranche? Why did it have to be Ville-bloody-franche?

She tugged at her hair with a brush and began to search in her bag for her lipstick.

Back at the table, the other three had settled in. Siobhan pulled out the chair beside her. 'You were a long time.'

'Was I? I just got to thinking I suppose and—'

'Well, never mind that. Tomato or mushroom?'

'What?'

'The choice of soups.'

One of the cousins recommended the mushroom. He said he had noticed a bowl of it on his way in and it looked very nice with a dollop of cream on top.

The cousins were from Longford and anxious to get back before the traffic built.

'I'm not used to city driving,' Bill said. 'Not any more, though I lived in Dublin for twenty years.'

The soup was hot, the coffee strong, and the sandwiches generously filled and made with thick slices of brown bread.

'I wish I had a local like this,' Siobhan said. 'And the staff are so nice.'

They chatted with the cousins, who said that they were closer, really, to Rosemary's mother, but that they remembered Rosemary so well when she was growing up. A lovely girl, they said, and always so kind.

Patrick came round to the tables to see that everything was all right. He stood between Paula and Siobhan and put a hand on each woman's shoulder. 'It was so good to see you there today. You two.' He shook his head as if in wonder. 'I remember the first time Rosemary brought you home, smart, city girls. I think I had a crush on both of you for a while.'

The women smiled across at each other, remembering too. Paula saw again the big, square kitchen and the gangly teenager who blushed whenever she caught him looking at her.

What age was he now? Mid-fifties?

'You both meant so much to Rosemary – like the sisters she never had. Now, I'm going up to the bar. Are you sure I can't get anyone a drink?'

The cousins smiled at his retreating back.

'He's a grand lad,' Angela said. 'He'll miss her – not indeed that you two won't. Friends are so important, I always think.'

Bill leant forward and plucked the bill from the middle of the table. 'This is on me,' he said. 'It's nothing, a couple of quid – I mean euro – I just can't get used to calling them euro.'

'Yes, we don't want to get stuck in the middle of Dublin,' Angela said, 'but it was so nice meeting you both. We'll all miss poor Rosemary.'

The pub was emptying now, and young men and women dressed in wine-coloured waistcoats were starting to clear tables.

'I suppose we should be off too,' Siobhan said. 'Are you

going home? I can take you, I'm in no hurry.'

Paula cleared her throat. 'You know, I think I'll go for a bit of a walk. I've been in cars all morning.'

'Are you mad? It's raining, and where are you going to walk? Out on the road and get yourself killed?'

'I don't mind the rain, and there are side roads. Really, Siobhan, I need to clear my head.'

Siobhan stood up and leant across the table to hug her friend. 'You were always a bit weird – I'm glad to see that that hasn't changed. But listen: we will keep in touch, won't we?'

When Paula left the pub, she found that the rain had stopped. She crossed the road onto the footpath, and, after a while, turned left, up towards the mountains. They had walked here as girls on Sunday afternoons, heading off for a hike, sandwiches in their pockets. None of them had had proper boots, and they usually didn't get very far. There was a field, just up ahead, where you could stop and look down on the city.

At first she thought that she might walk up to that field, but it was unpleasant walking here, with the cars far too close. The sky was dark, and the wind was whipping sweet wrappers and worse into her face.

She stopped when she came to a gate. There was no view of the city here with the road curving away. The grass was rough and bleached after a long winter. Beyond, there was the dark evergreen of a wood, and beyond that, the peak of a mountain. Which one? If Siobhan was here she would know. That was another annoying thing about her, how she always remembered what you had forgotten. Maulin, she would say now if she were here. Or Djouce or Kippure. And she would stick out her chin and look pleased with herself.

Paula turned back towards the Yellow House and the uncertain bus ride home.

It had been a strange, dislocating day. Up above her in the slanting graveyard, Rosemary lay buried in the yellow earth. The thought didn't fill her with horror or despair and, instead, kept slipping away from her. She couldn't hold onto it, though she wanted to, and she felt bad about deserting her friend.

Now she was anxious about being home late. And she had to go to the shops yet, and she hadn't even washed up the breakfast things. She should have taken that lift, and she would have if it hadn't been for bloody Siobhan and her announcement.

Villefranche. Why did they have to choose Villefranche? Anywhere else and she wouldn't have cared at all. In the car, she had actually begun to feel generous towards Siobhan – the two of them left, Rosemary dead. Her oldest friend now, not a bad old stick, and what did any of it matter, anyway?

But then she remembered the sly, sidelong glance Siobhan had given her as she had said the name. The scarlet-painted lips (at a funeral, on a sixty-year-old woman?) had parted, and the enunciation had been creamy with self-satisfaction: Ville. Franche.

Oh, she knew what she was doing all right. No doubt

about it: Siobhan always had been and always would be an eighteen-carat bitch.

In the gathering gloom, Paula began to feel more cheerful. She stopped and turned back towards the mountain, just about visible now as the clouds came down.

She smiled, hearing again Rosemary's voice as she stood at the door of the flat, the collar of her coat turned up in the fashion of the day, her handbag on her arm. 'We are going to be late if you two don't hurry up. For heaven's sake, aren't you ready yet?'

The clouds were further down now, completely covering the mountain, and it had started to rain again.

Paula peered, trying to see through the murk.

'Not yet, Rosemary,' she said. 'Not just yet.'

Queen of the Night

Natalie Ryan

'HE CAN HARDLY KEEP HIS PAWS off.' Mum sniffed into her gin and tonic. Her tongue chased an ice cube around the inside of her mouth before catching it in her teeth and biting down hard.

It was the annual company barbeque. Flemming stood in the corner, his big carpenter mitts stuffed into Jasmine's back pockets, the denim seams stretched to the point of ripping as he squeezed. Jasmine remained doll-stiff, her mouth twisted in a faraway smile that didn't reach her eyes.

'Quite the promotion, I'll say.' Mum's friend Ingrid rubbed a handful of roasted groundnuts between her fingers. She flattened her palm and blew the dry skins, which floated onto the grass like autumn leaves. There are certain things I miss about Ireland, like autumn. Out here there are only two seasons: wet and dry.

Jasmine was the garden girl for our first year in Ghana, and then all of a sudden she moved in next door with Flemming. I remember her days in our garden: body bent low with a cutlass, raising the blade back and forth over the dry grass, its sound the stroke of drum brushes. Despite her smallness, the muscles in her arm swelled to the size of an apple with each lift of the knife, deflating as she swung back down – a breathy sigh with every swipe. The other hand sat on her thigh, clutching a rag. Every now and then she stopped, stood up straight and mopped her brow, neck and chest in one movement. I took her hand in mine – just once – the day we met. Her palm felt rough as concrete, with welts from gripping the cutlass handle. Her fingernails were stubby and broken.

But at the barbeque, her nails were long and manicured, varnished to match her lipstick. Blue eyeshadow made her look much older. She sat on her own while Flemming loaded his plate with chicken wings at the buffet table. I studied the white clogs, the socks pulled high on his calves with shavings of sawdust from the factory clinging to his ankles. I wondered how he might appeal to someone as pretty as Jasmine.

Dad smiled furtively as he passed her to get to the bar. He was being watched by the huddle of expat women in the other corner. They sat discussing, amongst other things, how lemon juice was a natural highlighter and where to get the best meat in Kumasi. The tone dropped a note when they spoke about Jasmine.

'Lucky she didn't sink those talons into one of *our* husbands.' Ingrid's cheeks flushed. She clinked her glass against Mum's.

'I'll drink to that.' Mum sniggered and wobbled a little in her seat. She looked over to where Jasmine was sitting, chewing the end of her straw as she leant against the low walls of the bar. 'I remember Greg telling her she needed to water the grass every Thursday, and one day we arrived home in the lashings of rain, and she was out there with the hose!' They all started to caw. I looked over at Jasmine, but she was concentrating on a plaster that was coming away from the back of her heel.

'Shouldn't you be in bed by now?' Dad ruffled my head with a heavy hand, despite my being beyond the age of head-ruffling. 'Come on. Say goodnight to Flemming.'

A boozy-cigarette kiss landed on my cheek, as Flemming's beard scratched my skin. His eyes always had a reddish rim to them as if he'd been crying, but this time they actually started to water.

'You know, I have a girl too, called Stine.' His beer slopped all over my foot. 'She's coming out here in a few weeks with her brother. *Virkelig!*' He took Dad's arms and started singing and swaying.

'I'm your private dancer, za za za za za za . . .'

'Jesus, Flemming.' Dad broke free and motioned to Mum that he was taking me home. Jasmine smiled and blew me a kiss. I didn't dare blow one back.

Flemming and I passed each other in the evenings as I cycled home from the pool. He tooted the horn of his white Beetle when he saw me, elbow resting on the open window, waving on his way to the clubhouse. He just about managed to squeeze his Viking frame into the car, head skimming the low ceiling and the seat pushed back as far as it would go. It was lucky Jasmine was tiny, because he took over most of the passenger seat too. I had overheard Ingrid telling Mum he was divorced.

'A bit fond of the old sauce would be my guess,' Mum had replied, sipping a little white wine.

Ingrid lived on the other side of the compound, near the entrance. Boredom drove me to her house most days. That and a cupboard full of home-made biscuits in a place where biscuits could not be bought. She was only too happy to have an audience as we walked about her garden, reading aloud the unpronounceable plant names from her encyclopedia.

'You see these flowers are *my* children,' she smiled, stroking my hair one Saturday morning as we stopped in front of a large gangly cactus that looked as if it were on its last legs.

'Where are you, Night-blooming Cereus?' she said, thumbing through the hardback. 'This one is very special. It only flowers for one night a year. Here she is – look!' I followed her down to the grass where she laid the book on the brittle blades between her legs. 'I prefer its other name: Queen of the Night.' She pointed to the picture: a burst of white petals layered like a courtesan's skirt around a yellow centre. It was beautiful.

'This plant is native to the Sonoran Desert in North America and is quite inconspicuous during most of its lifetime. However, for one midsummer's night each year, its exquisitely scented flower opens as night falls, filling the desert with an exotic, inviting smell, then closes with the first rays of the morning sun. Pack rats often eat these blossoms before morning, so catching a glimpse can be difficult.' She closed the book as I took the rubbery leaf in my hand and stroked it for a bit, imagining the pure white of its flower.

'It's due to come out in a few weeks. I might have a party to celebrate.' She groaned as she stood up, brushing the dust off the seat of her shorts. We walked towards the house, the smell of warm sugar wafting from the open kitchen window.

'I don't want her getting ideas.' Mum pouted as Perfect left for the evening, taking the empty salad bowl into the kitchen on her way out the back door.

'You're being unreasonable.' Dad shook his head and nibbled the edge of a cucumber slice. 'They worked together for years. Of course they're going to be friends.'

Perfect and Jasmine used to meet at the top of our driveway, Perfect after her day of housework and Jasmine dressed for drinks at the clubhouse. Mum stood up from the table and looked out the window at Jasmine, who slouched on an upturned plant pot wearing massive hoop earrings and tight jeans.

'You can't ban them from talking to each other.' Dad pulled Mum away. Perfect had changed out of her white uniform, and, taking the net off her head, she combed her hair out while they chatted. Jasmine's hair was straight, sitting out from her head like that of a Lego figurine, from too much relaxer.

'She'd better pull her act together is all I'm saying. Look at the state of these.' Mum lifted two wine goblets out of the glass cabinet and held them up to the light.

'Why don't I find something nice to rinse them out with?' Dad took them out of her hand and headed for the fridge. I peered out the window. Jasmine was on her own again, leaning against the wall and pulling at her fringe.

'It's not right, eh.' She frowned when she saw me walking towards her. 'Come, help me small.' We cut through the bamboo to Flemming's veranda where an iron and board stood beside an ebony table.

'Jasmine! What are you doing?' I asked as she laid her head on the ironing board and, placing a tea towel over her hair, brought the soleplate as close as she dared.

'I am iron my hair so it's nice and straight like yours.'

Flemming's Beetle rumbled in the distance, stirring up a halo of red dust as it accelerated towards the house. Unplugging the iron, Jasmine ran to the top of the driveway. He gave the horn two short toots and waved as he swung around in a semicircle, two cigarettes hanging out the side of his mouth. Jasmine got into the passenger side and took one, pulling deeply on it. He kissed her full on the lips, and they drove off towards the compound gates.

'All she wants is a visa and a flight, and then she will run for the hills. Poor idiot.' Ingrid and Mum were drinking coffee on the veranda. I came out from the bedroom, attracted by the hush as their voices dropped. Outside, the atmosphere was chirping; birds unseen in the trees seemed to be complaining of the heat. I knelt on the terrazzo and listened, peering over the sill as the conversation trickled through the mosquito net. They were squinting over the bougainvillea into Flemming's back garden. Four gigantic pairs of white underpants billowed on the line.

'Oh, the vanity of menfolk; she's half his age. I suppose he thinks it's that sexy beer gut that's driving her wild!' They cackled and drained their coffee cups at the same time, like synchronised swimmers.

'At least he's divorced, not like Mark. And Karen such a beautiful woman. I wouldn't leave mine alone here, I tell you. Not for a second.'

I ran my fingers between the slatted windows, my nails making a whirring sound on the net. Mum coughed, and they stopped talking.

Ingrid stopped me on the way to the pool. My back tyre skidded as she came out onto the road, chopping the air with her gardening shears. I climbed off the saddle to have a closer look, laying the bike on the grass with its handles pointing into the gutter.

'The buds are long enough. I think it'll be tomorrow night.' She took me over to have a look. The stalk and bulb had turned purple-pink, grizzly like the pustules on a turkey's neck.

On my way home, I saw her parked outside the club-house while the watchman loaded her car with crates of beer and soft drinks. It looked like the party was going ahead. After putting my bike away, I wandered around the garden, collecting palm leaves to weave. Jasmine sat on Flemming's veranda, chewing cane. She looked ghoulish, her face white, with dark sockets and lips.

'What have you got on your face?' I stood at the fringe of their garden, brushing my legs with the palm. Jasmine sucked her cheeks, shooting saliva over the hedge, where it landed and glistened on the grass.

'It's skin bleach, so it will be nice and light like yours. Don't tell Flemming, he will be crazy-o.' As she started to laugh, the white powder fell off the creased parts of her face, landing like snowflakes on the floor, as if she was disintegrating.

'My mum lies in the sun so her skin goes dark – like yours.'

Jasmine laughed even more, so much so that it seemed a betrayal. I decided not to mention that Mum put rollers in her hair.

'Do you miss gardening?' I said, as Jasmine held a bowl of pared sugar cane out. I crossed the grass and took one, chewing and sucking the sweetness.

'You dey touch? Sweating all the day in the sun?' Jasmine took a damp cloth and started to wipe the white off her face.

'Do you know the Queen of the Night flower?' I turned the cane round and started to gnaw the other end. Jasmine shook her head as she rinsed the cloth in a basin of water. She was beginning to look like herself again. I told her what it said in the encyclopedia.

'Closed all the day and coming out in the night. Clever flower, eh?'

'It's closed all *year*. Ingrid is having a party. You'll see it then.' The cane was warm and sticky in my hand. I didn't know what to do with it. There was a small pile of them at Jasmine's feet, but it didn't seem polite to leave it there.

'I like to see this flower, but maybe I don't get invited,' she said, collecting the debris on the floor, holding her hand out to take mine.

'Of course you'll be invited.' I turned and dragged the palm branches behind me, with the disconcerting realisation that she might not be. 'I'll let you know.'

They promised if I went to bed for a few hours after dinner I could stay up late to see the Queen of the Night. I lay awake in the darkness until Dad came back to fetch me. He smelt of beer and barbeque smoke, laughing at his own jokes as he sprayed the backs of my legs with Autan. I picked up my torch, and we headed across the compound towards No. 7. Flemming's Beetle roared as it turned onto the road and drowned out the party noise floating towards us. Dad pulled me up over the gutter as the car dusted past, inches from where we stood.

'For Christ's sake, Flemming,' he coughed through the dirt. 'Drunken lunatic. Are you all right, pet?'

At the party, the men drank beer and talked about a new timber contract while the women gathered around Mark's wife. She had just returned from a month in England and stood holding her hand out in front of the group as they admired the diamond on her middle finger.

'Mark had it sent from South Africa,' she said. 'It was here when I got back. If this is ten years, I can't wait to see what I get for twenty!'

I turned back towards the garden where the cactus was

starting to blossom. Everybody seemed to have forgotten the reason we were there. The music grew louder, and I saw Heinrich spinning Mum round and round to 'I Will Survive'. Dad slouched on the wicker seat and flicked through a collection of *National Geographics*. Ingrid went round the room with a tray of ice, dropping fresh cubes into drinks.

I stood guard over the cactus and watched the giant white buds as they slowly unfurled. Minute by minute, petal by petal, the flowers were beginning to show themselves. The outer leaves – long green fingers – opened their palms to reveal a shower of broad white petals surrounding the yellow centre. Around quarter to ten, the first one was fully open. I laid my torch on the grass and stood still for a while, holding my face in its mouth, soaking in the radiance as if some of its beauty could be passed on. The smell was intoxicating.

'An exquisite fried egg. What do you think, pet? Does it smell like breakfast?' Dad crept up behind and tickled my waist. I didn't laugh. Something had been stolen, a precious moment lost. The revellers were making their way through the grass, led by Ingrid with her camera.

'Watch out for snakes! Karen, those shoes aren't made for the bush, you should have left them in England,' Dad said as Mark steadied his tottering wife.

'Happy anniversary, darling.' He picked a flower, dropping to his knees as he offered it to her.

'Ingrid, take a picture, will you?' Karen held the flower against her breast, her husband kneeling with his arms around her waist.

'Oh no, please don't pick them.' Ingrid stood by the plant, caressing each flower in her cupped palm. The group made their way back to the house, the broken stalk left discarded on the ground. I picked it up, remembering Jasmine. Nobody would miss me for a few minutes. My torch danced on the grass as I took the shortcut past the badminton court and through the bamboo towards their house.

The light was on in Flemming's porch, his clogs parked at the threshold of the half-open door. It was dark and silent inside, except for a whistling snore and the low whirring of the air conditioner. Two large feet hung off the edge of the sofa where he slept. I searched the rooms for Jasmine. Down the corridor in the master suite the bed was empty and unmade, but through the window I saw a lone figure sitting in darkness on the veranda.

I shone my torch through the glass and saw Jasmine framed, halo-like, in the reflected light. She was wearing a vest and shorts, her body curling into the seat. She was lovely without any make-up, her hair in fine cornrows and a small silver cross glinting on the tip of her breastbone. I looked at the flower in my hand, already wilting, the long petals starting to droop down the stalk. She wouldn't get to see just how beautiful it was.

I moved closer to the window, waving my torch, but she twisted her head away, and, as she turned, I saw her eye socket, swollen into a grotesque bulge. She held her hand up and out as if she could push me away through the glass. The other hand wrapped around her stomach. I didn't stop to look at Flemming as I ran out the door, through the bamboo and back to the party. I sat on the wicker seat beside Dad and didn't venture back into the garden. I had no heart left to fill with the Queen of the Night's beauty.

I cried the whole way through breakfast.

'I told you she shouldn't have been out so late. Look at her, the poor thing is wrecked.' Mum wagged her toast at Dad. He leaned over and cupped his hand on my forehead.

'Do you feel hot, pet? I hope she's not getting malaria. Remember last time she got very weepy.' Dad's hand moved under the sleeve of my T-shirt towards my armpit.

'I'm fine. Just . . . poor Jasmine.' I told them what I had seen. Mum left her toast down and pushed her plate away. 'Are you sure?' she asked, drawing her head into her hands when I nodded.

'That's terrible, poor Jasmine.' Dad drank his coffee in slow gulps, staring out over the rim of his cup. He passed me a paper napkin, I wiped my eyes, and we sat in silence until Perfect came to collect the breakfast dishes.

They both agreed while it was a very bad thing that it was none of our business. We couldn't possibly know the full story. We wouldn't be doing anything about it.

Jasmine didn't leave the house for two weeks. I looked across the grass to Flemming's veranda every day, but if she sat outside it was always with her back to our house. Her mother called in to the compound once with an elderly man, said to be a fetish priest. I thought I heard wailing of some sort, but Mum told me to come inside. I cornered Perfect in the kitchen, but she answered none of my questions as she chopped onions on a board, wiping her eyes with her sleeve.

After a while, Jasmine began to appear at the top of the driveway, but again she always faced the other direction. If I passed on my bicycle she would pretend to study something on the ground or on the wall or on herself. It was a relief not to have to talk to her. Something had passed between us, and it was obvious we both wanted to forget.

And then, one day, I heard a screeching noise coming from next door. A little blonde girl ran around the garden while her father chased her with the hose. It was a delighted, little-girl scream, and Flemming's laugh rocketed up through the branches of the giant odum all the way to the sky. The boy was quieter. He sat on a chair in guava-tree shade, reading his book. Jasmine stood at the edge of the grass, enjoying the play. The girl ran into her lap every now and then, burying her head to stop Flemming from soaking her. Jasmine stroked her hair and smiled, this time with her eyes.

I heard the cook call that breakfast was ready. Flemming dropped the hose and walked inside with the children. My own breakfast was ready too, but I stood there for a moment watching Jasmine as she bent to pick up the heavy garden hose. She tugged and curled it around her arm before dragging it across the lawn, putting it back where it belonged.

They'll Best You with Fun

Kathleen Murray

WHEN I GET INTO WORK ON Wednesday, there's a note on my desk saying the Boss wants to see me at twelve. You usually know what's going on before you end up in a meeting with him; that's my experience so far. But it doesn't say anything else, and no one in the office seems to know what's up.

His office, on the front side of the City Council building, is getting the full blast of midday sun. Before I knock on the door, I check my watch. Two minutes to twelve, so I've timed it bang on. It feels a few degrees cooler in the room than in the corridor outside; he's got his own micro-climate going on. The way he has the blinds half-closed is sending big slats of shadow across the room. They climb up the far wall, slicing up an old map of the city.

From behind his newspaper he extends a finger, indicating a chair.

'You remember that thing they had,' he says, 'outside the Archbishop's Palace? A kind of vigil, the whole abuse situation.'

I try to picture what he's going on about, the Archbishop's

house, north side. You can't see the building itself from the road; it's set well back behind a high wall at the end of a curving drive.

'Oh yeah,' I say. 'Well, I'm not a hundred percent sure.'

'Look at what I'm showing you, Brian.'

He's pointing at a picture in the newspaper in front of him. I lean across to have a good look, keeping my elbows close to avoid the towers of files on his desk.

There's a photo of a road bordered by a grassy verge, bushes. It's all upside down; he doesn't turn the paper my way. I can make out a footpath, and, at the far side of that, a wall. Must be the Archbishop's property. The odd bit is at the bottom of the picture. A railing, separating the road and the grass, seems to be covered in stuff, maybe. No people. No people in the picture, and nothing actually going on.

'Can I have a look?'

'Of course.'

He lifts the paper up and hands it over to me.

Now I get it; the railing is decked out with shoes, loads of them, attached the whole way along, blurring into the distance.

'The steam's gone out of it now,' he says. 'All the shoes left behind.'

'They don't seem to be blocking the path?'

'Not at all. Tied to the railing.'

'Where is it again?'

'Ribbons and shoes. Sweet Jesus knows what's next.'

I'm still looking at the paper; the article above the photo

has a headline about a fire in a chipper. It's near where I live, part of a local family feud. I thought there was a similar incident a while back. Then I notice the date; the newspaper is nearly four weeks old.

'What's the push on now?' I ask.

'It's the airport road, isn't it? Big contingent in and out for the EU presidency gig and they want it sorted.'

'It's not really my patch, I'm north-east. Will I have a word with Anthony?'

'Need to keep it low-key. The optics.'

'If the local depot sent a truck out, they'd sort it in a morning.'

'Realistically, who calls their house a fucking palace?' he says.

'It mightn't go that smooth. I could get a Polish crew in.'

'Can't subcontract it, Brian. The unions will rip us a new arsehole. You'll have to get the lads to do it. A few reprobates who might need something to clear their slates.'

'Right.'

'And you won't mind taking the brother?'

'What?'

'Your Denny'd be the man for the job. Alongside yourself of course.'

I haven't seen much of Denny since I got the promotion. But the Boss is right: he's good for this kind of thing.

'No bother.'

'As they say, no good deed goes unpunished.'

The sweat is starting to dry in my armpits; the shirt is lifting off my back for the first time today. There must be two fans going, creating a cross-draught in the room. I nod, and the Boss goes to give me a little salute on the way out.

When I ring Denny after the meeting, he's in St Anne's Park, waiting for a delivery of new summer stock. I want him to drive over with me to the shoes, to get a suss. He's not too keen on it at first; he's looking to get his hands on a few specimens for his own garden. Eventually he says he'll collect me some time after lunch, depending on how things go in St Anne's.

When he picks me up, he's all talk about the plants and shrubs in the back of the van. Heading out the north side, we pass the lads putting up flags along the canal.

'They'll have to get a new one made up,' he says, 'for Croatia.'

'What?'

'The EU flags. They're made in Waterford. Each colour has to be an exact tint, then treated with non-flammable chemicals. What's the Croatian one again?'

I lean out the window to try and pick up a bit of a breeze. 'What about this shoe thing?' I say.

'Wait till we get there and see what we're dealing with first.'

After the flowers and the flags he gives it a rest until we get to the Archbishop's Palace. He parks up on the footpath just where the grassy verge begins.

We walk up along the railing together. It's all children's shoes, runners and sandals, new and worn ones, some black, mostly bright colours. They go on and on, pair after pair, on the top, middle and bottom bars. We walk down the length of it until we get to a few people, three or four, sitting outside the high, ornate gates.

'Anybody missing a shoe?' Denny says. That's one thing you can say about him; he has a way of not getting people's backs up. He not dissimilar to the Boss; each man, lord of all they survey.

'Yeah, the lost children.'

A woman wearing a Red Indian headdress gets up from a deckchair.

'The shoes, stolen innocence you know. You're not a journo?'

'No, Dublin Corpo.'

Although her clothes are regular enough, her boots have fringes. She might have picked them to go with the head-dress, or not. I reckon the stripes on her cheeks are the same purple as her lipstick.

'Did you leave Tonto at home?' Denny says.

'I could be a fucking alien tomorrow. I'm in charge of me own destiny now.'

Denny nods to me, and we walk down the path a bit.

'What do you think?' I ask.

He lifts a couple of shoes, as if he is weighing them. He's not attempting to take them off the railing or anything.

'What are youse doing?' someone shouts.

'We might have to look at taking these down,' Denny shouts back.

'In yer fucking hole. This is a legitimate protest.'

They're up in our faces now, me and Denny, coming at us from all different angles. One bloke starts off civilly, then he gets going: 'What cunt'd want your job? I wouldn't piss on you if you were burning, youse are no better than the Brothers.'

Worst of all is this auld one that turns out to be the mother of some fella who committed suicide. She's trying to explain to us, but she's no grasp of the big picture. I start to get into it, but Denny says we'll be sure to pass the message up the line and he heads back to the truck.

On the way back to the depot, Denny's going on and on about the Chelsea Flower Show. He's planning a surprise trip, bringing the missus over. 'And I've booked a show,' he says. '*Mamma Mia*.'

'You're going with her? To a musical show?'

'"The winner takes it all",' he sings.

'If I didn't know better, I'd swear you were a fucking gay.'

He just highers up the radio, whistles along to the tunes.

A few phone calls the next day, and I pull a crew together for the shoe job; the usual shit-shovellers and serial offenders. Graveyard shift, double-time, meet at Marrowbone Lane Depot; no one asks more than that.

We assemble around 2 a.m. that Thursday: myself, two lads – Ger and Manus – and Denny. There's one no-show, but we only wait for a few minutes. It's Mick McLaughlin, and he has a habit of starting his weekends early.

As we head off in the truck, everyone's going on about holidays.

'We're heading over to the brother-in-law's apartment in Greece,' I say.

'Food like out there?'

'Beautiful, anything you want foodwise: Chinese, Indian, full Irish. All-you-can-eat buffet ten euro.'

'They'll have the hand out now for our fucking handout.'

'I'd never eat a kebab there. They put any auld shite in them.'

'Keep away from anything with fucking ice.'

'Souvlaki.'

'Sue who?'

'Fuck off.'

'Why would you leave here,' Denny says, 'in the middle of a heatwave? There's a postman in Donegal says it'll last till September.'

'Mumbo fucking jumbo, muckers examining sheep shit to tell the weather.'

'You can't beat a Sunday afternoon, sitting in the back garden,' Denny says. 'A suntrap.'

'You'd want some fucking trap to catch the sun in this hole of a country.'

'The roar coming from Croker and the match on the radio. Can't beat it, Costa del Cabra.'

That gets a laugh.

When we pull up outside the Palace gates, they all pile out, looking around for the job. Manus goes over behind some shrubbery to relieve himself, and then walks back to the truck.

'Story?' he asks.

'Get the stuff off the railing,' I say, 'and load it in the back.'

Manus pokes at the shoes, with a padded glove. 'Open the laces or cut them?'

'Cut them off or use a fucking blowtorch if you want. Just get on with it.'

Straight off, Denny notices something, over beside the entrance gate. He gets out a lamp and points it in that direction. There's someone wrapped up in a sleeping bag. With the beam shining directly at the bedding, there's a bit of movement; a woman stands up. She's not too steady, full of pills or maybe still dreaming.

'What are youse up to?'

'A bit of street cleaning,' Denny says.

'All in it together, all the powerful men.'

'We're just the Corpo.'

I recognise her now; the Red Indian, the only one left.

'I left those nuns with so many scars down the back of me legs I had scars on me fucking scars,' she says. 'There'll be a riot if you try anything.'

'How's that?'

'We're doing a perpetual vigil. If I send one text, there'll be loads here in a minute. Photographers, papers, everything.'

The other lads have sparked up and are settling themselves on the near side of the gate, watching her. Old-fashioned lamps, casting fuck all in the way of illumination, drag their shadows up the walls, drawing storybook monsters.

I go back over to the truck to find something. When I get in, I'm not sure what I'm looking for, maybe my phone. I see Denny go up close to the woman, have some quiet words; she seems to be listening to him. He walks off, and the woman follows into the darkness, near some trees. Now I can't really see them. I should be party to whatever's going on; even if he's older, I'm senior now in terms of grade. I'm just about to go over to them when he comes back to the truck. I still can't see the woman.

'Where's Hiawatha?' I say to him through the open window. My voice doesn't sound funny like I meant, it sounds tight.

'You owe me fifty squids,' he says.

I think about it. I'm the only one here with the authority to make decisions regarding payments of any kind. There's a figure walking towards town, must be her. Fifty notes. Seems a lot, but still.

'Okay, I'll sort you out later.'

'Lash through it, lads,' Denny calls out. 'She'll be gone for about an hour.'

Once the lads get going, Denny takes a ladder from the back of the truck and disappears over the wall, procuring cuttings from the Archbishop's garden. I should've known, with the secateurs in his jacket and a bag tied to his belt.

Barely twenty minutes in, Manus comes over to give me something he found in a shoe. It's a tiny note, handwritten, and an old coin, a sixpence, stuck to the paper.

'What about the rest?' he asks.

'Check them as you go along, and if you find anything, bring it over to me.'

'What about the ones we've already done?'

At this stage, they've a skip bag nearly filled. Ger drifts over, to see what's going on.

'Don't worry about them. Just check the rest as you go,' I say, 'and I'll deal with whatever turns up.'

As they head back down the railing, a discussion starts up in low voices.

'I'm not sure that's the way to go, Boss,' one of them calls back – Ger, no doubt, with his fucking appetite for a dispute.

'It's hardly anything,' I say. 'Don't worry about it.'

'I think we may go through them all again,' Ger says, and he has Manus behind him, looking at me. 'I just think we may.'

'He has a point there,' Manus adds.

'If youse want to go through them, do. It's all the same to me if we're here till next fucking Christmas.'

Ger gets Manus to give him a hand dragging the bag over to the grass where he tips the shoes back out. They form a little mound, and he takes his time, starting from the top, checking each one. Turns out there are these notes in a good few of them, little mementoes as well. I have to get a plastic bag from the truck to put them all in.

I take a quick look at one or two of them:

Still thinking of you Derek hope things came good rob and mac

or,

Sean your gone
they robbed your life but never ownded it
free as the wind

I can't read the next bit, someone and someone Dwyer.

Then this one:

> *always thinking of you May*
> *you will never be forgotten in our hearts*
> *we'll never let go of you again*
> *love Anne and Paul*

And, in red pen down the side,

> *suffer little children*
> *may ye burn in hell*
> *for what ye did*
> *daughters of satan burn.*

Occasionally, headlights swing around the corner and light the men up. A few cars slow down, but no one stops. Manus heads over to the shrubbery again for a piss, stopping for a smoke on the way back.

'My brother was in that report,' he says. 'You know, the industrial schools.'

'That right?' I say. I'm standing out of the truck now, glad to have someone to distract me.

'Yeah, you might have heard him on *Joe Duffy*,' Manus goes on. 'Over in Scotland for years. I don't know why he was sent to the Brothers after me mam died. The rest of us stayed home; the sister raised us.'

'Different times, I suppose.'

'He's an awful resentful bastard. Got the compensation. I heard he fetched up in Florida. Left a wife and kids behind.

Well for some.'

He waits for an answer, but I say nothing. He flicks the butt and walks off.

When they've filled the skip bags, they put the last few shoes loose in a toolbox.

Going home in the truck, there's not much chat bar Manus, who's always down in the mouth, going on about his prostate. The smell of flowers is unreal, like a hearse or something. Not only did Denny take a few cuttings, he put together a bouquet for his missus. Holding them in his lap like a baby, as if they were precious, telling us the names: gladioli and delphiniums and some purple flower like a ball, Alison or something.

By the time we get back to the depot, the lightest of rain has started up; maybe it's the break in the weather we're all expecting. Ger reverses right up to the door to let us out.

'What'll I do with the bags, Brian?'

'What?'

'The shoes. The recycling sheds are locked up.'

'Just bring 'em in for the time being, I'll deal with it tomorrow.'

While Denny and the lads take care of the bags, I start to brew up the tea.

They amble in after a few minutes, settling themselves down at the usual table. Except for Manus, who's up and down, in and out to the lockers.

'What's up with you?' I say.

Everyone's getting a bit tired; it's going on four in the morning.

'Nothing. Just going for a slash.'

'What's in your jacket?'

'Nothing.'

'Take it off so,' Denny says.

'Fuck off, Denny.'

As he tries to head out, Denny steps in front of him, puts his hand inside Manus's jacket. He takes out a pair of kids' shoes, black patent with silver buckles shaped like bows.

'What the fuck are you at?' I say.

'They're brand fucking new. I'm just bringing a few pairs home for the granddaughter.'

'You can't. They could belong to some, I don't know, someone who's been through the wringer.'

'I fucking doubt it,' Manus says. 'That bunch of tossers, just looking for an issue to hang their fucking hats on. If it wasn't this, they'd be marching over some shite about fuck knows what.'

I'm trying to work out how to go with this; I was thinking we'd dump the lot, but I wasn't given a clear directive from the Boss. One way of making sure the shit stops with me.

In the end, Denny proposes three pairs per man if they want them. They need the nod from me, so I make the decision, three pairs max, and the rest to be left over to the recycling sheds tomorrow. The lads sift through the shoes, trying to pick out matching pairs. Denny watches them while he's heating up the sausage rolls.

'Bad fucking juju there,' he says to me. 'If I had kids, I wouldn't put them near their feet.'

'But you don't, mate, do ya?'

As soon as it's said, I'm sorry, but it's a fact, no kids, living on easy street with his missus, house paid off, doing his gardening nixers. Sitting on his high horse. He keeps looking in the microwave, watching the sausage rolls turn round and around.

'I'd love to get in around the back of that Archbishop's Palace,' he goes, as if what I said disappeared into thin air. 'Hear there's a beautiful pond. I'm beginning to appreciate the merits of a water feature.'

After the tea, the lads hang around playing a couple of hands. Denny takes out some plant book, matching up his new cuttings with the pictures. Sitting there, you wouldn't think a day has passed since he was at our kitchen table sticking stamps into an album, head buried in worthless bits of coloured paper. Da, passing by, would give him a clip on the ear, 'put that shit away, do something useful', or stand him in the corner for backchat. Denny'd whisper over to me, 'I'm after finding a treasure map in the wallpaper', or pretend he could see through the floorboards all the way down to Australia. No matter how far Da went with the strap, Denny'd get back to himself quicker than me. He'd have Ma and me laughing at something stupid, even if we were crying. 'Kids,' Ma'd say, 'they always best you with fun.'

I spread my paperwork out across the far table in the canteen, signing off the overtime, the requisition forms. The plastic bag of notes is leaning up against the ketchup in front of me, not as off-kilter as the shoes, but still.

They're a mess, scrunched up, jumbled together. God

knows what I'll ever do with them; I should put them at the back of a drawer for the next fucker who warms his arse on my seat. Anyway, I unfold them, lay them across the table. I turn each one the right way up; even the ones that have no writing, just a drawing or a keepsake stuck on. Once I have the sorting finished, I push them along the table with my hand, sweeping one on top of the next, then on top of the next, to keep some sort of order. If nothing else, they're neater looking. That's all I can think to do. It's all anyone could do.

Ceremony

Sean O'Reilly

DRESS IT UP WHATEVER YOU WANT, go all Eastern or Muslim, go fucken quantum or dance around with the pagans in the forest, but it's still bloody terrible what can befall people who don't deserve it, I was saying to Siofra one evening back in ours after work. This guy Ringo had rung me during the day and given me some perverse news.

There's no point worrying about the future, Siofra said, throwing me a quick scolding look over her shoulder. She was chopping vegetables for another of her high-fibre soups. When she moved in a few months back, the first thing she unpacked was her soup pot; it was a magical pot blackened by a thousand fires and cured hangovers and colds and soothed all sorts of modern anxieties. These soups, and fruit and seeds and gallons of water, had kept this girl alive in the city until the early morning on Capel Street when our paths had crossed. She was young and vegetarian and unemployed.

I poured us some more of the wine, said, I'm actually in a state of shock. It's just fucked up. You try to live the best way you can, you try to make a life for yourself, pay the bills, don't ask for too much and your fucken reward is what?

There's no fucken justice. There's none fucken left. The cupboard is empty. We're like junkies after our stash is gone.

Is your stomach any better, babe?

My bowels were clogged up again; it was obviously connected to the painkillers for my shoulder; I was popping my way through a pack and more a day. The nausea had lifted since I got that call at work, I told her.

Poor Ringo, she said, and then shrieked and started hopping around on the kitchen tiles because a stray bit of carrot peel had landed on her silvered toes; she was trying to shake it off like it was a slug or something disgusting. Siofra liked to exist barefoot when indoors.

I waited for the drama to pass, said, Poor Ringo, why? Poor bloody Danielle more like. She's the one suffering here.

But I've never met Danielle.

What the hell had that got to do with it? One time only we had run into Ringo together on the street, the big junction at Fenian Street; a brief minute or two nodding along to his pompous crap from the bar of his new bicycle, and now these two were on sympathetic terms and humanity was saved. Ringo was involved with Danielle, who was an old ex of mine.

Anyway, I said, I'll have to show my face at this thing. I can't get fucken out of it, can I really?

Siofra put the spark gun to the gas. The coven of thin blue flames, tipped with orange, roared in our small kitchen. The darkness was earlier every evening now. She scraped the vegetable shavings from the chopping board into the bin, left a trail behind her on the floor. I was hit again by flashes of the first night she came home with me; only twenty-three candles to her name, a low heavy fringe the same moist brown as her wide-set eyes, the washed-out underwear and the jolt when my hand touched a hairless pussy.

I'll have to put in an appearance, I said.

She stopped, tilted her face, squinting: You're actually thinking of going?

They bloody asked me, Siofra.

After what happened? I mean, after how much they hurt you?

Choking on the wine, I said, That's years ago. Ancient history now, sure. You have to let things go or they'll kill you. You move on and grow. The past can become a cage if you let it, Siofra. One day you'll see what I mean. She looked at me sceptically, like I was exaggerating. What was I supposed to say to him then? No, thanks, I don't want to take part in your ridiculous love-in healing session for Danielle. And now there's this new baby. Listen: you don't have to come if that's what you're worried about.

She chose not to react, went back to her soup. I began to tell her more about Ringo's surprise call, how his parting shot was that he hoped I was mature enough to appreciate how important this event was for Danielle. Like, what the fuck was he insinuating?

Of course you are, babe. I'm sure he knows that deep down.

Too bloody right I can appreciate it. And so what did I say back to him? Ringo, I've no hatchet to bury, as you well know. I'm an unarmed man.

I'm coming with you, Siofra announced.

I won't have seen many of these people in years, you know. I'm not going to paint a pretty picture for you. It could be tricky.

You always think the worst of people, she said, and added, dreamily, I've never been to a christening.

It's not a bloody christening. It's a naming ceremony. They're going all non-denominational and secular with it. And that's Ringo's doing. They look down their noses at centuries and centuries of faith. Casting out the demon isn't necessary any more. It isn't fucken trendy any more. Ringo is having his way here.

I totally agree with him, she said.

Do you now? But her phone kicked off, and, as usual with Siofra, the thing had nearly rung out before she found it, under a tea towel this time. Hearing her speak in Irish meant her mother was on the other end. Her parents weren't happy to hear that she had moved in with the likes of me. I went out to the back garden with my drink to let them at it.

Danielle and myself lived the suburban life for nearly eight years in a house in Raheny. Her parents and two brothers had houses nearby, and every evening one or more of them would come tapping at the front window. I used to wonder if they were secretly disappointed Danielle had shacked up with a man with no family to his name, nobody to bring to the party. They are a tight-knit crowd, the Nixons. The lot of us went to mass together every Sunday on the Howth Road. Even if Danielle wimped

out, I'd join the rest of them in the pews. We all went on
holiday together one time, to a big campsite in the south
of France. I used to get on well with the youngest brother,
a quiet, gentle guy called Philip; he often dropped in to
my work on a Saturday afternoon, read the papers and sat
around listening to the punters' stories in the one and only
Atlas Barber Shop. I'd say it hit the Nixons as bad as it did
me when Danielle and myself broke up. I took it hard, they
say; even God must have heard about the state of me and
had a peep down at the antics.

Sometimes you are given the chance to save the world,
to carry the message to the king, to kill the monster. Then
you wake up and try to go to work, and you realise the
dream isn't over yet; it is spreading out across the city from
the bell ringing in your soul. Some people hear it. They
follow you, gather outside your place of work, peering in,
waiting to hear your plan. The people you really need to
explain it to, the dangerous bells, pass you by like you never
existed, and the faces you'd be happy never to see again
come frothing and spewing and all stuck together around
every corner – that's what Dublin became in the aftermath.
Not once did I run into Danielle in the years after we split.
Ringo, however, seemed to be enjoying the sound of his
own voice in the centre of every room I passed through,
both his paws reaching out for an extra-long firm shake
of mine. A man a few years older than me, near the fifty
mark anyway, who, despite the belly, still stuffed himself into his old punk T-shirts, a greying brush cut with
a receding hairline, divorced from an old work colleague

of Danielle's, some kind of engineer and a self-appointed atheist intellectual from near the castle at Rathfarnham. And before he released his overeager double grip, the man would already be expounding to me about the perfection of Danielle Nixon, what she was doing and thinking, how she'd quit another job, had a new hairdo, bought a new bed, the Nixon family update, then, eventually, that she was pregnant, a lot of stuff I didn't need to hear, and he shouldn't have been telling me.

When I heard news she had a baby girl, I sent a text to Danielle to say congratulations, heard nothing back, and thought no more about it. Maybe I wondered if it would have her mother's wild corkscrew hair, the big feet and problems with her thyroid gland. Maybe, one day, walking along a Dublin street, I'd spot Danielle coming straight towards me, pushing the pram, and maybe we'd be able to talk civilly together, and let what happened drop away into the past like a penny down a well. So, it was a shock to hear from Ringo on the phone that she was suffering with post-natal depression. Even so, he told me, they were forging ahead with the naming ceremony for the child, the idea being that Danielle might benefit from a day surrounded by all the people who loved her.

We were out in the back garden, Siofra and myself, after she was done arguing with her mother. The soup had been abandoned. It didn't matter to me; I had no appetite for anything other than the white wine and the chance to sit outside on maybe one of the last decent evenings of the year, enjoying our little terraced house in Kilmainham, with its strip of neglected garden about the length of a bowling lane, my old Vespa rusting in the ivy, and the prospect of bed later with my soft, enthusiastic, young girlfriend. I was pretty happy to stay in these days, just Siofra with her joints and me with a drink, but felt I had to hide that fact from her in case it led to secret thoughts on her part that I was becoming lazy and vaguer.

She was wound up so tight after the row with her mother there were tears in her eyes. She was too young to be in a relationship with someone my age, the mother and father, two Irish teachers who had met in the Connemara Gaeltacht, had always advised her, and yet they were proud of how they had managed to tolerate the relationship, giving her space to find herself, hoping and praying meanwhile that it would fizzle out quickly. But God hates the whingers. And now they were worried sick by the knowledge that their daughter was a full-time captive in my filthy lair. The phone battle went on every day with the same intensity and the same outcome, which was Siofra ranting about the boredom of her youth on the outskirts of Monaghan.

This night, it was a yarn about a family day trip to Dublin when Siofra was fifteen or so – if they had trooped down Capel Street together she might have seen me at work through the window of Atlas Barber's. The reason for this expedition was the fat furry mole on her mother's cheek and the appointment she had that day to have the thing removed after years of gentle persuasion and saving. The Ó Fiaich family had lunch somewhere, probably the safe bet of the old Bewley's on Westmoreland Street. Towards the end of the meal, the mother went off to the toilet. The minutes passed, the coals burned in the Victorian fireplace, someone famous went by, and Mrs Ó Fiaich had still not returned. Siofra went to find her. No sign. The woman had done a runner. She couldn't go through with the operation. They wandered the crude smeared streets of Dublin, searching for their mam. It got dark. They went back to the car; silently, the windows steaming over, they waited.

It's not funny, Siofra said, holding out her glass for more wine. My father just sat there. He didn't know what to do. It was, like, he had already given up. It was disgusting. So, I jumped out of the car, and there was, like, a guard, who happened to be right there; I almost knocked him over. She switched her glass to the other hand and dabbed at her lips with her fingertips cold from the wine. Guess where they found her . . . No, don't. That big cathedral in town, Christ Church?

As the sound of an ambulance siren came closer, she stared upwards at the sky, and I took the opportunity to gloat over her profile, the strong jaw and stretched throat, the lily and the rose at war in her pigment. The siren stopped suddenly, probably at the gates of the hospital. Maybe, Siofra said softly, musing, maybe they are only trying to be nice, Ringo I mean, and they're expecting you to offer a polite excuse. You know, for not attending? A white lie? She said there was a great phrase in Irish for it, wanted me to repeat it after her.

I wouldn't; instead, and maybe I was annoyed because the thought had already crossed my mind, I said, Now who's the paranoid one?

I have a past too, you know, she snapped back at me. I've been hurt too, you know.

I wasn't sure what was bugging her. This isn't about you, I said. This is about Danielle, the woman I spent most of my thirties with. The woman who now has post-natal depression. Can you imagine for a minute what that must be like? She can't even be in the same room as her own baby.

I know it must be horrible, but it's not your concern any more. Aren't you always saying you wish Ringo wouldn't try to be so friendly all the time with you? She seemed to freeze for a moment, her breath caught, like she had been pricked by an insect, then said, crossly, When Simon nearly died in London I didn't go rushing over to him, did I? I couldn't even talk about it to you because you got so angry.

That's totally fucken different, I said.

He was my first love. And stop shouting at me.

You want to hear me shouting?

It's the truth.

You wanted to borrow the money from me, that's the real truth, isn't it? You wanted to ask me for the money to go to London, but you didn't have the guts.

Her face emptied of blood. I was right on the brink of telling her a few more home truths, to have done with it entirely, all of it, with us, with myself, with trying to keep calm and included day after day, with the bluff of survival, with the sudden high angle on us sitting far below on that scratch of turf. I did the control routine, the breathing, brought myself down to ground level again, focused on the grass blade by blade, my moped, the soft wooden table between us and the seasons it had endured, tried to remember the good times. The threat got squashed. I'm sorry, I said, with no idea how long I'd been in a struggle with myself. Maybe you're right. I should avoid the whole fucken thing. Fuck them. What do they need me for anyway?

Siofra sprang out of her chair and dropped to her knees beside me, took my hand, always the dramatic gesture with her. No, you should go, I'm being . . . I don't know what's wrong with me.

I don't want to feel like a coward or something. I'm not running away from any bastard on earth.

You're not a coward, she said, her wild eyes offered up to me completely. We'll both go. Together.

Only if you buy the present for the kid, I said for a joke. She nodded, but she probably didn't hear a word: she had gone very serious, intense. Let me make it up to you, she said, and her eyes moved down my face and down my shirt to my belt buckle. She even tried to lick her lips. She was getting better and better at that.

For the next week, hunting the perfect gift, Siofra ran all over town. She would ring me at work with, I'm in Blanchardstown, I'm on Clanbrassil Street, I'm out in Dundrum, wanting my opinion on some toy or little hat or whatever. Every day she came back empty-handed, defeated, hating herself; she couldn't make up her mind, she said, she was useless, so immature. I lost patience with her a few times, told her neither of us were going anywhere, it was too much hassle. I meant it too. But pretty soon, I'd start to worry I was hiding from something, that people would be thinking I hadn't really got over what had happened, and I couldn't handle that idea. I was trying to cut back on the painkillers as well. Years of stooping over punters' necks, years of scissors and combs and buzzing electric razors was the probable cause. It must be my brain is wrecked too after the years of listening to the opinions and bizarre lies of the men of Dublin.

We have this saying at work: other than behind the curtain of the voting booth, a man is at his most conservative up on the stirrups of the barber's chair. Danielle's brother, Philip, came in with his shyness this one morning just after I had opened up. He took the middle throne. We did our spiel about Danielle, of course, how bad it must be for her, and who else might be attending the ceremony in Wicklow the next day, but I had the sense he was agitated and had more on his mind than his sister and babies. Taking a few inches off his wiry Nixon hair, I tried to draw him out of himself with a story about a regular customer, a married man, five kids reared, who on the first day he was making use of his free travel pass had fallen head over heels in love with a young gay lad on the train to Galway. Philip's response was to blush right down to his large Adam's apple and confess that he was bored to death of his civil service job; he had reached a decision to pack it in and start his own landscape-gardening business before it was too late. He got a hold of my eyes in the mirror as if my advice was desperately important to him; he had found what we all need, a dream, a reason, a rock to smash overselves against.

Clumsy, weak, painfully shy, Philip, the landscape gardener; a wheelbarrow and a spirit level, a skivvy for the decadent – it was so preposterous it had be true. The road less travelled is empty for a reason, was the best I could do, and it seemed to hit the spot, because he smiled with his eyes shut the way his big sister did. It was a nice moment between us, which the clatter of the cowbell above the shop door brought to an end. I turned to see who had come in, and there was this tall, middle-aged woman with a badly cut bob stepping onto the green and black tiles. Good day, she said in Irish, and then in English, I'm looking for Nathaniel McWilliamson.

He's not working today, I replied, before the ugly sound of my full name had stopped bouncing around the mirrors and walls. The woman muttered to herself, perhaps repeating what I had said. The mole was on her left cheek, near the crease of the nostril. No, he's not on today, I explained, the way you might do to the infirm. These little pouches at each corner of her mouth swelled and deflated like gills. From her neck to her ankles, she was concealed inside a puffy mustard-coloured overcoat, and the laces on her trainers didn't match. He mightn't be working tomorrow either, I continued. The lucky bastard won the lotto. Maybe you'll catch him at the airport, love. Do you want to leave a message for him in case he drops in to rub our noses in it? Her mouth puckered, and I may have noticed a slight tightening of the eyes before she announced in Irish, I shall return, or something like that. She paused in the doorway, thought better of it maybe, stepped onto the pavement and turned left towards the river. Philip, whose presence I had forgotten, lowered his eyes when I turned back to our reflections in the mirror.

After work, I went out for a few pints. I was belching gas from the compost heap in my guts. I didn't like what I had done, but that didn't stop me trying to justify it to myself. What the hell did Siofra's mother want with me anyway, coming into my place of work, in her Dalek's puffa habit? To plead with me to take my grim arthritic hands off her meaty sweaty daughter? And then there was the prospect of seeing Danielle and the swarm of mild-mannered ghosts the next day. By the time I got home, after two on the clock, I had made up my mind they would have to do without me in their circle of love, they could bloody find somebody else to gape at. Also, I was all set to come clean with Siofra about her mother, deny I knew who the woman was at the time, say it was a joke that had got out of hand, tell her anything, get it out in the open, stop the rot – but only after I had plucked the clothes off her back and pressed and shaped her body under mine like it was my own imprint.

Far below, propelled by some mysterious urge, a single drop of blood moves silently along the crust of an endless, winding black scar. That was us, Siofra and me, down there trying to make up lost time as we drove across Wicklow the following day. The tarmac was the only human route through this high bog land of heather and stone and monster ferns. I had Siofra's purple shawl over my shoulders against the cold; even my hands on the wheel were aching.

We didn't seem to have a word to say to each other. Neither of us were in the mood for music either. I accidentally let one off inside the car, a pure stinker, and Siofra pressed the window down, stuck her head out into the ballistic wind. Hours of work had gone into her hair and face, and now she didn't seem to care. I caught myself checking her skin for any new marks, scratches or bruises on her neck or upper arms. She sat back inside, blinking her eyes like a child after a rollercoaster ride. Maybe we should break up, she said, like it was one word. What are you even doing with me? I can't manage a simple thing like buy a little baby a present. I told her it didn't matter what you bought for them, that she was making too big a deal out of it, and she asked me why I hadn't bought the bloody present then.

To keep the peace, I agreed it should have been me. Arriving home the previous night, before I had my jacket off, a very distraught Siofra announced she had failed to get a gift for the kid, she had been to every shop in Dublin but just hadn't been able to make up her mind. It didn't matter; it shouldn't have mattered, but I still lost my temper anyway. Siofra fled the house, returned after a few minutes, and we did some talking, and calm was restored. She showed me what she was planning to wear, danced barefoot around the room for me in her short green dress with nothing else underneath. I grabbed her, forgot everything I had planned to say, and a lot more.

Under a sky of jammed-up cloud, the road took a dive down from the hills and miraculously straightened out across the bottom of a valley. Our little red blob of blood trickled along faster. I didn't like the idea of arriving late, attracting attention to ourselves. As if she was reading my thoughts, Siofra said, I tried to wake you. I tried to wake you three times. You couldn't wake up. I know how nervous you are and on edge about today and seeing all those people again, I really do, but don't take it out on me.

She had kept away at a safe distance, over by the bedroom door, while she called my name a few times early that morning, and I hadn't moved. I heard her voice each time, knew she was there, and couldn't find the will to lift my head from the pillow or show her any sign of life. I had a cruel hollow feeling in my chest, that sourness you can taste after a big row, after the tongue has nearly torn out its root and your eyes are sore with what you've seen. I knew it well enough by now to be sure it wasn't a hangover or the constipation. I'd stayed up after Siofra went to bed, doing nothing, drinking a bit more. She must have come down to me later on, maybe tried to get me to come to bed. I couldn't remember what had happened, but I could guess I had gone too far, crossed a sacred line. That morning, the three times she tried to wake me up, afraid to lay a hand on me, my name in her mouth was barely more than a hint, a little question to see if it was really me under the duvet.

The first drops of rain to hit the window were thick and distinct enough to have their own names. Up ahead I saw there was room enough at the start of a hiking trail to pull the car in. Siofra said, rapidly, I had this terrible dream last night about my soup pot. It was so disgusting. What are dreams really, Nathan? I had the impression she was only talking to keep me away from her, like she thought I was after a bit of dogging. Listen to me, I said. That's when I told her about the unbalanced phase after the split with Danielle, how she took a barring order out against me, how there was a voice in my head with a message from someone who knew the son of God, how I woke up during a bed bath in a state-of-the-art mental ward.

We were over an hour late by the time we found the right hotel and pulled into the car park. Siofra had jumped out of the car before I turned the engine off; I watched her staggering in heels across the gravel, the shawl over the head. I took a minute to clear the gas out of me. A tiny Brazilian girl showed us to the hotel's back entrance and pointed to a paved path running downhill towards a line of old sycamores. No one had bloody bothered to tell me the ceremony was taking place outside; we weren't dressed for the weather. A few metres down the path, we saw people coming towards us the other way, about thirty of them in small groups, children and adults in bright rain-coats and wellies. At the front were Danielle's parents, the mother in a wheelchair and a baby in her lap wrapped in a white blanket, the eldest Nixon son sheltering them with an umbrella. I stepped onto the grass to let them pass, and Siofra did exactly the same, stood by my shoulder with her hands joined under her chin like she was at a tear jerker. I doled out the nods to every familiar face, and a few were returned, just about enough. Danielle, as she passed, seemed to be in a world of her own inside the hood of her coat, surrounded by a chorus of ecstatic women. More people trooped by us. Finally, at the very back of the procession, there was Ringo in a pair of red brothel creepers and a fisherman's waterproof cape. He approached us, took both our hands wordlessly, too full of emotion to speak, supposedly, and, after he had lifted his face and felt the succour of the rain for far too long, asked Siofra, Did he manage to get you both lost? Shame about the weather, I said. Nothing, absolutely nothing, could spoil this day, he said, and put his arm around Siofra and guided her ahead of me back up the path into the hotel.

I followed them, slowly, through an empty bar into a reception room. The next act was already under way; at the long white-draped tables, the different family units were feasting en masse in a steamy incense of gravy and stuffing. I spotted Danielle at the main table; she was staring into space, her back as straight as ever, but her hair was shorter and a harsh red colour. I felt stranded, wrong, an extra thumb; I went to find a toilet, sat in a cubicle for a longish time without any success. I came back to the reception room. The feeding had eased. Kids flew deliberately against the windows. Siofra waved at me to join her table, but it was made up of lads I'd probably known before they were legal. Danielle was looking in my direction. I waved but it didn't warrant a response. She looked ten years older than her thirty-seven winters. Ringo was showing off the baby. Right from the start, from the first time I met him, when he was going through that divorce from Danielle's friend, I never took to him, the self-importance, the fake cameraderie. You did the right thing, this guy Ray said to me, with a dessert in each hand. An Armagh man, he was married to another friend of Danielle's. We used to know each other well, head out for a few pints together without the women. Maybe, I said. Fair play to you for coming, he said. We looked around the room. Philip received the baby from Ringo. Terrible about Danielle though, Ray said. I followed his gaze and saw her beside her mother now. I better get these back or there'll be murder, he said, waving the desserts. Good seeing you, I said. He came back and said, I never felt right about what happened, just so you know. You were in a bad way, and I should have stepped up. I shrugged it off. Siofra was coming toward us, tottering in her heels. He gave me a dirty wink on the sly. Catch you inside for a pint in a while, he said and returned to his family. Siofra threw her arms around me extravagantly, tried to kiss me, but I leaned my head back. She gave me the what's-wrong-now look. There were a lot of possible answers to that. I don't feel well, I said.

I got to sit alone with Danielle at the end of a table while the dishes were being cleared away. A gang of her protectors stood at the other end: Ringo, the elder Nixon brother who was in the army, other men I used to know. Siofra was probably outside smoking with her peers or arguing with her mother. Hello Danielle, it's good to see you, I said, not knowing what to do with my hands, and she replied with a sound blown from between her lips, which I took to mean Don't be fucken ridiculous, look at the state of me. I grabbed a seat. Up close, her hair, which I used to slag off as an Afro, was a weird metallic red, her lips were chapped, and her eyes almost black and sealed over, maybe to do with medication. Even so, her cleavage was on full display. Congratulations, it's what you always wanted, Ellie is a great name for her, I said. Danielle stroked the knot she had made in her napkin. Some kid must have taken a bad spill because there was inconsolable screaming for the next few minutes.

My eyes moved from stain to stain on the tablecloth, and every time I braved it, glanced at her, she was gawking at me with those unholy blind eyes. Philip had joined the wise men at the top of the table, his tie loosened under the inflamed Adam's apple, avoiding my eye. Ringo rang me and asked me to come, I said, in the hope of a sign Danielle wanted me there. I really needed to know she hadn't been forced into it. I needed to know what I was doing there as well. There's no hard feelings here, Danielle, I said. I've moved on. If that's of any use. Forgive yourself.

Nothing happened on her face, and her voice was monotone as she said, Are you for fucken real?

Maybe that came out wrong, I apologised.

You want to forgive me?

You're taking me up wrong.

Am I? Her eyes moved in close, and her hand touched mine under the table. I knew you'd come, she said. You were always a glutton for punishment.

I wasn't sure you'd be too happy to see me.

I couldn't tell you who's actually here or not, she said, removing her hand and gazing around the room and then up at the ceiling. I saw my granny earlier, and she died when I was three. You know how she died? A thing fell on her. What's the godforsaken word for it again? One of those things, she said, pointing at the ceiling. Yes, a roof. An ordinary roof fell on her and crushed her to death. There's not a mark on her though, which makes you wonder. So, anyway, I don't have a clue who's here. I'm off in la-la-land. Sure, you know all about that place.

I'm trying to forget.

Last time I saw you, what? I can still smell the petrol. She leaned forward, her breasts had always made me crazy, and whispered, You were threatening to set yourself on fire, you prick.

I wasn't too well.

Would you have done it? She didn't appear to be joking; she wanted an answer. She was close enough for me to smell the lavender in some lotion on her. From above I saw our two heads touching, the long table and her protectors moving in a circle.

Would you?

Of course bloody not, I said.

That seemed to really annoy her; she sat back, folded her arms, said with a disappointed sneer, I heard you won the lotto.

Nabbed, I hung my head. For some stupid reason, I suppose I'd been hoping Philip might have done me a favour and kept the sorry tale of the visitor to the shop to himself like he seemed to do with everything else. Danielle didn't like lies; even when she started fucking Ringo, she would come home and tell me. I reminded myself she was on meds, wasn't responsible for what she was saying. You must be exhausted, I said. You don't have to be here, you know.

Ringo, come here, she called to the other end. Come here quick.

I waited for whatever was going to happen like it had happened before, again and again, and asked myself why I was still no nearer learning what I had to grasp to make this the last time. Ringo stood behind her chair, put his hands on her shoulders. Nat is here to forgive me, she said. Isn't that nice of him?

He's a saint, said Ringo.

And you're a fat pompous bastard, I said, jumping out of the chair. She should be at home fucken resting or something, not here in the middle of this farce.

A saint with a temper, Ringo said.

I had landed a few on him years ago outside Danielle's, and he drove straight to the Guards to make a complaint. He had no witnesses, but they gave me a warning. Maybe that was it, where I had lost myself; I had missed my one big chance, my true moment, and I would have to pay for it for ever. I couldn't tell how many might be watching us this time in the reception room. A counsellor once told me I had a problem letting my anger out as if the mayhem would burn itself out fast like a scrap in a pub and everybody would go home to the safety of their beds. His arms open wide, Ringo was coming towards me like he was walking on the water. Let's not do anything to ruin this special day, he said. Danielle bored already; I think I wanted her to order me out of the place. Then I heard Siofra sing my name; it distracted me, this image of her running barefoot through the maze of tables across the reception room. Before I could stop him, Ringo took me into his arms like he was saving me from the deep, and a blast of fumes got expelled from my arse for all to hear.

A while later, most people were in the hotel bar. Things had calmed down. If something had needed to happen, it was over with now, and out of the way. People seemed more relaxed as if they were backstage after the show. Anybody who wasn't driving, they were enjoying the free tab. I stuck to the weak coffee. There was a game on the big screen so you could stand by yourself and act absorbed in the action if you needed a break from the banter. The bar area's French doors banged repeatedly in the wind and with the comings and goings of the kids with armfuls of flowers and twigs and feathers like they were building a wacky new creature in secret in another room. Every now and again, there would be a song in the corner, and a round of applause. Siofra and another girl brought the baby for me to see and then rushed off to change its nappy, the lucky thing. Ray stood with me for a while, reminiscing about our nights on the pull in town, then Philip and his elderly father, who shook my hand; one by one, most of the old faces from Raheny found their way into my orbit and we exchanged a few good-natured words. When the soccer finished, I disappeared to the toilet, one far away from the children on the other side of the hotel, near the pool. It was another fruitless session. On the way back, through a deep circular window, I watched a man who was missing a hand bless himself with the stump and disappear into the brimming pool.

It was a very special moment, Ringo was telling my girlfriend at the table where I'd been sitting. You would have appreciated it I think, Siofra. You know, there's a pagan stone at the end of the path out there? Yes, well, that's where we all gathered. Now, I don't normally tend towards the superstitious – opium for the people, yes, of course, but this little island of ours is historically very prone to mass hallucination and groupthink for reasons we should leave for another time – but the place down there definitely has a power of its own. So, there we all are by this ancient stone, I have my speech memorised, and everybody is waiting, everybody who matters in my life, when what I can only describe as a kind of current of warm energy rises up through the ground into my feet and rushes up my body and wipes every word right out of mind, every single word. I was a blank slate, Siofra. A tabula rasa; you understand what I'm saying. Siofra gave him the Irish translation, which impressed him no end. So what else could I do but speak from the heart? And that's what I did. Simple, truthful, spontaneous words. Just let it flow. Have you read Walt Whitman? Of course you have. What a great man. A visionary. I don't know the words or have the facility to describe what happened out there, but whatever it was that flowed up through me was as real to me as the love I feel for that beautiful new citizen of the world over there.

Thank fuck Ray appeared with Philip and two other men, barged in with, We are discussing the pros and cons of barber shops.

We get plenty of cons on Capel Street, I said. They come in for a trim before they head to the courts to hear their destiny.

Siofra put in with, Nathan is in constant pain in his elbows and his shoulder especially. It's repetitive strain injury, but he won't listen to me. He won't talk to a doctor.

I gave her a look to keep it to herself, but she didn't catch it.

Who's the most famous person that's been in? Ray went for the comedy as usual. Somebody interesting now. Give us an aul story there Nats.

What's that actor's name you told me about? Siofra said, excitedly. Tell them that story about you and him. Was he Canadian? They went on a four-day bender. He was really famous.

He used to be an actor, I said. He gave it up. They pressured me for more, but I wasn't for telling. What happens in Capel Street stays in Capel Street, I said.

Tell them about the man who pretends he's a detective then, said Siofra.

Why is it so tempting to tell the biggest lies in a barber shop, Ringo couldn't resist wondering aloud. When I lived in London, I had my local barber convinced I was a chauffeur for The Clash. He was a big fan. He would swear on his mother's life he wouldn't tell anybody the stories I was spinning him about nights after the gigs. It got completely out of control. Eventually, I got so sick at myself I had to move out of the area.

I was about to tell him I didn't believe a word of that, only Siofra raised her voice again, her hands joined, to ask, Please? Just for me? It's so funny. Tell them about the man who wants to be a detective. She looked drunk; maybe she'd had a smoke as well. I wanted her to stop giving away stuff about my work I had told her in private.

He pretends he's a guard, not a detective, I said.

Whatever. She stretched out her legs and wriggled her toes.

Philip said, unexpectedly, It's all about men's grooming now. That's the way forward for your line of business. I'd say we're seeing the last of the traditional barber shop.

This man has his own illegal uniform and goes out every night on his bicycle, Siofra said. Stopping crime like Batman.

The man bloody lost his wife in a car accident, I reminded her.

Calm down, she told me.

Is he still feeling bunged up? Ringo leaned in to ask her.

I wanted him to repeat what he'd just said.

Siofra was telling me you're having some trouble with your stomach region, he replied. There was a spate of laughter of course and the usual riffs on constipation while I tried to catch my girlfriend's eye; she was too busy listening to Ray's mouth whispering in her ear, her hands joined, playing all amazed and easily shocked.

I caught Philip's eye, said, I hear you're spreading rumours about me winning the lotto.

He blushed, checked over his shoulder for the exit. I gave him the nod to encourage him to tell the story. I was in with himself on Capel Street the other day, he began tentatively.

He took them through it in his own way; added some new details I hadn't spotted, like the woman's classy emerald ring and a man who had been staring in the window the whole time. Ringo tried to change the subject, but the others were gripped. I watched Siofra's face harden into a mask when finally Philip mentioned the mole on the woman's face. She peered at me, her pink mouth agape, horrified.

I found myself outside, took the path down towards the line of trees. Off to one side, down three steps into a boggy hollow, there was this thin worn pillar stuck in the ground. I fingered the Ogham marks down one side of it. The path carried on into the trees, turned into a track. An idea tempted me to keep onwards: to walk deep into the woods, never come back. Never be found. Become a wild man. Despite what had just happened, I think I was hanging on to see if Siofra would come out to look for me.

Instead, it was Danielle who materialised in the space next to me. I was beyond feeling surprised by this point. What's it like to hate your own child? I said.

The worst of it is she knows I do. She's already afraid of me. Danielle sounded as indifferent as I did.

She probably doesn't. Even if she does, she'll forget.

What, like you did, you mean?

My guess was she was talking about me being adopted. Danielle used to blame anything she didn't like about my character on how I'd been adopted, even the fact that I was happy enough being a barber. She pushed and pushed me to find out who my mother was. Then, one Easter morning in Raheny, I open a letter from the agency informing me the woman didn't want to know. The entire Nixon clan had gathered in our house before lunchtime to commiserate.

I hope the day has done you some good, I said.

That's not even a real one is it? She meant the stone. I bet the hotel had it put there as a . . . what's the godforsaken word I'm looking for? Maybe it's these tablets, but I couldn't remember the word for toothpaste the other day.

I told her I thought the marker was real but Ringo was an asshole to call it pagan because the Ogham alphabet was early Christian. Danielle said, elbowing me, Do you still say your prayers every night? and the stone seemed to darken suddenly and tremble like a barometer, and a shower of rain swept in over the trees. Neither of us had coats on, but I asked if she fancied a walk into the forest. She was knackered, she said, suggested we sit in the car out of the way of people.

She clicked on her seatbelt as if we were taking a drive. I launched into the story about selling our old car, a funny story to lighten the mood, but she cut me short to say, It was me told Ringo to invite you, okay? He was against it, so I made him do it right in front of me in the kitchen. He does anything I tell him. She held my gaze like she wanted me to witness the cruelty in her.

The man's only trying to look after you, I said. Why though? Invite me?

Again, she seemed disappointed by the question, by me. She put her hand on the belt as if she was about to get out of the car, changed her mind: It's like this is all an act. It's like

I'm pretending. But I've no choice. I have to. I can't stop, because, you see, if I do, if I don't behave like this, exactly like this, there's going to be a lot worse will happen. A lot worse, you know what I mean? I'm being watched day and night, and if I'm caught not playing along, not pretending, it's going to be worse than horrible what happens. You understand, don't you? she said, nodding her head so I had no choice but to agree. As long as I keep doing this, nothing can happen to anybody, we're all safe, that's just the way it is.

Well, keep doing it then. Until you're ready to do something else. Things only change very slowly.

Then the other day, she went on, reaching for my hand, I came downstairs to look for her, and I heard Ringo in the thingamajig feeding her. The kitchen. And for a moment I just stood there in the hall listening, Ringo was whistling to her as he fed her her bottle, and I forgot and put my hand to the door handle, and I just froze. I couldn't go in. I wasn't allowed in. So I went back upstairs. Other than that, all I think about is sex.

We laughed together. Just hang on, Danielle, was all I could say.

Says the man who pissed through my letterbox. I always thought you were just pretending to be mad too, that's why I didn't take you seriously. I thought if I just ignored you then you'd get a grip and do one, Danielle said, and yawned. Please let's not get into the if onlys and what ifs. We couldn't have done it any differently, not a single day of it – that's the way I see it. We'd no choice. We played it out to the end. Five years ago though – can you believe it?

A gurgling racket started in my stomach that felt to me like a plug being pulled and the past five years of dead time glugging away down a hole. Through the windscreen, the afternoon was fading around the hotel, the trees bristling in unison and the sky busy with all sorts of birds. I had this other sensation of having been catapulted forward in time and that I had just landed and caught up with myself again, here in the car with her. There was a definite relief in just seeing her, actually seeing Danielle in the flesh, and a kind of shock too that she had aged, that her body was done with me. I used to console myself after we had finally split with the idea that nobody would ever fuck her like I did and nobody would ever make her laugh as much either. Sitting behind the wheel now in the car with her, I knew I was wrong, and suddenly I was relieved to be wrong. Turning to say some of this to her, she seemed to have dozed off; her face leaning towards me on the seat, her mouth open slightly, the skin on her breasts goose-pimpled. I turned on the heating. She would be okay; she would fight her way through this bad patch. We would both be okay. We could be friends now from this moment on. I started the car, as a joke really, switched on the lights. I wanted it to be funny. I thought Danielle would open her eyes and have a fit but enjoy the cheek of it all the same. She only mumbled something, licked her lips and sighed. Then I was reversing. I'd no idea where we were going. Where the hell was there for us to be headed for? Then I was taking the car towards the gate barrier when Ringo and her brothers and Siofra and even some of the children ran out in front of the car and made a brave line to block our way.

Back in Dublin, hours afterwards, Siofra cleared her throat to show she was behind me in the garden. We had run out of words by the time we came down from the dark hills into the streets, even Siofra's Irish curses on my head for abandoning her among strangers had died away. Of course, I tried everything to make her understand I wasn't sick or mad enough to kidnap my ex-girlfriend; that it was a bit of a joke and I was just taking us on a scenic spin around the roads. Then we would switch to the issue of her mother's visit to the shop and what type of person was I to keep it from her. Then back to Danielle, and the darker suspicion of what I was planning to do to her; she was too afraid to come right out and ask me, but it was on her mind I might want to hurt Danielle. Inside the walls of our little house in Kilmainham, I couldn't find a corner to hide myself, so I evacuated to the garden with the end of a bottle of vodka.

I need to go, Siofra said. She had changed her clothes, put on the baseball cap I hated, and there was a bag over her shoulder. I think you need some help, Nathan, she said. A few seconds later, the front door slammed behind her.

I knew a big thing had happened and wasn't over yet. The repercussions were only taking shape. I had crossed another line. Hunkering down, I ran my fingers through the grass and tasted the dew. A thunder rumbled in my guts. What I did next was a brand new one: straightening up, I started to dig out a hole in the ground with the toe of my shoe, then with the heel. Then I got to work with my fingers, gouging and scooping up the soil. It was hard work and took a while. When I was satisfied, I dropped my trousers and shorts, squatted down and out in a long roll without any effort whatsoever came the dump which had been living in me for nearly a fortnight and dropped into the hole. Even when I was emptied, I remained squatting over the hole, inhaling the stench, as I stared up into a corner of oblivion.

Eventually, after belting the trousers, I scraped the loose soil over the steaming pit, pressing down on the surface with my foot, covering my tracks.

It was a good experience out there. For as long as it lasted. One day every soul will be found.

The Widow's Ferret

Frank McGuinness

SHE DISLIKED ANIMALS. THEY HAD THEIR place. Not in her home. They were not welcome. They could be responsible for fleas. Fleas were an affront to any civilised person. This was not being swanky or rare. And it would take a rare man or woman to have sex with a ferret. She was not that rare, thank you very much, mister.

She said that sentence to herself, and she really had to laugh. It sounded northern. And it had stopped sounding foreign. She had lived in this area so long you'd swear the strangeness of its sounds would not matter – would not make her cry – and it didn't. She now loved this place. If they showed John Betjeman's documentary on Dublin's architecture as an archive treasure on the BBC, she did not get on the first bus south the following morning. People were friendly in Coleraine. They were so kind. She did not even mind the many silly suggestions she get a pet. She resisted – she bit her tongue instead of telling them to go fuck themselves. In the silence she once nearly tasted her own blood in her mouth.

She should not have taken the advice so seriously. People were ridiculous, but it was understandable. Males especially, they meant well. Cautioning her to go for the best – buy a pedigree dog or a finely bred cat. A cat particularly would be company. For her, cats brought to mind Egypt. Armies of them, guarding the pyramids, or marching in phalanx through ancient cities of Mesopotamia. Lovely names, Ur or Baghdad, like a mouse in a heaving paw, flattened, eaten. Had she been fighting the Iraqis, she would have come across weapons of mass destruction. Even one would have been sufficient. She was not a greedy woman. She had always been lean as a greyhound. A whippet. A well-trained thin spaniel smelling out bombs on the platform of Belfast Central station. If she had been turned into an animal, a dog – she would not have wasted time smelling her own shit, depositing her piss about the streets of Coleraine. No, she would have hastened to the centre of conflict, carrying that particular device which could destroy the entire feline population of this town. Not the people nor the buildings. They would, like herself, be left standing. Trembling, traumatised, but still on our feet. And of course she would spare the bridge over the River Bann that cut through the heart of Coleraine.

When she first moved there, one drunken neighbour whispered a terrible secret. He was a well-known queer, always after policemen or rugby players, a red-faced ghost she thought him, renting out rooms to students, most of whom he sucked off in lieu of rent. That's what the word was, she saw no reason not to believe it. Nor did she not believe him when he whispered that if civil war ever does break out in this province, you're stuck in the worst possible hole for a Catholic to find herself. I beg your pardon, he simpered, I know you've shifted sides – since you tied the knot, you're now crossed over to our ones – but I tell you, some are savage, and if they ever indulge their bloodlust, if they free their fists from beating the bastarding drums, they'll tear down that bridge and cut off each and every Fenian or Free-Stater from escape. No one will be able to do a runner. They'll shred you to ribbons – I'm warning you.

She looked at this man as if he were mad. How long since she'd been called a Free-Stater? The red ruin of his face matched the red of his tie. She made no acknowledgement of his nonsense. She simply vowed she would never drink in any pub in this quarter ever again. She kept her vow. But if push came to shove, in the dark days – even before he died, there were dark days sometimes – she thought of that bridge. She saw it demolished stone by stone. Men, women, children, bound hand and foot, green ropes paralysing them, blood from their mouths hurled into the innocent Bann, the river weeping to receive them, trying to soften the blow of their death at the hands of their neighbours, drowning them as swiftly as possible, taking the little ones – stop this now, stop. Only being silly.

Silly and stupid. Deeply ungrateful. She lived surrounded by friends and acquaintances. A lot of her neighbours were in the police themselves. None of them were widows but they would surely never see her harmed. They were friendly. Friendly as could be. Sociable. But those who had mentioned the cat – she wished they hadn't. Yet they kept on and on, bringing back to her time after time school books where she read of cats worshipped in Egypt. She never got that out of her head. It just stayed there. Don't imagine she ever went to that pagan country. Still, she was always there in her daydreams.

God's curse on daydreams. As for night-time – it was fine if you could sleep. She couldn't. So often she just could not. She'd lie awake letting the most ludicrous things slip into her mind. It had happened on so many, many occasions she stopped trying to control – let it flow – no harm to it – anything to stop seeing him dead. It always happened at three in the morning. That was when she'd imagine skiting off to Egypt, landing there, not letting herself be scared to death, doing the sensible thing, covering up completely, more bandaging herself against the utterly destructive heat of the sun. It ate you up. Everybody knew it dried your skin, but it also drank your bones. The sun fed on your marrow. It took its pink and turned it into gold. The sun spent your gold like water. She never went out into its heat, day or night. That was why she was intensely white, com-pletely immune to the melting temperature of Thebes, of Coleraine, of Egypt as she walked along marvelling at the sights and sounds of this civilisation, when she suddenly realised she was carrying on her person, discreetly hidden in her handbag, a machine gun.

Wherever she found idiotic Egyptian folk on their knees praying to a cat, she shot them. She'd open the bag, search for something the heathens believed she was looking for, say a compact to powder her pale skin, the compact in the shape of a crocodile – had she thrown it at them they'd scream and step back, imagining it might bite them – but no, out of the handbag came a weapon of sufficient destruction, and she shot them. No mercy, I'm afraid. She was utterly cruel in that way. She'd learned to be. Even if it was only in her dreams. Had she ever been transported in person to those faraway, foreign places, her weapon would have been money in her purse. Bestowing it would have seemed like a miracle. They would have proclaimed her a goddess, ascending into heaven. But she would have kept her bearings. She would have ended back in their own bed. Where she slept with him. Without him. Ronald. Who believed—

What did he believe? That they would be safe. She would never be without him. She would never have to resort—

What was it she would never resort to? She couldn't as yet say. Nothing could be said. Never answer how they expect you to answer. Trust nobody.

That was the way of working in this part of the world. So everyone believed. She didn't. She found the people very direct. Straight. Look at the lovely row of Georgian buildings down at Hanover Place. They were simply demolished. The council had put a protective order on them. The builder knocked them down. There were a few who raised eyebrows. A string of letters in the *Chronicle*. But they were gone for ever. Who missed them?

In her way, she did. Her first hairdresser was in one of those buildings. Tina's. She chose it for no reason other than the name. Neither one tribe nor the other. Innocent. She liked the owner, a Limavady woman, two kids, husband drove a lorry – his own business. In all her years going to get her hair done she had gleaned only that from scraps of conversation.

Okay by her. Tina could do her hair well. All that mattered. But her head grew a little sore, strangely sore, when she was told this would be her last visit likely to the salon. No more would she push open the maroon front door. Glance in to see if anyone had taken over the bankrupt solicitor's office on the floor below the salon. There was a big poster of Rory Gallagher peeling on the wall, his guitar elegant in his hand. The boys on the bus coming home from school loved his band, Taste. Practising his blues song, making the words more indecent, they used to tease her, once asking what Rory could sing to shock her. She had a piece of chalk in her schoolbag. She took it out and wrote, on the back of the bus seat, Thank Christ for VD. I'd like to hear him sing that. They were shocked. One of them put spit on his hands and rubbed it out. She was rarely bothered again on the way home, though now her nickname changed from mousy to scabby. She looked at Rory Gallagher and smiled. For old times' sake she scratched the guitar peeling on the wall. She wondered what had happened to those lads who'd tried to torment her all those years ago. Dead maybe, married, fled somewhere, to the States, to Spain, to Majorca. That was where he'd done a runner, the disgraced solicitor. No one else she knew had ever done that. She wished the cheating robber well. It was only money he took. But now it was time to ascend the stairs – rickety stairs they were, ready to collapse. She thanked God she wasn't a heavy woman.

She wanted to take up a question with Tina she'd not dared answer – not dared ask – before. What would Tina do if there were ever a fire in this house? It would go up like matchwork at the hint of a spark. Tina laughed. She said she'd throw herself out of the window and into the Bann. Her assistant said – she joked that if Tina were to dive into the river, the size of the splash would put out the flames of the fire imagined in the salon. Tina roared laughing. She called the girl a bad bitch. Tina was the boss, but she could take a joke – she would give the young one the road, if they weren't all for the push.

But seriously, the man upstairs – they were soaking her hair. He must have been four storeys up – I will die gasping for breath as they drench every root and residue of dandruff. Tina knew for a fact that he kept a rope – a big rope tied to his bed. She was released fresh from the basin. If something did happen, he'd climb out and down the building. If she had vomited while her head was tied back into the drenching basin it would not have been funny. Woman's windpipe torn by her own puke. Stop thinking about yourself. Think of the poor man suspended by his rope while fire rages. The blaze might devour him. He could easily burn to death if that was all he planned for his safety. But you could not talk to him, he was English. They knew it all, didn't they? Tina concluded.

Straight away she was imagining the poor man swaying on his rope, his pyjamas singed and torturing him. Maybe he slept in the buff. So long had she not thought of a naked man she actually blushed under the dryer, feeling the skin of this fellow, the fine hairs on his English arse, his sweet purple cock. God forgive her, this dying creature was a human being, and all she wanted to look at was his private parts. Dirty bitch she was. The assistant shocked her out of her pleasure. Did she want a cup of tea? No.

When she took out her purse to pay, Tina closed the clasp of her bag. She was a bit shocked – it was as if the purse was going to be snatched. Of course, the opposite happened. The kind woman was saying, 'You owe me nothing – nothing – not this time. I've valued your custom. In all your years coming here, you've never taken as much as a drink of tea. This is from me.' There was no danger of the woman kissing her. Not done here. They shook hands and wished each other well. It was as she was leaving she noticed a bundle of stuff packed in a big box. At the top of the mess there was a tiny statue of the Sacred Heart. So she found out at long last. Tina was a Catholic. And she still had some generosity to show for the turncoat widow of an RUC man. No – no tears, not a chance, not after so long. But she found herself looking back at the two of them – I'll miss you, I will.

What had possessed her to say something so stupid? The women looked at her as if she was – what was she? Some kind of tinker woman who was begging for a free haircut? She could feel lice on her scalp, but she would endure the itch and not give them the satisfaction of scratching the vermin. Did she smoke of dirty gypsy clothes, or what? Were they expecting her to pull a shawl from her bag and throw it over her stinking head? Was there something in their minds that she needed – no, it was worse – she expected charity? She took eight pound coins out of the purple purse – purple like him hanging there – control yourself – but she couldn't. She started to laugh as she counted out the precise amount it would have taken to pay for what she owed. She watched them watching her, shaking their heads. She was leaving the money on the chair she sat on. She left them saying nothing, not looking back at them mocking her, the poor, deserving, dirty bitch. She banged their door shut. Climbed down the shaky stairs. Wanted to light a match and then a cigarette. Drop both on the ground and rush out before it burst into lovely flames. But she didn't smoke, she never had. What was she thinking of? Could somebody be kind enough to let her know what?

The fresh air did not settle her. She didn't want to be settled. How dare people make any kind of concession to her. They all tried to do so. They all seemed to be in the know. Except herself. Something was afoot. She was not party to it. What was it? It seemed that people on every side of the divide were suspicious of happy marriages. If you loved your wife, it might become a rule of law that you were certain to get it in the back. It was always the good and loyal that got plugged. You heard it every evening in the news. It was beginning to dawn on her that maybe they were all in cahoots with the murderers. She could not bring herself to admit what she'd long suspected. RUC, IRA, British Army, UDA. Fuck it, the whole shebang in Northern Ireland – it could all boil down to a very effective way of making sure you don't need a divorce. Everybody is killing off an unwanted partner. That is why murders go unresolved. They are all in this together.

She was putting such things behind her. Slowly but surely. It was a kind of grief. She wouldn't excuse herself like that. She was ashamed for entertaining notions that such baloney would ever be true. What was she becoming? Ronald would be . . . he would be understanding. All the more reason to get a grip. Keep that grip. Firmly. Such rubbish about divorce. It was something left behind to fester from her rancid Catholic childhood. Against her will, she was still controlled by the catechism. God made the world, God is our father in heaven, we should love God above all. Her world had broken into bits, no one heard her crying and helped her on heaven or earth, and she had loved her husband above all others. She had committed the sin of pride – why could she so exactly recollect those ridiculous lessons? Warped, hateful. She had to leave primary school behind her. She had to grow up. It was time to take stock and see the good side. Be sensible. It was sensible to remember that many people change partners. It can all be for the best if a marriage were to end. The new couples that create themselves after they separate, they can even meet without a battle, particularly if there are children. If the worst comes to the worst, they can rise to an exchange of pleasantries.

But her marriage had not ended calmly and legally in any court. No. He was blasted to kingdom come. The vision turned her stomach inside out. His face – what face he was left with, it was a stick of stewed rhubarb. His eyes were custard. She insisted on identifying her husband's body. She smelt frying off his flesh. It was as if some god had wanted him for his dinner and dessert. But the touch electrocuted him. Left him near to a cinder. Now, he was discarded, bone picked clean down to pink marrow, waiting to be shovelled into the earth of the province he died defending. All she said on seeing him was, here is the man kissed me this morning.

She was declared to be a brave woman. A tough lady, some judged. She'll survive. She never cried either. In fact she was always on the verge of bursting out laughing, as she'd done . . . wherever it was she'd last done that. It was one of the reasons she avoided cafes and restaurants. It was not that she was in purdah. It was just that any mention of the Ulster fry made her want to giggle. Want to accuse these people that they were a gang of cannibals. You are damned in this country because you eat your own. You down the blood of your brothers. You devour your sister's skin. She had by necessity to keep her mouth shut. And so she never smiled. Never gave interviews. She was asked to do photographs with others who were touched by grief. By disaster. By murder. She was not that keen. The government understood, but could she not reconsider? The police would put no pressure, but did she not realise – I'm afraid I do and I don't care, let that be an end to it. An end to it now, she insisted. She always fiercely refused. The mood towards her changed. The tough lady became a hard piece of work. The brave woman was maybe a wee bit selfish.

Too fond of her own mourning. Too much harping on her loss, after a certain period of time, well, for want of a better word, she was spoilt. Some called her heartless.

She could immediately scan her own body and watch it without a heart. A beating heart. Instead it was lying quite daintily, quite deliciously, on a white plate beside her. Dainty in that it was so small. Delicious it must be, for there was a knife and fork set prettily beside it. Someone must have cut it from her, with the precision of a surgeon, as she slept deeply for the last time on the night her husband was being blown to the four corners of the earth in a nondescript village no one had ever heard of before or since. What clever engineers those bomb-makers proved themselves to be. How expertly their fingers had constructed such a truly sophisticated piece of work. In the very instant they dismembered three living men, miles away, tens of miles away, scores of miles from the epicentre, a shard had travelled through the stench of the air, breaking its rotten eggs, and that shard jagged her, entering the breast of one wife. Maybe it even entered through the finger, the imperceptible space between flesh and wedding ring. It exploded inside with such remarkable energy that her heart had cut itself cleverly from her, and she was left to live without this vital organ, keeping alive by supping daily on the merest fragment of that food placed so considerately on the white plate, knife and fork neatly folded over each other, waiting for her to dine. If she ever met Ronald's killers, she would amaze them when she thanked them for the delectable sustenance they had so unexpectedly provided her. This would be immediately before she disembowelled them.

She could get away with that, she reasoned. Walk off, unidentified, scot-free. No one could trace her. Not even the most complete police procedure. To hell with DNA. It had no fear for her. And here's a good one – here's one to make you howl – take this on board, boys – it was the killers – they were responsible for this extraordinary gift. If they had left her a heartless woman, they had also made her invisible. She could have marched for miles, walked through walls, without benefit of arms and legs, without breasts and head, hair or feet, if she could survive without a heart.

This power pleased her. She wondered would Ronald have fancied his invisible wife? Would he have found the space where her ribs had vanished, the vacuum in the centre of her face, the hole where her tongue should be – would he have found her repulsive? As his body had turned to meat and jelly, now her body was nothing, without stain or smell. What wickedness worked its magic on both of them? Wife and husband were transformed entirely, transformed beyond recognition. Taking to an early grave, one was put in the earth. The other took to the sky. She realised that if she so desired, she could spread her unseen arms and fly. Dear Christ, she could fly. But this was to be resisted. Resisted for a reason. And it was all explained by a comic book she'd read as a girl.

She remembered that specific story in *Bunty*. This was about a disappearing schoolgirl. Her dad was a scientist who'd discovered some miraculous potion. It was for the British military's use and was only to be employed for world peace. Wasn't he – the father – kidnapped by foreign spies? His daughter alone kept a sample of the elixir. Only she could free her father – she drank it and could vanish. But who would believe her? She realised she had to ration the magic. If she swigged a few drops, only part of her vamoosed. To prove this, she did a strip in front of her friends. Her head and legs were there for them to see. The rest of her was hollow. Her clothes were covering nothing. There, behind her pink bloomers and black schoolgirl boarder stockings – nothing, nothing at all. A blank body.

She had never seen knickers of any shape, size or colour in *Bunty* before. Maybe it turned her on a bit, she was just hitting puberty. But it was as if in losing her stomach, her arse, her woman, her knees, the girl was so misshapen as to be something alien – even something beautiful. And her name was Ira. Honest to Christ, that's right. Her stomach churned when that hit her. IRA. Had she read in that child's comic some hideous prophecy of what would destroy her life? Not merely would she lose her husband, his body, his soul be taken, they would also want to take something more from her. In making her invisible, they wanted her to cease being a woman. No man could literally set eyes upon her. No man could find her attractive. The only ones who would have done so were the bastards who killed her husband. Those malignant fairies would have been enthralled to remove her from womanhood. It was this that convinced her absolutely that the night they did away with Ronald it was no accident her heart was cut from inside her. They had tried to remove her as well.

They had really tried to murder her. But she would remain visible. She would not take flight. She would continue to let her heart beat outside her body, hearing it gallop as she lay awake through each and every paralysed night, her new heart her new husband, now her constant companion carried beside her, beating out the message, I am alive, I have not stopped, I have defied them, and I want revenge.

God forgive her, but she did know about revenge, although one thing she didn't know was, where did the time go? Things she thought she'd believe for ever, she kept forgetting the ins and outs of them. Did they play Abba's 'Super Trouper' on her wedding day, or did she hear it the evening – no, it was at night, late – they first met in the disco at Portrush? She was with a crowd of other teachers. This strapping fellow – not her immediate type, she'd hasten to add – he asked her to dance. That gentle Tyrone accent so complimented her own – didn't they make such sweet music, love took possession of them, they had to tie the knot. It was decided – as quick, as terrifying as that.

Still and all, she made him wait for the great pleasure. And the first night together it didn't hurt, it was lovely, and he told her she was beautiful. That was as good a way as any of proposing. In fact she asked him. He refused. Can you believe it? It was on Valentine's Day, and she had a perfect right to pop the question. He burst her balloon, saying he needed time. She laughed it off, insisting it was a joke. He didn't believe her. That was the worst thing about him. He never did believe her. And he wouldn't now if she were to walk into the living room where he was sprawled on a couch, watching ice-skating, laughing at the men, spinning themselves silly, if she were to walk in and tell him there was a ferret in the garden.

But there it was. A ferret the colour of gold. It smelt of meat and wet clay. It was quite tame. It came into her hand and licked her face. She let it touch her fingers. It chewed on them gently, not so hard as to frighten her. Her flesh delighted in his taste. He started to move about her body, leaving her hand, clinging to her arm and going into her clothes, lying against her breast. She carried it into the house, going upstairs, lying on the bed as the ferret moved down her tits, between her legs and sucked her clean.

She did not call the police. She did not have to say, my husband is dead, my beautiful husband, and in his place, in my bed, there is a ferret. Please, come to my house and kill it. Shoot it dead. Blast its brains out. Take its neck and wring it. I want to hear its fucking bones crack. I want this ferret dead. I demand revenge on it, for it has violated me, a poor widow, a woman it has tricked into trusting, because I might believe it to be an innocent animal. But it is not innocent. Nothing will ever be innocent again. If this creature survives, I will place it in a cage. I will never release it until it dies. I will never feed it. I will never let its soft lips touch water. I will never speak into its strange ears. I will keep it under lock and key for ever. Key – I will throw away the key. It will never smell the day of light – never see the day – it will die in its prison from thirst, starvation. Let it die of hunger, die of want. Let me watch it end its days and do nothing. This is the way I will prove I do not need rescuing from a ferret. Yes, I am a widow, I am alone. But I can still deal with this.

It was then the ferret found her throat. Its skin caressed her mouth. She patted her face, pointing to her mouth. He kissed her. She could feel the filth of its breath. She was going to be sick. But the ferret was now caressing her shoulder. She noticed the smell of drink, whiskey, brandy, it stank. The breath. But whose? His or hers? Before she could answer, the ferret raced from her bed. She did not scream. No fuss. It was all finished now. And who would believe her? They would think she was mad. Worse than mad, they would think her a pervert. She wondered if it was all a joke? A foul joke – blasphemous, a mockery of her mourning, a Protestant way of telling her, even in death you are not fit to be one of us?

Perhaps that was why the following morning she was tempted to go to Holy Communion. Walk into the silent, damp church and have a feed of Christ. She did not believe in the body and blood of the Saviour, but if her husband could come back in the shape, the smell, the size of a ferret, then anything could happen. If she had taken Communion, it would have to be in the Catholic church in Coleraine. When she'd first arrived in the town, young and not giv- ing a damn, this was how she'd ask for directions about this loyalist stronghold. Can you tell me where the hospital is – how far from the Catholic church? The hotel that serves tea on a Sunday when everywhere else is closed – that's right, the Lodge Hotel – is it near the Catholic church? The locals might look at her with distaste. They might think she was dangerously bonkers. Still, they all knew where their enemy congregated. They told her exactly where it was located. That's what made her go there today, to get back her bearings, putting her hand in the holy, ice-water font, feeling him where he was waiting in there, drenched, freezing her fingers, stopping her making the sign of the cross, his fur wet and soft, his teeth grinding into her. She was about to squeal, he was hurting her. About to let her rabid voice fill that hollow church. He was leaving her to bleed in that stagnant, blessed liquid. She did nothing. She just knew exactly what she was up against. She had to be rid of this animal.

The advertisement in the *Coleraine Chronicle* was simple. It read: Ferret found in garden. Good home required. She waited for replies. The answering machine delivered. She listened to them as she bathed, enjoying the strangers' voices filling the hall. The first woman said she was a sixty-seven-year-old grandmother. I have always wanted to cherish a ferret, please let me give it the good home required, she slurred on the phone. Country and western music played behind her. Take my heart, hearts get broken. Steal me blind, money's just a token. The king of hearts always takes the queen. The old woman was joining in the song, forgetting she was still on the phone. Drunk as a skunk, the poor fool. Next was a farmer with a rough Antrim whisper of a voice. He had a grandson, a bit of a sissy. I would like him to get an interest in ferrets. Toughen him up. If it bit, all the better. He needs to learn that life is not soft. My grandson. Jesus, who answers these advertisements?

The last call was from a ferret farm away in the wilds of County Down. Should she wish to dispose of the creature, they would respect and rear it in an environment where it would thrive and learn to appreciate the ways of its own species. Our emphasis is on treating the beast as it should be treated. Go on, give in. Give us the ferret.

That was not possible. She found him dead this morning. Some of his golden hair lay in a puddle of blood. Who'd got him? A fox – a pair of hungry cats – or was it herself? The widow woman? Had she turned into a beast and could no longer be trusted? Should she be muzzled? Did she take the ferret by its neck in her mouth? Did she shake it till it howled for mercy? Did she swear, I will be revenged on the animal kingdom – I will tear this fucking house down – I will leave this town laid waste – I will bomb this cursed country into kingdom come – I will blow the bridge to bits. I will be revenged for my husband's death. My husband with no arms, no legs, no hands, no ring, no stomach, no face, nothing but a handful of golden hair in a puddle of blood, torn to ribbons, smashed in pieces, nothing left. Where has he gone to? My ferret, was that him? Was that you? If you think so, then let me think so as well. Let me. Let me. Let me.

Beneath Green Hills

Eileen Casey

CLAMPED BETWEEN HER LIPS, IMELDA BRENNAN'S electronic cigarette flashes neon blue. But there's no smoke and definitely no nicotine.

'Don't know why I bother,' she mutters to her daughter. 'If that quack ever tells me I'm on a hiding to nothing, I'll puff my way into the next world.'

Lucia frowns. After the stroke, Dr Coady's list of possible scenarios indeed included a trip to the cemetery, an event Imelda roughly translated as 'pushing up the feathers in Mount Jerome'.

'At least you won't need to redecorate this place so often now, Mother,' she remarks, looking up at the stain-free ceiling. Growing up in this Corporation house on the south side of the city, Lucia had so hated stale tobacco clinging to curtains and furniture. Imelda used to joke that between cigarettes and hair lacquer, it was a miracle they didn't all combust.

'Wonder where that sister of yours has got to?' Imelda asks, not for the first time that morning. She wipes away the mark her bright lipstick has left on her cigarette device and tucks it into her cardigan pocket.

'She'll show up,' Lucia reassures her. 'Her festive drinks party was last evening, remember?'

'Drinks party my backside, hah!' Imelda says, propelling her wheelchair nearer the window where a miniature tree is practically obscured by flickering lights. 'I'll kill her if she swans in here without that bedspread . . . or pockets the money and delivers a no-show. She's a smooth operator that one when it comes to style, and style doesn't come cheap, Lucia, we both know that.' The flush on Imelda's cheeks is clearly visible despite the newly applied foundation and powder. To calm her agitation she turns her attention to a straggle of Christmas cards on the sideboard near the metal-railed bed where she sleeps each night.

'These seem to get fewer each year. I guess some people think I've already departed this vale of tears.' Fluorescent white from the fairy lights on the tree flares across her face. 'What did you make of the funeral yesterday?' she asks, after a pause.

'What funeral? Who's dead?' Lucia casts about in her mind for a mutual acquaintance, recently deceased.

'Mandela's funeral. Nelson Mandela. Papers are full of it. There's nothing else on the box. Or the radio,' Imelda says, raising her eyebrows. 'What planet have *you* dropped off, girl?'

'He got a great send-off,' Lucia acknowledges, 'no mistaking.' She's glad Imelda is distracted from the half-price bedding extravaganza Joan is supposed to be availing of in the city. Perhaps 'supposed' is a bit unfair, Lucia concedes. No matter how hectic her Friday night, Joan would rather crawl to the shops than miss her Saturday outing to the shops. A particular trait that wasn't licked off the ground: Imelda too had always been very fond of the department stores on Henry Street. Lucia is glad she herself doesn't have these spendthrift tendencies and likes to think she's careful rather than having the 'short arms, deep pockets' her mother sometimes credits her with.

'Death comes to all, even the highest and mightiest,' Imelda remarks, arranging the cards in order of size and shape. 'Is there nothing to buy except robin bloody redbreasts or bleary-eyed Santas?' She sighs and purses her mouth.

'We're nearly down to the quick with this one,' Lucia observes, swivelling the panstick foundation back into its case.

'We must be if *you* say so, Lucia. I never saw anyone to eke out the last drop the way you can.' It's the same porcelain shade Imelda has worn since Lucia's maxim *quality always pays its way* finally persuaded her to switch from the cheaper brand. She prefers when Lucia or Joan apply it because she herself can't always tell if skid marks streak along her neck or under her chin.

'Lucky for us, Helena Rubinstein is still in business,' Lucia observes, tidying away her mother's cosmetics into the big floral-patterned vinyl bag. She rises from the couch and, in a few brisk strides, crosses over plain brown carpet tiles to stand beside her mother at the window.

'One more panstick should see me out for sure,' Imelda says matter-of-factly, staring intently at the bus stop straight across the road.

'She'll be on the next one, Mother. She knows you have your heart set on that particular design,' Lucia says, conscious of the melancholy edge creeping into Imelda's voice. Not that she can blame her. The street outside is practically deserted, lined with skeletal trees and a gusting easterly breeze. This raw Monday in an Irish December causes Imelda to complain about being colder since being 'stuck in these wheels'. Hardly the ideal description for her mother's condition, in Lucia's opinion, but to her immense relief she's stopped calling herself *Imelda Ironsides*.

'The neighbours have made a great effort this year,' Lucia says, gesturing to ornaments twinkling in some of the windows.

'I suppose,' Imelda concedes, but with little interest. 'For the life of me I don't know why we bother. It's all over in a few hours. And that shower over there,' she says, pointing across at No. 43, where a very large Santa with a full sack perches on the ridge tiles near the chimney, 'well, they have no shame at all. They better hope the real one comes down that chimney because their father is nothing but a lazy scrounger and a scourge to his poor wife.'

Lucia does not reply and thinks instead of little Eva, her granddaughter, celebrating her second birthday on Christmas Eve. Only a few more days before herself and Frank go to Mayo. They haven't seen Ruthie, their only daughter, in months, and this will also be their first Christmas in years away from the city. Though Lucia sometimes feels disloyal for thinking it, she'll also be away from the responsibilities of her invalid mother. Joan will be spending Christmas Day and St Stephen's Day with Imelda, but to make up for it Lucia is shouldering the bulk of 'Imelda time' over these coming weeks.

Imelda focuses on the postman, newly arrived into the street. Lucia's thoughts stray to the falling-out with Lucy Doran. An unwelcome development as the feud, skirmish or whatever it is, has left a severe dent in a rota that has to be kept going day in, day out, all year round. Although Imelda sometimes jokes that her schedule is a conundrum, like Dr Coady's surgery hours, even thinking about it sometimes makes Lucia feel tired. Mondays and Fridays, laundry and cleaning; Tuesdays and Thursdays, the Old Folks' Centre. Imelda hates the centre, but it's either go or be marooned from the time of the home help's morning visit until Joan calls in on her way home from work. From what Lucia can gather, Joan's visits end almost as quickly as they begin. Now that Lucy Doran is off the list of helping hands, Lucia crosses the city from the north side most Saturdays too and replenishes Imelda's supplies. On Sundays, Fr Joe Kinsella, or Holy Joe as Imelda calls him, comes to the house with Communion and to hear Imelda's confession if she's in the humour. More often than not she'll tell him that the only sins she's capable of are in her head and don't count for much. A home help comes twice each day: she gets Imelda out of bed and dressed, and then later in the evening she calls again to make her comfortable for the night. Having to be put to bed early with nothing for company but the television or the radio is one of the two things that Imelda Brennan resents the most. The other is the fact that she hasn't seen her own bedroom upstairs in over three years.

A bus pulls in, but when it moves off again it's obvious that Joan isn't among the passengers deposited at the stop.

'Your sister's probably lying in state, hungover, like half the country,' Imelda says, and slumps a little in her wheelchair.

'I'm sure there's nothing to worry about; let's have a cuppa instead.' Lucia gently squeezes her mother's shoulder.

'I suppose . . . and those little cakes you've brought,' Imelda adds, her face brightening.

'Mandela was brought home to his own bed in his old village,' Imelda says a little later when Lucia places a cushioned lap tray across her knees. 'They wrapped him in the skin of a lion, you know . . . and sang and danced for three days so his spirit could be released to the Holy Souls.' On the tray is her favourite mug, which has 'I love Gran Canaria' written across it in orange. Joan brought it from holidays to her a few months before. 'His tribe did him proud, bringing him home like that to his own oul shanty. Wasn't that a lovely touch, Lucia?' she adds, before biting into an iced fancy.

'It *was* a lovely touch,' Lucia agrees, and then nibbles at the edge of her own cake. 'Have you made up with Lucy Doran yet?' she asks, in the companionable silence that follows.

'No way,' Imelda splutters. 'There'll be white blackbirds on the moon before I speak to her again. And if anything happens to me, she's not to set one foot inside my front door.' Drawing herself up in her chair, she pushes the last bit of the Mr Kipling's into her mouth. As far as Imelda is concerned, that's the end of the subject. She busies herself brushing away the hail of crumbs that has fallen onto her shawl. Her wedding ring glints under the light but is barely visible in the folds of her fleshy fingers. She has never taken off the ring even though it's now over thirty-five years since Sam Trainor walked out on her.

'Promise me, Lucia,' Imelda says now, her voice dropping to a whisper, 'you and Joan will lay me out upstairs when the time comes, won't you? You know it's my wish to spend my last earthly hours in my own home. It's not like I'm asking you to slaughter an ox or anything. But I feel the same as Nelson about the spirit world. Your own bed, under your own ceiling is the best place to be if there's to be any chance at all of finding eternal peace. Promise me, daughter.'

'Ah, Mam, we've been through all that. Let's not hear any more talk of dying.' Lucia swirls her tea around her cup before draining it.

Imelda's wishes concerning her funeral were first mooted some months ago: extensive plans which covered who to ask to her wake and, more importantly, who not to ask. They include instructions as to the clothes she wants to be dressed in: nothing too garish but nothing mawkish either, definitely no mutton dressed as lamb, which might happen if Joan got her way. Although Imelda is proud of her younger daughter's stylish image, she's made it clear that a nice respectable two-piece suit and tailored blouse is more in keeping with her age. On no account is she to be buried in white, no matter what, as a fat lot of good that colour has done her. She's adamant too that she wants to wear the peridot birthstone necklace her daughters clubbed together to buy for her seventy-fifth birthday the year before, which, of course, is to be removed before the lid is nailed down and given to Eva for when she's older. Her wedding ring is to be left on her finger as it would need a ring-cutter to remove it, and, from what she's heard, those folks aren't too particular about what gets cut. The scapulars she got when the reliquary of St Thérèse of Lisieux came to her local church are to be laced around her fingers, because they're the only thing free that she ever got off 'that lot'. After an amount of deliberation, her crowning glory is to be allowed hang loose around her shoulders. Although all trace of its original light brown is gone, she still has a thick head of hair, and 'it would be my last chance to show it off'. Under no circumstances are there to be plastic flowers anywhere near her, especially not on the grave, as she could never, in her own words, 'tolerate anything that wasn't real'. But being laid out at home, in her own bedroom, well, that's the coveted prize for sure.

'You know it would take a lot for me to break a promise,' Lucia reassures her. What she doesn't tell her mother is that Joan is very much against the idea and has said more than once that when Imelda 'bites the bullet' she has no intention of putting on a show for folk who only go to these events for a nosey and who wouldn't call round from one end of the year to the other. Lately, Joan has even gone so far as to intimate that maybe it's time their mother went into full-time nursing care. Especially as property prices are picking up again.

'We have the same namesake, you know, only different versions,' Lucia says now, glad that her mother is unable to read her mind.

'Who? You and Mandela?' Imelda replies, pretending ignorance.

'You know very well I mean Lucy Doran,' Lucia says with a sharp edge to her voice, but there's warmth in her brown eyes. Lucia's own birthday was three days earlier, on the feast day of the saint she was named for. Imelda had been deeply affected by the tale of courage a nun told her in the maternity ward in St James's forty-seven years before. She'd been affected and romantic enough, back then, to name her firstborn for the young girl who went down into the dark catacombs of Rome to help perse-cuted Christians, wearing a crown of light to guide her. It was a story she'd regaled the neighbours with at Lucia's christening party and with different variations ever since, depending on her mood.

'It's Winnie I feel sorry for,' Imelda persists, dusting off the last of the crumbs and refusing to be drawn on Lucy Doran. 'Having to take a back seat. After all her years of loy-alty. No one really knows what that tortured soul has gone through, do they, Lucia? Under the full glare of the public eye as well. You know something? I think she should be canonised. She's as much a candidate as a lot of them saints on the roll book.' She takes out her linen handkerchief and blows her nose. 'And poor Madiba,' she says then. 'They made out, you know, that a great tree had fallen. Imagine

227

that, Lucia. But who could ever forget his suffering? All those years confined in a prison cell. Hah! No one knows better than I do about mouldering away behind four walls.' Imelda sighs, then glances down at her empty plate with a look of amazement on her face. 'There's hardly a mouthful in them fancies,' she says and gives Lucia a reproachful stare for not putting out all the cakes. 'There's no tow bar on a hearse, girl,' she mutters under her breath.

'Remember how Joan used call me "Melda" when she was little, Lucia?' she suddenly remembers, her voice rising with pleasure. 'Sometimes she still does.' Imelda's eyes mist over.

'There didn't seem to be any hard feelings between Winnie and Mandela's widow. I'm sure the great man is pleased with how things turned out, wherever he is,' Lucia says, ignoring her mother's remark about Joan. Her sister could always turn on the charm when she wanted something.

'No one knows what's between two people,' Imelda counters, nodding her head sagely. 'Perhaps Mandela regretted to his last breath not staying with Winnie. Who knows? When all's said and done, that woman can hold her head high. She's done no wrong. Always such dignity in the face of busybodies . . . and nosey parkers with nothing better to do than rummage in other people's lives. God knows there's plenty of them around.' She tightens her shawl around herself and shivers.

'It's a pity you and Lucy stopped speaking to each other all the same. Over a cat, of all things,' Lucia says, ignoring the warning look that rises briefly in her mother's eyes.

If only Joan had kept her mouth shut when Lucy Doran's black-and-white cat was discovered, some weeks ago now, lounging on Imelda's bed upstairs. But out it came, Joan omitting the fact that it was she herself who hadn't closed the window, and naturally, cats being opportunists, it wasn't long before the intruder had curled up in the feline equivalent of Trump Towers. The thought of cat hairs and a cat smell all over her bed had almost given Imelda a heart attack to add to her stroke. But there must have been more to it than that, Lucia thinks.

'Look at Obama, didn't he shake hands with Castro,' Lucia argues.

'The eyes of the media were on him. He probably wouldn't give a thrupenny toss otherwise, the two-faced git.' If Imelda's legs have become heavy as iron weights, her tongue certainly hasn't.

For the next five minutes or so, a torrent of invective flies from her mouth. She leaves Lucia in no doubt about her feelings regarding low deeds in high offices. But still, Lucia is surprised. Her mother's old friend and neighbour from two doors down didn't in any way fit the bill as far as subterfuge was concerned. She wonders if her father's tenth-anniversary notice some weeks ago, around about the time of the cat incident, has anything to do with it. Perhaps Lucy had read it in the papers and mentioned it to Imelda, without any guile or hidden agenda.

The clock on the mantelpiece chimes the hour and plays a few bars of 'O Holy Night'. It was bought in New York on one of Joan's frequent shopping trips there, but Lucia thinks it a tawdry object, a total waste of good money. Adorned with sprigs of prickly holly and robins, it remains on the mantelpiece all year round. Try as she might, Lucia can't persuade her mother to disable the carol-playing element of the clock: 'Jingle Bells' in July doesn't strike Imelda as being odd in any way. Before another word can be said, the front door opens, and Joan sweeps into the room.

'Look what the wind's blown in,' Imelda says, still miffed, but a smile soon follows. Lucia nods to her sister and indicates the pot of tea and the third setting.

'Thank God. I've taken enough painkillers to bring down a wrestler,' Joan says, lowering her bags and then removing her black faux-fur hat. She runs her newly manicured fingers through platinum-coloured hair. The cost of its upkeep is shocking to Imelda, and then there's the damage all that peroxide must be doing, but she's learnt to hold her tongue. Joan could be as volatile as herself; the apple definitely hasn't fallen far from the tree when it comes to her younger daughter. It's part of the reason mother and daughter have so much in common but can also provide the flint to spark more than a few rows. Imelda can barely contain herself as Joan lifts out the bedspread and a cascade of satin flows over the sofa.

'It's . . . blue,' she says, after a pause, somewhat crestfallen. 'But I said cream or beige.'

'It's all that was left, and sure you can easily change the curtains in the January sales,' Joan says, tossing off her mother's disappointment with her usual aplomb. 'Your favourite son-in-law will throw a lick of paint on the walls come spring. Frank won't let you down. One of the pluses of having an in-law in the trade, eh Lucia? Before you know it, you'll have a brand-new room.' Joan winks at Lucia above her mother's head.

'I hope I won't pop my clogs before all that's done. But surely, it'll take a stick of dynamite to get that wallpaper off?' Imelda's face creases into a worried frown.

'It'll fall off, sure it's ready to give itself up at this stage,' Joan says, and again winks at Lucia behind her mother's back.

'Here, give me the bedspread and I'll put it on,' Lucia says, ignoring the gesture.

'Don't forget the camera,' Imelda reminds her. 'I can't wait to see how it looks on my bed.'

Lucia grabs her handbag from the floor and goes into the hallway, leaving her mother and sister to rake over the coals of Joan's night out and any other gossip in storage since they've last been in each other's company. Out of habit, she mentally counts the thirteen steps, as she always did as a child, before arriving at the landing, where the large embroidered sampler hangs: 'Learn of Me, for I am Meek and Humble of Heart'. The frame had been purchased years ago at one of the winter fairs held in support of the Poor Clares, whose convent was a few streets away. The image of the foundress of the order had been replaced by the sampler Imelda had made as a child in primary school. Lucia shakes her head. Her mother could make her mark with a needle all right, but as for being meek and humble?

As usual, Lucia takes a quick inventory of the upstairs rooms. The bathroom and front bedroom are cleaned and aired regularly. Cobwebs are swiped off the ceilings, and the oval-shaped mirrors in the dressing tables polished. Blankets are neatly rolled up at the ends of the beds. Occasionally, the net curtains are taken down and bleached. Although the carpets are regularly hoovered, they have a faded look about them. In the bathroom, the shower curtain is mildewed, and some of the floor tiles have cracks. She makes a mental note to ask Frank to take a look at them. If the lower part of the house maintains a comfortable degree of heat, upstairs is freezing, and a damp, musty smell is beginning to insinuate its way into the rooms. Lucia feels the drop in temperature keenly, but she has a task to do, and standing on the landing isn't going to get it done.

When Lucia opens the door of her mother's bedroom, the heavy scent of wax furniture polish makes it seem as if she is stepping back in time. Whatever about the rest of the upstairs, this bedroom is given the same attention as if Imelda still climbed the stairs each evening. Lucia goes to both windows, rolls up their blinds and opens them out so some fresh air can circulate. Getting two windows in the one bedroom is 'posh' as far as Imelda is concerned and one of the pluses of an end house.

When the new bedspread is in place, Lucia takes her camera and photographs it for her mother to see. As she feared, the bright blue fights with the pink wallpaper and floral green curtains. Lucia focuses on the deep frill along the hem in an effort to draw the eye away from the obvious clash. In her prime, when she took in sewing from the neighbours, Imelda could probably have run up a quilt just like it.

Lucia's gaze comes to rest on the mahogany dressing table. Amongst talc boxes and powder puffs, there's a picture of Lucia and Joan taken at around the age they were when their father left. In the photograph, both girls wear the same navy gabardine coats with saucer-size buttons. Their knee socks are so white they are almost luminous. Lucia stares at her thirteen-year-old self. Joan, two years younger, has the fattest ringlets, like 'big, thick sausages', their father used to joke.

Tall, slim, Sam Trainor was very handsome, especially so that Saturday morning on O'Connell Street that Lucia remembered from so long ago. Not at all the 'long streak of misery' Imelda subsequently dubbed him. Their father hadn't been on his own, though. As the bus drew nearer their stop, Joan and Lucia saw him on the corner of the street talking to a beautifully dressed woman, whose hair shone like burnished gold in the midday sun. She seemed much smaller than him, barely reaching his shoulder, and she smiled at whatever their father said to her before he bent to kiss her full on the mouth. They'd never seen him do that to their mother, yet there he was, in broad daylight, kissing a complete stranger. Before they got off the bus and walked the short distance to him, the woman was gone. Lucia could smell her perfume, though, it was all around him, a smell that reminded her of fresh cut roses. Soon they were all three seated in a booth in Woolworth's on Grafton Street. They each got a bowl of ice cream with a cherry on top which Joan promptly popped into her mouth and practically swallowed whole.

Lucia goes to one of the windows and looks out onto the long length of garden that seems to stretch like the years before her. So far, it's well looked after. Frank, even after a hard day decorating other people's houses, does more than his share. Lucia knows she has a decent man in him. Little did he realise that he'd be taking on Lucia *and* her mother. If he sometimes calls Imelda a 'battleaxe' instead of Joan's wheedling 'Melda', she knows she can rely on him completely. And Lucy Doran has been a very trust-worthy friend. Hopefully, when the dust settles on Imelda's imagined affront, she will be again. Plus, her mother's immediate neighbour, Anthony, is very obliging, mostly on the basis that Imelda keeps a memorial card of his mother in her handbag. She often takes it out in his presence to marvel at the likeness between himself and the woman she praises as an angel. Once he is out of earshot, however, she is not so complimentary. Anthony has even planted some spring bulbs directly in front of Imelda's kitchen, secur-ing them from the neighbourhood cats with wire netting, probably on Imelda's instruction.

Lucia's body sags against the windowsill. An image of her mother's white face swims before her, a ghostly reminder of their return home that Saturday. Although Lucia had warned her not to, Joan told their mother anyway about the woman their father had been with. Imelda had gripped the table for support, her eyes widening in disbelief. Some of her hair tumbled from the clips holding it back from her face, and she had a wild look about her as she slowly gathered together the facts. After a long time, she finally sat at the table and looked directly at Lucia.

'What happened to your coat?' she'd asked, in a voice devoid of any feeling. Lucia explained about the ice cream and how she had squashed her cherry against the spoon. The liquid sprayed against her coat, and her efforts to clean it had only worsened the stain.

'It's ruined. No amount of cleaning will get that right' were the only words Imelda said about the entire incident.

The following week, their father moved out of the house. Imelda would not tolerate him once she found out about his other woman. Apart from the odd let-ter and card over the years, contact had been minimal. Lucia sometimes wonders what would have happened had Joan held her tongue. But was it fair to blame her sister? Joan was little more than a child at the time. And how pretty her father's companion had been that day, Lucia remembers now. Her admiration is tinged with guilt, however, for being disloyal to Imelda, a woman who, over the years, had to face down the neighbours 'at every hand's turn'.

Lucia takes one last look at the garden, at the wire netting under which bulbs are already taking root. Come spring, they will pierce upwards through the earth, tiny spears of colour after harsh winter. She thinks of Mandela, of the sound of drums and of mourning rituals, of the green hills where he now lies at peace.

She closes the windows and rolls down the blinds, checking

they are each at the same level, about three inches from the sill, exactly the way Imelda likes them.

Before she leaves the room, Lucia bends down and touches the wallpaper where it is beginning to unpeel at a join. One good pull is probably all it needs.

The Journey to Galway

Colm Tóibín

SHE REMEMBERED AN UNUSUAL SILENCE THAT morning, a stillness in the trees and in the farmyard, and a deadness in the
house itself, no sounds from the kitchen, and no one moving up and down the stairs. But she wondered if the silence
had been real, or, instead, if it had been something she had
merely imagined afterwards. She was unsure if getting the
news had not actually changed her memory of the hours
that came before. At times she thought that it hardly mattered, but at other times, especially when she woke to dawn
light and dawn birdsong, the details of how word of Robert's
death came, and precisely what the period before was like,
belonged to her life as much as her breath did, or her heartbeat. It came to her as a story that had been told and retold
rather than a brutal single fact, as though placing it in time
and remembering how the news had spread would come to
soften what had happened, ease it, edge it away. The details
of her journey to Galway to tell Margaret, for example, and
what she thought about on those two trains. Or where she
was sitting when the word came, and what went through
her mind in the seconds before she saw the telegram.

She lay in bed some mornings, living it all from moment to moment, knowing that she would go on doing this until she died and that nothing she could do would make it change. For her, there was a line between the time before she heard of her son's death and the time after. In the time before, she had wondered, if bad news were to come, where she would be, what room she would be in, at what time of the day it would come. She had even pictured herself receiving the news, her own face in shock, her voice gasping. And every evening, as she walked upstairs to bed, she had marked the day just ended as another one that had come and gone without news and thus a day to be savoured, to be thankful for. These thoughts seemed as different from the thoughts of later as land was from ocean, as air from water, as a death in a play in a theatre from a real dead body lying in a pool of blood in the real street outside.

When Robert had written letters, they had been read with care and attention. She knew that there was much he could not say, which meant that a stray phrase carried weight, perhaps even hidden meanings. But how much was often unclear because his letters seemed to be written in haste. Perhaps he had intended his letters to mean nothing more than what they said. Yet it must be true, she thought, that unintended words gave away something. But when he wrote, 'I sometimes awake feeling as if some part of me was crying in another place', it hardly mattered whether he had meant to alarm her or not, whether he had meant or not to let her know how afraid he was despite his efforts to be brave, and, as an airman in a war, how much daily fear he lived with and how much he masked. 'The other place', where he was crying, she thought, was here, where she was now, the house which he owned, which his father and grandfather had also lived in. If the crying was hidden, then it was hidden here and in the woods and fields around here. The thought almost satisfied her as she read the letter again and again.

It occurred to her afterwards that what he did in those few years when he was a fighter pilot was merely an exaggerated version of what we all do as we live: we swagger, we are full of pretence that there is no real danger coming towards us, we talk as though the enemy is in flight, or under control. As time moves, however, it drags us with it until the time for pretending ends and the body lies spent. When she saw him in London, and later when he came home to Coole, she noticed the swagger. She made sure that she gave no sign that she was watching all the time for a break in it, gave no sign that much of it seemed to her closer to bravado than bravery. He could hardly have put his fear on display for her when he came home. He had not come home to frighten them but rather to reassure. She hoped he believed his own pose some of the time at least, but she wondered when night fell for him and he was alone, how much he knew, how much he could foresee, and how little peace he got when the prospect of being helpless in a burning plane thousands of feet above the earth insinuated itself into his waking time as much as into his dreams.

She wondered about luck. He would need to be lucky;

but not everyone could be lucky. Forces no one could control, or almost no one, decided which pilots died and which survived. Each morning it occurred to her that this might be the day, the day when Robert's luck ran out, and then she thought that the very act of thinking this meant that it would not happen, this would not be the day. It would never be the day she imagined it would be; it would be some other day. Thinking would, or might, or should, keep it from happening.

When she wrote letters to him, she thought too about chance. This letter, she imagined as she wrote to him, might be the last word he will read from me, or it might be the letter from me he will never read; it will arrive too late and it will be returned. It will be the special letter, written in hope, maybe even confidence, written to be read by some-one who was alive, who would recognise the writing and know that when she referred to Margaret and the children, she meant his wife and Richard and Catherine and Anne. These things would not need to be spelled out for him, since they were written in the quickened spirit of being alive, but they might never be read like that, they might become, unknowingly, last words, or they might be words that came too late, or they might be ordinary words glossed over, taken for granted.

The days before she heard the news were days that seemed to have passed in slow time and lodged in her memory with sharpness and perseverance. What hopes she felt then that the war would come to an end and Robert would survive later became bathed in irony, almost in bitterness. How foolish she had been! And also, as she thought about it, how foolish she was now to think or imagine sometimes that if she had known he was going to die, if she had been sure, she could have done something to prevent it, she could have written a letter to some high-ranking official or stayed in London and made contact with those who decided on which pilots went out on what days. How foolish she was to think that the future could have been known, or that anyone would have listened! How hard it was to realise how powerless she was!

She had gone to Dublin, stopping off on the way at her sister's house in Galway where Margaret and the children were. Both she and Margaret were happier that Robert was now in Italy. He had written to Margaret to describe being cheered all along the line as they crossed the north of Italy, how the people brought fruit and flowers. He had loved Italy on his visits as a tourist, and now, as she left Margaret and the children, the thought came to her that, if anywhere was worth fighting for, it might be Italy.

In Dublin, she spoke at a meeting in the Mansion House calling for the paintings which had belonged to her nephew, Hugh Lane, to be returned to Ireland, as he had wanted, or at least wanted at the end of his life, a life also cut short by the war. The meeting was crowded, and there was enthusiasm about the pictures and their importance for Dublin. The pictures were things that might matter. It was always what she had said, that the struggle for freedom in Ireland was nothing compared to the struggle that would come afterwards, the struggle to build on the freedom, and that was what she had been working towards. The pictures would inspire that struggle, maybe their return would symbolise it. Helping to bring them back from London would be the least she could do. From Dublin she wrote to Robert, saying that if the pictures came back, she should feel 'Now lettest Thou thy servant depart in peace'. She was not sure she meant it, but he might see the humour of it mixed in with the sense of this effort to get the pictures returned as the last one his mother would have energy for. And she gave him news about the trees she was planting, the formal rows of larch with inlets of elm and sycamore, and then some silver birch and broom. And she added what she thought might please him about the children without making him too sad, writing of Richard with a catapult looking quite the schoolboy, and then concluding with the thought of what a happy world it might be, 'with you back and the war at an end!' She concluded with 'God bless you, my child.' She did not know that he was already four days dead.

When she came back from Dublin, she went to the wood where she had been planting and was vexed that some timber had been given away and annoyed too the men were cutting the young ash which had come into sight after they had cut the spruce. She had imagined Robert coming home and seeing the ash trees and the blue hills between them and seeing also the broom and the flowering trees. She decided that she would spend the whole next day at the wood making up for her absence, making sure that everything was done according to her wishes. In the morning, she asked for a sandwich to be made for her and the donkey carriage made ready, and, while waiting, she decided to go into the drawing room and write a letter, some letter that was urgent, or that seemed urgent then, that morning. Her day ahead was fully planned, and it was easy to imagine how it might have been. She would have been well wrapped from the cold; she would have been decisive, thinking ahead to what things in the wood might look like in a year, and then in twenty years, and then in fifty years when other people, those not yet born, would walk here. That day could so easily have happened, and, if she had spent it making her wishes known and watching the work happen, it would have left her satisfied.

She was at her writing table when Marian, the servant, came in very slowly. When she looked up, she saw that Marian was crying. She had a telegram. But there had been telegrams before. Twice on her last visit to London she had received telegrams, and they were from friends about the breaking of some engagement. Marian could so easily have presumed that a telegram meant bad news. But when she was handed it and looked down and saw that it was not addressed to her but to Margaret, Robert's wife, she knew that it was bad. If it had news of Robert's death, it was to Margaret they would send it. The first words she saw were 'killed in action' and then at the top, 'Deeply regret'.

She turned to Marian. 'How will I tell Margaret? Who will tell her? Who can go to Galway and tell her?' She tried to stand up, but she could not. It occurred to her that she must not cry now or think about herself. She must fix her mind on one thing – on that scene she had witnessed a few days earlier, Margaret and the three children lodged with her sister, the ease and the peace in the house despite the worry. It was to be broken now. Who would break it? She wondered if she could send Marian and if Marian could hand Margaret the telegram as she had handed it to her. She asked about trains and was told there was still time to get a connection to Galway. She told Marian to order some vehicle that could meet the train in Gort. She sat there frozen until Marian came back to say that she had also had a note from Mrs Mitchell in the Post Office saying that there was only one person who should break the news of Robert's death to Margaret, and that was Robert's own mother, and that was why she had sent the telegram on to Coole, even though she knew that Margaret was not there.

She stood up then and nodded. Then she went upstairs and got some things for the journey, even changing her dress as though it might matter what she was wearing. But it slowed time down as she selected it. It slowed time down too as she took the other dress off and put this one on and then checked herself in the mirror and made sure that she had forgotten nothing. The carriage would be waiting. She wondered if there was one more thing she needed to do in the bedroom, but there was not. She had the telegram in her hand now, and that was really all she needed. She would have to show it to Margaret. Maybe that is what she would do, say nothing, just hand her the piece of paper.

In any case, she would have to set out on her journey. As she looked out the long window while going down the stairs, she saw one of the workmen with his head hanging, walking away from the house. The news would have spread.

In the carriage, she thought of nothing, forced herself to go on having no thoughts, letting nothing into her mind. The effort gave her some relief, or something that was like relief. Once they arrived at the station, she determined that she would not wait on the platform with others, people whom she did not know, or allow acquaintances come to exchange pleasantries. She would stay in the carriage until the last minute. John, the driver, told the porter the news, and the porter went and got her a ticket to Galway. As soon as she heard the train coming, she went to the platform. No one, she thought, no one in the world should ever have to do what she was doing now.

As she walked towards the train, she saw that Frank, her brother, was at the window of a carriage and was motioning her to come and join him. She looked at him and looked away and walked further down, away from him. She did not want his company. She could not speak. She went to some other carriage, where there was a woman, a stranger. As she sat down, she tried to picture the scene in Galway, her arrival, she tried to imagine what words she would use if she were asked why she had come. She bowed her head.

At one of the station stops, when Frank came to her window, she tried to tell him, but found that she could not speak and instead held out the telegram which she had in her hand. For a second it struck her that if she could only have something else in her hand, then this might all be nothing, that it was the telegram itself which was bearing down on her. Frank spoke softly. 'I know all about it,' he said. He had guessed from her face when he had seen her at the station that some dreadful thing had happened; when he sent someone to ask the driver of the carriage, the worst was confirmed for him.

As the train went on, she cried, but not much, aware of the other woman, the stranger, opposite her. She forced herself to sit up straight and steel herself. So this was what Robert's life had led to then, this death! It was like an arrow hitting its target. It would hardly matter now, or in the future, how cruel and thoughtless Robert had been in the year or two before he signed up. There was no need to judge him any more. She would remember him instead when he was a boy, or a young man she was proud of. Someone brave and talented, filled with daring. His dying meant that she would no longer have to judge him. Death would simplify him, and that at least was something. Margaret could mourn him, or some idea of him, and forget how, in the time before he joined up, he had been in love with her best friend. In that time, he appeared to enjoy the idea that Margaret knew that he and her friend had become lovers.

Perhaps it was easy, or too tempting, to be cruel to Margaret; she would, she thought, as the train moved towards Galway, find out herself soon since Margaret would inherit everything, the house, the land. There would be a struggle. Robert was already in a place where such struggles no longer mattered. She gasped for a moment when Robert's face appeared before her and the idea came that his body had been burned and that he might have suffered badly as his plane went down.

She put all thoughts of Robert away and just looked on stoically as the woman opposite her got out her lunch basket. When the woman offered her some food, she could only shake her head. She tried to smile, but she was not sure it was a smile.

Yes, she thought, going to war had solved so much, it had left things in abeyance, it had meant that all discussion had been postponed, it had made compromise impossible, but in solving what it did, it had solved too much. It had solved everything so there was nothing left. All their daily thoughts, all the differences between them, all their knowledge of one another, were nothing now and would always be nothing. Despite what had happened, Margaret had wanted Robert back. But he would not be back; he would not grow old or live to regret anything at all or be forgiven. Action had given him simplicity, as it must have done for others, an avoidance of having to deal with his own complexity. Death, on the other hand, would give him nothing at all. From now on, it would be all absence. For her too, everything she did or said in the future would be a way of distracting herself from the stark, simple fact that her son, her only child, had died in the last year of the war. There was hardly anything else to be said; the texture of what happened was reduced to a telegram, the telegram that she still held in her hand.

And he had died in a British uniform, a uniform that had seemed more and more the uniform of another country. In joining the British Army, he had been his father's son; he had followed his cousins. He had not followed her,

247

nor had she asked him to. She wondered now if he and those like him, the others who had died for this dream of empire, this large and abstract conflict between nations, would belong to the past, if they would not be shadows fading into further and deeper shadows. Their class would not hold sway in an Ireland of the future, she was sure of that. She began to imagine what it would be like instead if she were going on a train to Dublin to be with him on the night before his execution, if he had taken part in the Rebellion in Dublin. She thought of how proud she would be on the train, how there would be some people travelling with her who would feel exalted by her presence. But it would end in the same way. It would end in death, it would end in three fatherless children, it would end in a future in which Robert would only be a name and a memory. He would never come into a room again. It hardly mattered what cause he had fought for, or what his impulse to join had been. It was simple; he had been killed.

She was relieved that Frank kept away from her as she changed for the Galway train, relieved that Frank was not also going on to Galway. She looked around for Daly, the porter whom she knew. Someone would have given him the news. But there was no sign of him. She was glad that none of the strangers near her guessed. This was an ordinary day for them; perhaps there was comfort in that, but it was not a comfort that lasted long. When the train came, she sat alone and willed only that it would go slowly, or that it might stop somewhere for a while. In Margaret's mind, she thought, Robert was still alive. Maybe that meant something; it gave Robert some strange extra time. Although she knew that that idea was foolish, it helped her, but it also increased her dread. She was moving westward like cruel death itself, she thought. She was the one who had the news. Until she appeared in the doorway of that house, there would not be death. But once she appeared, death would live in that house. There would be nothing else except death. She carried death with her, she thought, as she had once carried life.

Later, every single thought she had on that train stayed with her as though she had written the thoughts down one by one there and then. But she did not remember the next part clearly. She moved from the light of day into a dream as she left the train that day. It was already dark in Galway, she was sure of that. She took a car across the city, or at least she must have, and they went to the house. She remembered the instant when she gave the man his fare. That too she was sure about. When a maid opened the door, she remembered wishing if only she could be back somewhere else now, in the woods, even in the train, even in the car on the way here. But she had arrived. As she went into the hallway, she asked for Margaret. The maid said that Margaret was in the study with the mistress and followed her as she walked deliberately into the room on the right, a room that was seldom used. She told the maid to ask Margaret to come to her, just Margaret. She stood there with the door open. When her daughter-in-law appeared, Margaret looked at her and asked 'Is he dead?' She handed Margaret the telegram and then turned away towards the window while Margaret read it. She had brought the news. It was done. It was over. The journey to Galway was over.

Acknowledgements

Sincere thanks to Angus Cargill at Faber and Faber, Madeline McGahern, Claire Keegan, Harry Clifton, Declan Meade and Éilís Ní Dhuibhne.

About the Authors

LUCY CALDWELL studied at Queens' College, Cambridge and at Goldsmiths, University of London. She has published three novels: *Where They Were Missed*, *The Meeting Point* and, most recently, *All the Beggars Riding*, which was chosen for Belfast and Derry's One City, One Book initiative. She has also written for the stage, and her first play, *Leaves*, premiered with the Druid Theatre Company in Galway before transferring to the Royal Court Theatre. Her other plays are *Guardians* and *Notes to Future Self*. She has won awards for both her fiction and her drama, including the George Devine Award, the Dylan Thomas Prize and the Rooney Prize for Irish Literature.

EILEEN CASEY is a graduate of Dublin City University and Trinity College, Dublin. A fiction writer, poet and journalist, she also works in adult education. Her poetry is widely published, including in the anthology *If Ever You Go*, a Dublin One City/One Book Choice 2014 (Dedalus Press). Her debut poetry collection, *Drinking the Colour Blue*, was published by New Island. She has received many awards, including a Hennessy Literary Award, the Cecil Day Lewis Fiction Award, The Oliver Goldsmith International Poetry Award and a Katherine Kavanagh Fellowship. In 2011, she was a Visiting Writer on Eastern Kentucky University's winter programme. *Snow Shoes* (Arlen House Short Fiction), 2012, was followed by *A Fascination with Fabric* (Arlen House literary essays and memoir), 2014.

ITA DALY was born in Co Leitrim, and studied at University College Dublin. She has published a collection of stories, *The Lady with the Red Shoes*, and five novels: *Ellen*, *A Singular Attraction*, *Dangerous Fictions*, *All Fall Down* and *Unholy Ghosts*. She has also published several books for children, including *Irish Myths and Legends*. She has won a Hennessy Award for her work. Ita Daly was married to the late David Marcus. She is a member of the Irish arts academy, Aosdána.

ANDREW FOX is the author of *Over Our Heads*, a collection of short stories. A graduate of University College Dublin and Trinity College, Dublin, he is currently at work on a Ph.D. at the University of Massachusetts, Amherst. His writing has appeared in the *Dublin Review*, the *Massachusetts Review*, *New Hibernia Review*, *New Irish Writing*, *Prairie Schooner*, the *Stinging Fly*, the *Daily Beast,* and in the anthologies *Sharp Sticks Driven Nails* and *Dubliners 100*. Born in Dublin, he lives in New York City.

MICHAEL GILLIGAN is from Sligo. He is a graduate of Trinity

College, Dublin, where he studied English Literature and French. He is currently studying medicine at University College Dublin. 'Absent' is his first story to be published.

SELINA GUINNESS studied at Trinity College, Dublin, and at Oxford University. She is a lecturer in English Literature at the Institute of Art, Design and Technology, Dun Laoghaire. She is editor of *The New Irish Poets* and co-editor of *The Resurrection: Manuscript Materials by W. B. Yeats* in the Cornell Yeats series. Her memoir, *The Crocodile by the Door*, about her life farming sheep at Tibradden in the Dublin Mountains, was shortlisted in the biography category at the Costa Book Awards 2012 and was also shortlisted for the Bord Gáis Energy Irish Book Awards 2012 (Best Newcomer).

DEIRDRE MADDEN (editor) studied at Trinity College, Dublin and at the University of East Anglia. She has published eight novels, including *One by One in the Darkness*, *Authenticity*, *Molly Fox's Birthday* and, most recently, *Time Present and Time Past*. She teaches on the M.Phil. programme at the Oscar Wilde Centre, Trinity College, Dublin and is a member of the Irish arts academy, Aosdána.

FRANK MCGUINNESS studied English at University College Dublin. He is a poet, playwright and novelist. He first came to prominence with his play about the First World War, *Observe the Sons of Ulster Marching Towards the Somme*, which premiered in the Abbey Theatre in Dublin and was widely performed internationally. His other plays include *Dolly West's Kitchen* and *Someone Who'll Watch Over Me*. He has also written new versions of classic works, including *A Doll's House, Three Sisters* and *Oedipus*. His work has garnered many awards, including the Rooney Prize for Irish Literature, the New York Critics' Circle Award, a Tony Award and the Irish PEN Award. His first novel, *Arimathea*, was published in 2013. He is Professor of Creative Writing at University College Dublin and is a member of the Irish arts academy, Aosdána.

BELINDA MCKEON was born in County Longford. Her debut novel *Solace* won the 2011 Faber Prize and the Bord Gáis Energy Irish Book of the Year Award. Her second novel, *Tender*, will be published later this year. Her writing has been published in many journals, including the *Paris Review*, the *Guardian* and the *Dublin Review*. She is also a playwright; her work has been produced in Dublin and in New York, where she has lived for the past ten years. She teaches at Rutgers University.

EOIN MCNAMEE was born in County Down. He has published seventeen novels, including *Resurrection Man, Blue Tango, Orchid Blue, The Ultras, 12:23* and, most recently, *Blue is the Night*. His first book for young adults, *The Navigator*, was a *New York Times* best-seller. He has also written screenplays, including *Resurrection Man* and *I Want You*. His work has been widely translated and has won many awards, including the Macaulay Fellowship for Irish Literature. He is a member of the Irish arts academy, Aosdána.

MARY MORRISSY is the author of three novels, *Mother of Pearl*, *The Pretender* and *The Rising of Bella Casey*, and a collection of short stories, *A Lazy Eye*. Her stories have been widely anthologised in Ireland, the UK and the USA. She has taught creative writing at university level in Ireland and in the USA over the past decade, and she currently teaches on the MA in Creative Writing at University College Cork. She has won a Lannan Literary Award and a Hennessy Award for her fiction.

KATHLEEN MURRAY is from Carlow and now lives in Dublin. Her stories have appeared in a number of anthologies, including *Davy Byrnes Stories* and *These Are Our Lives*, and in magazines, including the *Stinging Fly* and *Prairie Schooner*. She was winner of the Fish Short Story Prize 2007 and is working on her first collection of stories.

SEAN O'REILLY studied at the University of East Anglia and at Trinity College, Dublin. His first book was *Curfew and Other Stories*, and he has also published three novels, *Love and Sleep*, *The Swing of Things* and *Watermark*. His stories have also been anthologised in *New Irish Writing*, *Arrows in Flight* and the *Granta Book of Irish Short Stories*. He lives in Dublin and is a contributing editor to the literary magazine the *Stinging Fly*.

NATALIE RYAN was born in Ireland but spent her childhood

in Ghana, West Africa. She completed her undergraduate studies at University College Dublin, where she later obtained an MA in Creative Writing. She won the Bryan MacMahon Short Story Award and the Originals competition at Listowel Writers' Week. She has been shortlisted for the Francis MacManus and William Trevor/Elizabeth Bowen short story competitions. She has just completed her first novel, *White Lies*.

COLM TÓIBÍN is from Wexford. He is the author of eight novels, including *The Blackwater Lightship*, *The Master* and *The Testament of Mary*, all three of which were shortlisted for the Booker Prize, and *Brooklyn*, which won the Costa Novel Award. His most recent novel is *Nora Webster*. He has also published two collections of stories, *Mothers and Sons* and *The Empty Family*. He is Mellon Professor of the Humanities at Columbia University, and a member of the Irish arts academy, Aosdána.